Forsaken

In the Night

Book 3

Ellen Fritz

Forsaken

By Ellen Fritz
© 2016 Forsaken
Swartz Creek, MI 48473
Cover design by Clarissa Yeo

Tell-Tale Publishing Group

An Imprint of TT

www.tell-talepublishing.com

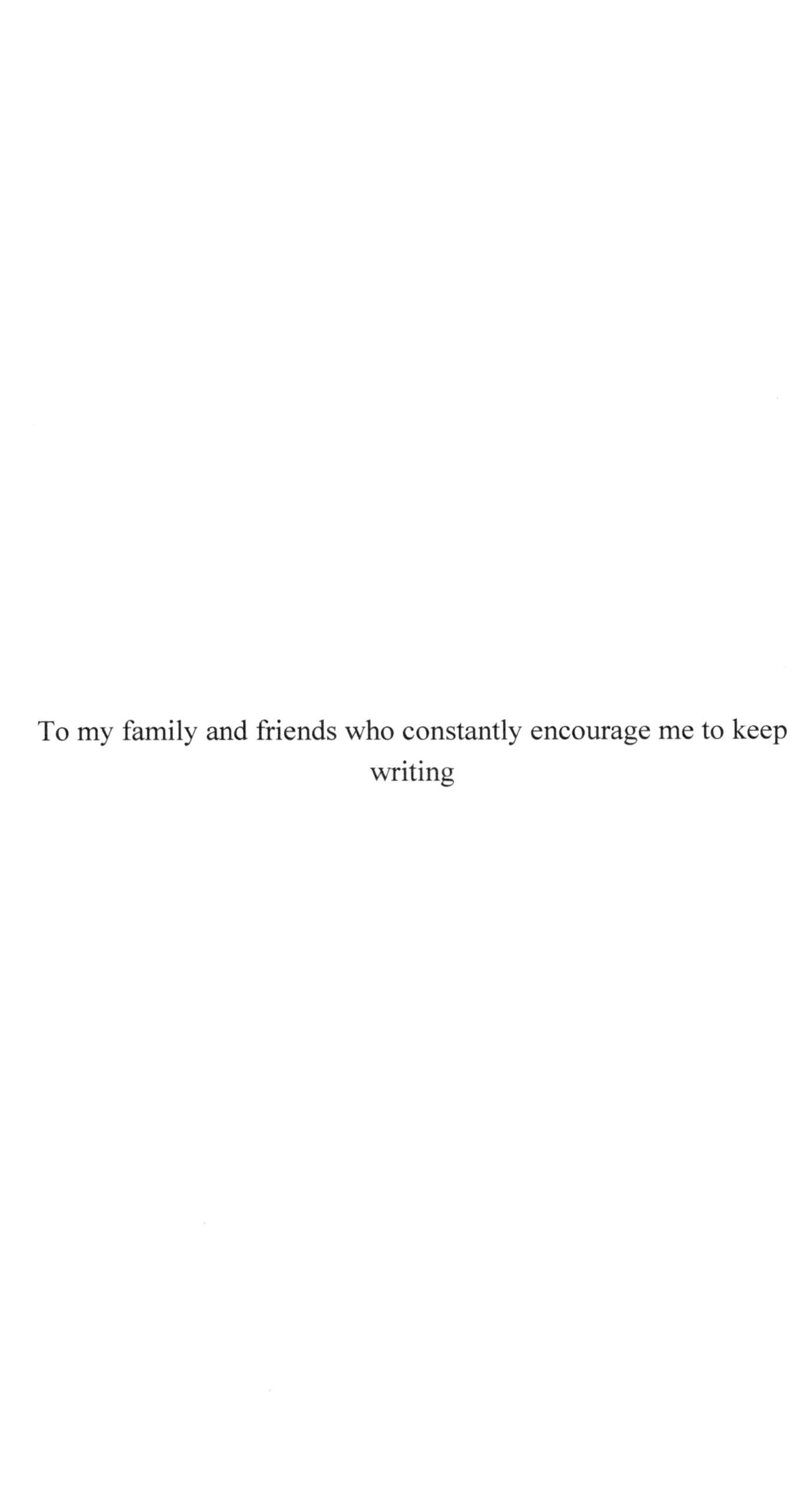

To my family and friends who constantly encourage me to keep writing

Chapter 1

Someone was shaking me.

"Holly. Wake up, Holly."

I opened my eyes from a very sound sleep to see Chris leaning over me with his hand on my shoulder. *Parker's dead!* I thought, even before I'd had time to move.

"Parker?" I asked. I didn't want him to say it. *Please don't say it.*

"No! We haven't heard anything about Parker," Chris said shaking his head vigorously. Then he held still and looked serious. "It's Mom and Dad."

"What?" I was still waking up and not thinking clearly with the dread of hearing about Parker in my head.

"There was an accident last night." He hesitated like he was trying to choose the right words. "They're dead, Holly," he practically whispered. "They were killed in the accident."

I realized then why Chris looked the way he did. His eyes were puffy and red, he was sniffing, and his lip quivered a little when he wasn't speaking.

"They're dead?" My brain was empty except for the need to repeat what I'd just heard. Could I have heard him right?

"The police called me this morning. I guess Mom got out of jail yesterday, and they went out last night."

"They were drunk," I sighed. I wasn't asking. I knew.

"Yeah."

"Uncle Steve driving?" Mom and Dad didn't have a car anymore, but Uncle Steve did. He was still living with them since Chris and I left, so it just made sense that he'd be driving.

"Uncle Steve told the cops that Dad said he was okay to drive, so he was driving Uncle Steve's car. He plowed into a tree. Uncle Steve was passed out in the back seat. He doesn't remember anything, and wasn't hardly hurt. Just scrapes and bruises."

"When did they call?"

"About 7:00. Someone found the car this morning along that road by the river. They didn't have seatbelts on. Steve was still passed out in the back, and they took him to the hospital and everything to have him checked out. The whole thing's a mess," Chris was shaking his head like he couldn't get a handle on everything the cops told him. "I just keep thinking that I'm glad he didn't hit another car and kill someone else."

That's when I started crying because I knew it was real. Neither Mom nor Dad usually drove when they were drinking. Drunk driving was Uncle Steve's specialty. Chips was close enough to easily walk home, and a lot of the time they drank at home anyway. I was always thankful for that because, that way, neither of them would kill someone else. But now, Dad had killed himself and Mom.

Chris hugged me and we just held each other for a few minutes, both of us crying.

"I can't believe it," I blubbered, looking up at Chris. "I've meant to go see them, but … you know. I never knew what to say, and Uncle Steve was always there. I … I just can't believe it."

"I have to go talk to the funeral home in about an hour and arrange things."

"What? God, I forgot about all that. Can I help you? I mean, can you do it at night?"

"I already asked them," Chris said shaking his head. "I wanted you to go, too."

"I don't want you to have to do this all by yourself," I whispered.

"I called Aunt Sarah." That surprised me. Uncle Steve's wife, in the process of becoming ex-wife, was not a favorite person to either one of us. "The cops already called her about Uncle Steve, so I figured she was the easiest, and he's still sleeping it off, so he won't be there. It won't be so bad."

"Oh Chris, I'm sorry," I said through a sob. I hated that he'd have to handle everything alone. My next thought made my voice stronger. "But don't let her think she's running the show. Remember how she got Grandma's funeral all out of control?"

"I sure do, but not this time," Chris said with determination. "I was thinking about something really simple. No calling hours. Just a simple prayer at the cemetery, if that's okay with you."

"Sure, that's fine with me, but it's what you want that counts. I can't be there, so make it what you want."

"Okay," he nodded. "But, you know, any funeral is really expensive, and, hell, this is *two*. I have some money saved, but I know it's not enough. Do you have any?"

"Sure. Most of my salary's still in the bank. But don't worry about the cost. Byron will loan us whatever we need until we sell the house. Unless you want the house?"

"Oh, hell no! And I don't think I want anything that's in it."

"Me either."

"I'd better go. I'm meeting Aunt Sarah at the funeral home. I told the hospital Carson-Grant over on Pine Street. That okay?"

"That's fine."

Tears started pooling in Chris's eyes again. "I don't want to do this, Holly. Even if you were there ... I just don't know what to do."

"I know." I hugged him again. "I wish I could help you. Did Lorna have any advice to give you?"

"She didn't hear the phone, and I didn't wake her up. Nobody knows, but you."

"They'll want to know. Come get me when you get back, and we'll tell them together."

"I don't want to wake you up again."

"You won't. I'll be thinking about you, not sleeping."

"I'm sorry, Holly. I didn't want to wake you up to tell you all this. It's just ... hell, I'm sorry."

"Don't say that. I'm sorry you have to handle everything alone. Just ..." I shook my head, not knowing for sure what I wanted to say. "Just stay strong with Aunt Sarah, and we'll talk when you get back." I reached up to touch the side of his face.

Chris hugged me again and left for the funeral home. I watched him walk out the door and thought about him being the only family I had left. And if Parker didn't come back ... No. I couldn't think about that now. Parker was missing, but that didn't mean he was dead.

As a young vampire, I'd someday have to face the death of every human I knew, but I really didn't think it'd be this soon. Then I started thinking about Mom and Dad. Dead. It was so unreal.

How long had it been since I'd seen them? I still saw them like they were when I left that night. I couldn't ever really see Mom in jail like Chris said she was. So unreal.

We'd have to get rid of all their stuff and sell the house. How do you do all that? And I was sure the house was a complete mess. I was the only one who ever cleaned the last few years and I hadn't been there since last fall. Where would we start?

Two hours later, I still sat there with my scattered thoughts, but Chris was back. "How was it?" I asked without even saying hello.

"Not bad," he answered, trying to smile a little. "The funeral director was cool. He explained everything. I had to tell Aunt Sarah that you and I'd decided how we wanted it, and he figured out really quick that I was making the decisions. So he pretty much ignored her and talked to me."

"That's good."

"We'll meet the hearse at the cemetery the day after tomorrow. One of the funeral home guys will say a little prayer, and that'll be it."

"Good."

"The caskets, burial plots, all that stuff really costs a lot, though. It'll be close to $10,000 for the two of them. And I didn't even pick out the fancy caskets."

"Thank you, Chris. I'm really proud of you for handling all this."

"Thanks. I guess you do what you have to, you know?"

I smiled at him and kissed his cheek. "Let's go tell Lorna and Byron. We'll let them tell the rest."

"Should we wake them?"

"They'll want us to," I said, nodding.

We decided to take Lorna with us to tell Byron because we only wanted to tell the story once. I couldn't face going through the whole thing multiple times, and I was sure Chris had had enough talking about Mom and Dad with Aunt Sarah and the funeral directors.

So we woke up Lorna and asked her to go to Byron with us. She was worried, and kept asking us questions from the bathroom while she got dressed.

"It's not about Parker, or anything, but it's bad news," Chris told her. "We just don't want to go through it a bunch of times."

"Are you two okay?" she asked, looking worried.

"We're fine," I said. We were fine, but I think both of us were pretty numb. I just couldn't get it to sink in and be real. Chris was probably doing better than me since he talked to the funeral home, but I didn't really know if he was, or not.

Byron and Crystal, like Lorna, were sleeping soundly when we woke them. It was about noon, the middle of the night for vampires, but we knew they'd never forgive us if we let them sleep. Again, we had to quickly tell them that it wasn't about Parker. He was constantly on everyone's mind.

They put on robes, and we all sat in Byron's living room to talk. I could feel the tension as we gathered. They knew it wasn't about Parker, but they all wondered why on Earth we would wake them like we did.

"Mom and Dad were killed last night in a car accident," Chris started without any intro. But what could you say? Except the blunt, horrible truth.

Tears came to my eyes immediately. I knew that telling other people would start to make it real, but I guess that's the way it should be. It was real.

Byron held us both. Lorna and Crystal cried. I cried. Chris cried. It was everything anyone would expect from telling someone both of your parents had just died. Horrible, but wonderful that our friends cared so much for us.

Eventually, we got to the money part. Byron said he'd pay for everything, and we said we only needed a loan.

"Byron," I finally said. "I think we need to pay you back so it's real. It hasn't sunk in, and I think it will if we handle stuff ourselves. We have to pay you back."

"Okay," he finally relented, "but I'll call my lawyer, Clyde Reynolds. He'll handle everything, and I have him on retainer, so there'll be no extra cost."

By the time we left Byron and Crystal, it was 2:00 in the afternoon. We all agreed to try to get some more sleep, but Chris and Lorna didn't want to leave me alone. They sat in my room while I crawled in bed, and we talked quietly.

I know they were both trying to get my mind on something else so I'd sleep. The surprising thing was that it worked. I felt myself drifting away as Lorna was quietly talking about when she lived in Paris.

I guess they left after I was asleep, because the next thing I knew I was waking up and it was almost 5:00.

That night Chris and I both worked because we had to do something. Byron said we could take the time off to do whatever we wanted, but we both wanted to work. The only thing there was to do was to go over to Mom and Dad's house, but we couldn't face that until after the funeral.

The day of the funeral came, and I didn't want to let go of Chris to go bury our parents without me. I wanted more than anything to be able to walk into that cemetery with him and hold his hand while the caskets were lowered into the graves, but that wasn't an option for me anymore.

"Don't let Uncle Steve and Aunt Sarah give you any kind of shit," I said. "You know they'll both try something. Stay strong and just do what *you* want."

"I will, little sis. And I'll feel you beside me the whole time."

"I'll be there," I said through my tears.

While Chris was gone, I paced around my room. The TV was on, but I didn't pay any attention to it. Crystal, Lorna, and Byron all came to be with me during the time of the funeral, even though they should have been sleeping.

We'd asked the three of them to tell everyone else what had happened. All the employees stopped to offer me a few words, but the hardest person to see was Sarita.

She stayed with me for about a half hour, even though she'd been really sick lately, and looked to me like she was getting older by the day. Dr. Jamison said she had the beginnings of Alzheimer's, but it seemed to me she was beyond the beginnings.

She remembered those she had known for a long time, but often forgot all kinds of things, even stuff that she knew an hour before. Byron had hired a vampire to help Anna with the cleaning, because we were just too busy anymore for one person to handle it. Sometimes, though, Sarita still went up and cleaned something just because it was what she had done for so many years.

Besides the worry over Sarita's health, the hardest thing was when she talked about Parker. She remembered everything from when he was a little boy and when he was a teenager, but she never remembered that he was missing.

We'd told her the truth about Charles taking him and about him running away, but she acted like none of it ever happened. She talked about Parker like she'd just seen him in the kitchen, or on his computer that day. He'd been gone several days by this time.

It broke my heart.

"Are you still sweet on Parker?" she asked as we sat on my bed talking to Byron, Crystal, and Lorna."

"Sure am," I answered.

"I knew all along you two liked each other. Is he at school?"

"I guess."

We decided there was no sense in telling her over and over that Parker was gone. It was like her brain refused to accept it. We just let her believe what made her happy.

Byron sighed deeply and closed his eyes while he listened to us talking. He knew it wouldn't be much longer before she needed round-the-clock care, but he'd hire whoever he had to, to help her. Dr. Jamison was already searching the country for a live-in nurse that knew about vampires--not an easy person to find.

Parker and Sarita were Byron's adopted children, and he was losing both of them. He couldn't do anything about Sarita getting old and sick since she chose not to be a vampire. But there had to be something he could do to find Parker. I didn't see how he could give up on that.

Chris finally came back and said everything had gone fine at the funeral. A lot of the guys Dad had worked with showed up, and even some friends Mom and Dad had gone out drinking with. He thought half the regulars from Chips were there.

While they were waiting for the funeral to start, Uncle Steve had brought up who was going to pay for his car which was totaled in the accident. I would have slugged him if I'd been there.

"I told him that Dad didn't have a car, so he didn't have any insurance," Chris said. "I said that he'd have to sue us, but since he handed the keys to a man obviously too drunk to drive, he probably wouldn't get very far."

"Good for you, Chris," I said. "He's not getting a penny of our money."

"I guess I should tell your lawyer about that when we talk?" Chris asked Byron.

"Definitely," Byron answered. "But, you're right. He won't get anything."

We sat in Byron's suite the rest of the day after getting Sarita back to her room to rest. She was so tired all the time anymore. Besides, she kept forgetting that we'd just buried our parents and kept talking about Parker. I could hardly stand it much more, even though I loved Sarita and knew she meant well.

Chris and I went to work that night, but Byron came to get us about 10:00.

"We're going for a walk," he said to Chris and me.

"I'm good," Chris said. "You two go ahead."

"No, you're coming, too," Byron said. "Crystal and Luke can handle the bar."

We walked through the warm night, and I immediately felt a little better. A little more normal. I was in the middle with my arm through Byron's elbow and Chris holding my other hand. It felt good to have that support, but I put my arm around Chris's waist so he could reach around my shoulders. Chris needed the support as much as I did. Maybe more since there was so much he had to handle himself.

We walked silently, and I wasn't paying any attention to where we were heading, but, before I knew it, we were at the gates to the cemetery. I figured out what Byron was up to, but wasn't sure I wanted to go to the graves.

I went anyway.

The cemetery workers had covered the graves with some kind of fake grass and a few bouquets of flowers that people had sent. I was glad the graves weren't bare dirt.

"It's nice here," I said as Chris and I stood there staring down at the graves, still holding each other.

"I didn't want them out by the road. It cost a little more back here, but I picked these anyway."

"Good. I'm glad you did. I'm so sorry you had to do everything on your own." Tears were slipping silently down my checks.

"I know. But it was okay."

"I can't believe Uncle Steve and Aunt Sarah didn't give you any trouble except for the car."

Chris sighed. "I wasn't going to tell you, but I guess you should know."

"What?"

"Aunt Sarah had this guy come with doves that he was going to let loose to symbolize their souls flying up to Heaven."

"You're kidding? They didn't have any religion. They wouldn't have wanted that." The tears had stopped immediately as my anger at Steve and Sarah flared.

"I kicked him out, and she was pissed off during the whole thing. Then, after the funeral, both of them started going on about where you were."

"Damn. What did they say?"

"You know," he shrugged. "Shit like the least a daughter could do was come to the funeral. I lost it and told them they needed to stay out of our lives. Uncle Steve started arguing, and I told him to go to hell."

"Good for you."

"I just wanted it to be peaceful, you know? And they had to start shit."

"Nothing is ever peaceful with Uncle Steve and Aunt Sarah involved."

He squeezed my shoulders a little and we stood there. Mom and Dad might not have been the best parents. I mean, they were both drunks, but they were the only parents I had, and now they were dead. I'd never see them again.

"Why am I so sad," I said through eyes that were tearing up again, "when I spent most of my life hating them?"

"You hated the stuff they did, and what they let drinking do to them, but they were still our parents. When we were little, we had some good times, didn't we?"

"Yeah, we did. I remember. I always hoped they'd somehow quit drinking and we'd get back to those days. I guess it's sad that that hope is gone now. Drinking actually killed them."

"Yeah, it did. You ready to go? We could stay longer if you want."

"No, I'm ready. What about tombstones? Are they expensive? How do we get them?"

"I don't know. We'll ask Byron if he knows."

I'd forgotten about Byron while we stood talking, but expected to see him when I turned around. He wasn't there. Looking across all the tombstones, I spotted him waiting at the gate. He'd given us private time and moved away to where even his vampire ears wouldn't hear what we had to say to each other.

On the silent walk back to Rule the Night, I started to think about how good this vampire family was to us. Who would have thought that vampires would be so nice? Why couldn't our real family have been so supportive and caring? I knew the answer to that. Alcohol.

Mom and Dad really were good people at heart, but they'd been drinking too much since they were teenagers. Even when we were little, and they were sober most days, getting drunk occupied too much of their time.

I couldn't stop thinking that I just couldn't take one more thing. Why did this have to happen now, with Parker gone, and maybe dead, because he'd been purposefully turned into a bloodthirsty vampire by Charles, the most hateful, evil vampire I could imagine.

Byron was as hurt and terrified as I was, living through each day, waiting to hear what had happened to Parker. He'd adopted Parker only ten years before, but couldn't have loved him any more if he'd been his natural son. Everyone at Rule the Night loved Parker.

Now, my parents. I felt so hopeless. Thank God I had Chris. He'd turned out to be everything that I ever hoped a big brother could be. But even though I had Chris, I didn't think I could handle it if one more thing went wrong.

Chapter 2

Parker and I prowled the deserted street. We were like shadows melting into the odd crevices between the buildings as we sniffed and searched for our next victim.

The incredible scent of human blood was faint, but we followed it, sensing it getting stronger. There! In the alley lay the body of a sleeping woman. Homeless, dirty, smelling of sweat, urine and alcohol, but none of that mattered to us.

What mattered was that her blood smelled delicious.

Parker pounced first, grabbing her shoulders, dragging her to her feet, and pulling her against his body. She struggled as the rough treatment woke her, and started yelling. She beat on his chest and called him every foul name I'd ever heard.

I'm sure she thought she was about to be robbed, beaten, and raped. She fought, but she was not anywhere near strong enough to affect Parker at all. He laughed before showing her his fangs. She looked confused as she stared at him.

"You're going to taste delicious," he said with a deep, evil voice.

She screamed while Parker laughed, and I laughed with him. He grabbed her hair to pull her head back, and plunged his fangs into her neck.

Then I moved behind her, pushed her dirty, matted hair out of my way, eased her head back even farther to give me room, and drove my fangs into the other side of her neck. We had what we'd been looking for. We drank, sucking hard and relishing every drop.

She didn't last long with both of us feeding so violently, but that hardly mattered. We were a team. It didn't matter if we got our fill from one victim because there were thousands, hundreds of thousands, to choose from.

We were predators. Strong, powerful, we took what we wanted and enjoyed the chase. No one could stop us as we moved among the humans, feeding at will. Two, three, or four a night. We drank and humans died.

We let the body drop to the ground, and reached over her toward each other, licking the blood from each other's lips. We left her body in the alley and moved on, tracking the next scent of warm, human blood that was calling to us.

I woke up sweating. Flat on my back, the covers were thrown off and my arms flailed out at my sides. I was actually breathing quick, shallow breaths as my heart strummed rapidly against my chest.

I'd had that dream, or some variation of it, almost every day since Parker left. Sometimes I had it more than once as I tried to get the sleep my brain and body so desperately needed, and sometimes it went on and on before I woke.

I'd tried staying awake to avoid the dream, but I was too exhausted to keep going. Yesterday, I fell asleep leaning against the bar and woke up when my arm started slipping out from under my head. I couldn't go on without sleep, and couldn't stand to have the dream anymore.

Top it all off with the whole funeral thing. It'd been days, and most of the time I slid it to the back of my brain like it hadn't really happened. But the truth was, when I wasn't thinking of where Parker might be, I was thinking of Mom and Dad.

Chris and I had talked to Clyde Reynolds about all the legalities of dealing with our parents' death. I had no idea about sending the death certificates to the insurance company, Dad's job, his pension company, and other places that I'd never heard of. Thankfully, Clyde took care of all that for us.

We'd gone over to the house and found it to be as big a mess as I'd figured. We were right that there wasn't anything we wanted except some photos. We had the opportunity to laugh at some of the ones from when Chris and I were little, but I couldn't stop thinking about how much I'd like to show them to Parker. Everything brought thoughts of Parker to my mind.

Clyde had a suggestion about the house that Chris and I jumped on right away. We hired an auction company that Clyde had worked with before. They would go in, clean everything out, and schedule an auction of everything. The house itself, all the furniture, appliances, even their clothes and dishes would be auctioned.

It was the easiest way, and I didn't mind paying the auction company a percentage of whatever money we got. I couldn't face getting rid of stuff myself and I knew Chris couldn't face it either. It would be a couple months before the auction took place, but then it'd be over. So sad that Mom and Dad's whole life would be reduced to an auction some afternoon, but it was all we could do.

On the morning after meeting with Clyde one more time to finalize everything, I went to bed as soon as the bar closed because I couldn't stay awake until dawn. But here I was again, an hour later, awake and feeling like my body was on hyper drive. The dreams were killing me.

I sat up in bed and tried to shake the dream out of my head. They were always bloody, nasty and, in every one, Parker and I were killing without any feeling for the humans that died.

That feeling of still being in the dream faded, I stopped sweating, and my heart slowed down to normal. Sometimes the dreams were worse and took me longer to recover, but, believe it or not, this one wasn't so bad. At least no one drove a stake in my heart right before I woke up.

I rolled over, pulled the covers back over my shoulders, and tried to go back to sleep. As I was starting to doze off, Byron called and asked me to come to his office.

I didn't let him know that I was asleep because there was still another hour or so before dawn, and I normally wouldn't have been in bed so early. I simply told him I'd be right there.

While throwing on jeans and a shirt, I had to try to clear my brain. I needed to fully wake up and get the remnants of my dream out of my head. I looked at the clock to assure myself that it was very early morning and I'd just gotten off work a couple of hours earlier.

It had been a long night in the bar, but every night was long and dreary since Parker'd been kidnapped by Charles and turned bloodthirsty. Crystal, Luke and I hardly spoke all night. Not because we were mad or anything, just because none of us had much to say.

Since the funeral, it was even worse. No one knew what to say to Chris or me. Everyone wanted to be supportive, but what could they say? We never mentioned our parents before they died, why suddenly start talking about them now?

It was hard to think of stuff to talk about when all of our heads were filled with so much worry and sorrow. Thankfully, the bar was busy these days and it took all three of us to keep the drinks flowing to the customers and clients.

Chris was back on valet parking duty with Lorna and Anthony while some of the new guards, Nick and Harlan, were on the door, so I didn't see much of him. He seemed so happy with Lorna, but I think he tried to hide it from me. I guess he thought it wasn't very nice to go around so much in love while I was so miserable.

We all felt Parker's absence, and we all knew that the odds of him surviving were really slim. Even if he got away from Charles, his plan was to turn himself into the Assembly, and they would execute him.

Byron didn't say why he wanted me in his office, but I had to guess that it was about Parker, and it probably wasn't good news. If it was good news, I think he would have told me on the phone, because he knew that I sure could use it. I would have at least heard the tone of it in his voice.

Instead, I heard the same profound grief that we'd all been living with since Parker left. That grief was like a living thing inside me. It fed on me every minute of every day, and I didn't know if I would survive it or not. It was there even before Mom and Dad died.

Parker'd been gone almost a week, and there'd been no sign of him, no word from him, nothing. He might have found Charles, and Charles might have killed him. He might have been caught by the Assembly, and they might have killed him. He might be living on the streets, completely lost to bloodthirst, and the Assembly would kill him as soon as they found him.

Byron had called Constance to tell her that Parker had left, which bothered me at first. I was feeling more and more like Byron was betraying Parker, but Byron explained that he couldn't let Constance show up to check on him, and find him gone.

Constance had given Parker one week to make some improvement, but he'd run away instead of working on the bloodthirst. When I thought about it, I knew that Byron had to call. He really didn't have any choice.

We were all surprised, though, that Constance didn't have much to say to Byron. All she said was to let her know if he came back or if we found him. I thought she'd blow her stack. I thought she'd suspect that Byron was hiding him and show up here to search or demand that Byron go to the Assembly to explain himself.

She didn't even say that they'd send hunters out to look for him, but surely that's exactly what she had done. After that call, I thought for a little while that maybe things would work out. Maybe we'd get Parker back safe and sound.

I tried to believe that but, when it came right down to it, I couldn't think of any likely scenario where Parker would be safe. Constance had probably just played it cool with Byron so she wouldn't give away what she was planning. Most of my thoughts ended with Parker already being dead.

After a week of TJ and Quinton searching for him, I was just waiting for us to find out how he died, and that's what I was afraid Byron wanted to tell me. I didn't want to go to his office and hear the news I expected, yet dreaded. I didn't think I could stand to hear him say it. Yet, I couldn't stand the not knowing anymore either.

"Come in, Holly," he said quietly.

TJ and Quinton were with him. That wasn't good. They'd been out looking for Parker since the night he left, and had only called in with reports. If they were back at Rule the Night, they'd probably found out what happened to him.

I sat in the empty chair next to TJ because I wasn't sure my legs would hold me up for much longer. *Say it, Byron. Just get it over with. No, don't say it. I can't stand to hear it.*

"There's no word about Parker, but there's something else going on that we need to talk about," Byron said as I stared at him.

There are times when the old adage, *No news is good news,* applies. This wasn't one of them because I couldn't think of how there could be any good news about Parker. Instead I guess this was like, *No news is at least not bad news.*

"What's going on?" I asked. What could possibly be going on that wasn't news about Parker?

"We were looking in Columbus," TJ answered me. "There was no sign of Parker, but we found something else."

I just stared at him.

"There have been several young women killed," he continued. "It's in the papers, on TV, and the police don't have any leads. I'm afraid it might be Parker."

"Were they drained?" I asked.

"Yeah," TJ nodded his head.

I looked toward Byron. His hands were folded on his desk and he gazed down at them. Lost in thought, or blank and numb? We all seemed to be pretty numb these days.

"What are you going to do, Byron?" I asked.

"TJ?" he mumbled without looking at me. I looked at TJ.

"I'm sorry if this is too personal, Holly," TJ said, "but … has Parker bitten you?"

"Yeah, he has." That *was* a personal question, like asking what kind of foreplay we'd done, and I didn't know why TJ felt like he had to ask it, but I had to answer.

"When a vampire bites another vampire, it creates a bond between the two. He'll sense you miles away, and will probably come looking for you. We want you to go back to Columbus with us. We haven't had any luck, but you will attract him, and he might be willing to let you bring him back."

His words lifted a heavy weight from my heart. I wanted to go with them from the beginning, but Byron wouldn't hear of it. He was right when he said how dangerous it could be, but I was willing to face that danger. Besides, I had to do something. I couldn't stand going through day after day wondering and worrying anymore.

"Yes! Of course I'll go with you. When?"

"Tonight. We have to get some sleep and feed. I suggest you do the same thing."

"I'll be ready as soon as it's dark. Can I sense him?"

"Did you bite him?" TJ asked.

"No, he bit me."

"He carries some of your blood in him, so he'll sense you. You won't sense him any more than normal."

I wished that I'd bitten Parker.

"Holly," Byron finally looked at me, but his expression was hard to read. I think he was afraid. "I'm not happy about you going back to Columbus with them, but I told them it was your choice." He hesitated for a moment. "It will be dangerous. Parker hurt you once and he's probably worse by now. I have to ask you not to go," he practically whispered.

I looked into his eyes. Into that fearful, sad, miserable expression, and knew my face showed him the same thing. But I was also determined. Determined to do everything I could to help Parker.

"I have to, Byron. I couldn't live with myself if I didn't. I think I was the reason he left, because I was pushing him to run away with me. So this is all my fault. I have to go."

"I want you armed," Byron said and never took his eyes off me. He knew I wouldn't change my mind, and didn't waste his time arguing with me. "You have to be able to fight him if you need to."

"I don't want to fight him, but I know I might have to. I'll do *whatever* I have to do, to get him back.

"The most important thing you have to do is listen to TJ and Quinton. Don't take any chances without them. If they tell you to back off, do it." His voice was so emphatic. I knew he meant every word.

"I will."

"You two are charged with her safety," Byron said looking back at TJ and Quinton. "Do not let her get hurt."

"We'll take care of her, Byron," TJ answered. "We'll bring them both back."

Byron didn't say anything. He just looked back down at his hands on the desk. I wasn't sure he wanted Parker back. I wasn't sure he believed Parker could be cured of bloodthirst. Maybe he never did really believe that he could be cured.

"Get to bed, Holly," he finally said to me. "We'll wake you when it's time to get ready."

I went back to my room feeling emotionally and physically exhausted, but relieved. Tonight, I'd help them search for Parker and I had to believe that we'd find him.

I'd had no idea that drinking my blood would leave a bond between us, and Parker'd be able to sense me at such a distance.

He'd come to me, I knew it. He had to. I wondered if he knew that when he took my blood.

Within a few minutes, I was on the edge of sleep, thinking about that one day when Parker and I'd been together. The day he'd bit me.

I would never forget even a second of that time, and didn't think he would either. His body against mine. The love we shared. Losing track of how many times each of us had said, *I love you*. Thinking about all that, helped me fall asleep much faster than I expected.

I slept through the day without dreaming, at least without remembering any dream. I finally felt a little better about Parker because I felt like I was going to be able to do something. After he left and the whole thing with Mom and Dad, I'd been feeling so helpless. It felt great to be able to have the chance to accomplish something.

I'd be able to help Parker and maybe bring him back with us. Then we'd find some way to cure him of bloodthirst. We had to be able to come up with something.

Quinton called in the late afternoon to wake me so I would get ready to go. I was rested and excited as I dashed into the shower. All kinds of thoughts floated through my brain. Could we find him as soon as tonight? Would he follow me? Would he come back with us willingly, or would we have to tie him up and throw him into the back of the SUV?

I didn't care how it happened, I just needed to have him back. He needed to get better, I needed to hold him again, and he needed to stop killing. Any little bit of hope was at least something to hang on to.

The longer he was out there, the more likely it was that Charles or the Assembly would find him. The Assembly was actually scarier, because they would kill him immediately.

Charles might let him live, hoping to use him to hurt Byron even more than he already had. But, after what Charles had done to him the last time, I knew it would be a battle to the death to get through Charles and save Parker. It was close to that the last time.

I packed a few changes of clothes and headed up to our meeting in Byron's office. I met Crystal on the way.

"Byron said you're going with TJ and Quinton," she said.

"TJ thinks he'll come to me." I couldn't help letting my happiness show a little on my face.

"Byron's afraid you'll get hurt or we'll lose you, too."

"I know he's worried, but I have to help Parker any way I can."

"I know you do. But if Byron loses both of you, I don't know if he'll be able to live through it. With Sarita being so sick, he's taking everything so hard. He blames himself for Charles being able to take Parker in the first place, feels guilty about not changing Parker when he wanted it, and he's torn apart by his relationship with Constance and the Assembly. I don't know how to help him."

Crystal sounded so sad and lost. She loved Byron and hated seeing him so upset, but what could any of us do except keep trying to find Parker?

"Oh, Crystal ... I don't know either. I wish I did. I just know that getting Parker back here and finding a way to get rid of his bloodthirst has to help. It has to help all of us."

"If the Assembly will let us continue trying."

"I know. But right now, all I can concentrate on is getting him back here. We'll face the rest of it when we have to."

"Be careful, Holly," she said and hugged me.

"I will. You take care of Byron."

Chapter 3

"Not again," Detective Joe Garrett said quietly to the universe as he stood looking down at the body. There were other people around, his partner, Karl Jennings, and many uniformed police, but he spoke to no one in particular.

"The ME's on her way," Jennings said hanging up his phone.

"Who found her?" Garrett asked.

"A jogger," Jennings tilted his head to indicate a guy standing with a uniform cop on the sidelines. "He's waiting for our questions."

Thinking out loud, Garrett mumbled, "Four nights, four bodies. A pretty strong pattern."

"Yeah," Jennings answered. "Fully clothed, not a mark on her except the throat torn out. No blood. Killed somewhere else and dumped here."

Garrett pulled out his latex gloves, and Jennings did the same. They didn't need to talk about what they were doing, because they both knew the information they needed. While Jennings held the victim's head so it would stay in the same position in relation to her body and preserve any evidence, Garrett placed one hand under her shoulder and the other under her hip.

Rolling her slightly, it was easy to see that there was no blood trail on her clothing, the back of her neck, or in her hair. Just like the other bodies they'd found the previous nights.

"Damn it! How the hell does someone lose a throat and bleed out without getting a drop on them?" Jennings said as they lowered her gently back to the ground.

"Maybe Valerie will find something on this one that will give us some answers," Garrett said aloud, but inside he felt those words as a prayer. They had no clues, no evidence, and all he could think of was asking God to send them some kind of a lead.

"Detectives," Dr. Valerie Clark, head Medical Examiner, said as she approached. "I hear we have a repeat performance."

"You could put it that way," Jennings answered.

"We'll try to have something for you by late afternoon." She shook her head as she looked down at the body and knew that she wouldn't find anything more here than she had on the other three bodies.

Garrett and Jennings moved under the yellow police tape while the forensics team started looking for evidence and taking pictures. They still needed to question the jogger, but didn't think they'd get any more information than the uniforms had gathered.

The body was stretched out so close to the path that the pre-dawn jogger had practically tripped over the victim's foot. Someone had placed it where it would be found quickly. The jogger used his cell to call 911 while moving away to avoid looking at the ripped out throat any more than he already had. That was it.

The jogger didn't see anyone else, didn't hear anything, and had never seen the victim before. There was nothing he could tell the detectives that gave them any hints at all.

While the forensics team searched for footprints, tire tracks, pieces of fabric, hair, or anything that could be evidence, Garrett and Jennings did the same thing in a wider perimeter. Before long, the body was removed and everyone went back to the station except for the victim and Valerie Clark's forensics team.

She went to the ME's lab to begin the autopsy that would hopefully show something that could help them begin to solve four murders in as many nights. She started with fingerprints, hoping this one was in the system and could be identified. The other three weren't. Once again, Valerie would be at it all day.

The two detectives went over the information from the crime scenes again, hoping that they'd discover something they missed the first thousand times they'd gone through it. They spread out the file on each victim: pictures, locations, times of death, everything, but still couldn't find anything they really had in common.

All the victims were female and under thirty. Other than that, they didn't have any ties to each other. The bodies were found all over the city, so there was no location they could concentrate on, and each victim was dumped where she would be easily found.

None of them had been robbed. None of them were beaten or raped. No one had seen or heard anything. None of them had been reported missing, which probably meant they were runaways, hookers, or just on their own and no one had noticed them missing, yet.

If Valerie didn't come up with something, Garrett had no idea where they'd go with the investigation next.

Finally, they moved on to other case files that were sitting on their desks because there was nothing for them to investigate unless Valerie found something. There were other crimes that needed to be solved. Still, they couldn't get their minds off the murders of the last few nights.

Columbus had its share of murders, but this was different. Most killings were gunshots or stabbings by rival gangs, spurned boyfriends, or ex-spouses. They were crimes of passion that weren't very well disguised and fairly easy to solve. Usually neighbors heard the shots, saw someone running away from the scene, or witnessed the escalating fights that had gone on in a home for weeks.

This was so different and left a sick feeling in the detectives' stomachs. The whole department knew that these murders were the kind that could go on. The words "serial killer" were hard to face, and those cases often weren't solved until they'd gone on long enough for the psycho to make a mistake.

Serial killers followed their own pattern of viciousness and kept at it until they got out of control and did something that would get them caught. A lot of victims could die before that happened. A lot of innocent young girls could die horrendous deaths while the police looked for anything that would give them a lead.

Serial killings became big news in any city. People would begin to panic, one innocent weirdo after another would be turned in to be investigated, and lonely people would claim to have seen something that led nowhere.

Concerned and scared citizens would start calling the chief of police and the mayor to complain and demand that something be done. Then the chief and the mayor would push the detectives to find something. As if the whole homicide department wasn't already itching to solve those cases.

After all that, the killer might never be caught. He could move on to another city to start again or might be arrested for some other crime. Any number of things could happen, but serial killers didn't just get their fill and stop.

The city would settle down after a time and most people would forget about the murders, but the unsolved cases would still be on the books, and the detectives would still live with the victims tormenting their minds. The families of the victims would mourn, and try to go on with their lives with no answers.

Jennings started searching the FBI database for similar, unsolved murders in other cities. Nothing had come up, yet, but it didn't make sense that a killer like this one hadn't killed before. Whoever it was, this monster was good at it.

It took practice to leave no evidence, to completely drain a body without making a hell of a mess, and to blatantly leave the body where it was sure to be found. This killer was taunting the police, daring them to try to find any evidence. He had to have done the same thing somewhere else. Hopefully, finding other cases would help solve these new ones.

Finally, the ME called and asked Garrett and Jennings to come to her office. They only hoped that meant she'd found something.

"You guys know as well as I do that these victims were murdered in exactly the same way and by the same person," Valerie started as the three of them gathered in the lab. "On first glance, the wound looks like a large animal bite, but we know it had to be a human killer. A wolf, coyote, or bear would tear up most of the body and leave a bloody mess."

"Yeah," Garrett said trying not to let his impatience show in his voice. "We know that." Inside he thought, *Tell us something we don't know so we can solve this shitload of a case.*

"So I started at the beginning trying to determine what could cause this kind of wound," the ME continued. "The only thing I can come up with is some kind of biting instrument. Looking very carefully, I can see the puncture marks on one side as if very large canines plunged in. The rest is simply ripped out without a pattern at the edges. But that doesn't really get us anywhere, because no human has the teeth to cause the wound and no animal would leave the body this neat and clean."

"Is all that just to tell us you still don't know?" Jennings asked. His impatience was clear.

Valerie sighed. "In a way. But I do have a kind of half-assed theory. You know the huge claws they use at dump sites? The ones that look like a gigantic jaw with teeth that they use to pick up tons of trash? If someone made a similar tool, only smaller, it would make this kind of wound. It could plunge in, get a hold on the flesh, and tear it out."

"So our guy is someone who made his own murder weapon? A machinist, metalworker, auto-body mechanic? Someone who had the knowledge and tools to make a weapon that would rip out a throat," Garrett said.

"That's as close as I can come."

"What about the lack of blood anywhere on the body?"

"It had to have been carefully hung or laid out horizontally so gravity took the blood away from the body. The killer would have had to get the victim in the right position and slit the throat before letting the blood drain onto the ground or into a container. I don't know, maybe the killer collects the blood."

"And tears out the throat afterwards?" Garrett asked.

"Tearing out the throat like this would splatter blood and tissue all over her face and clothes. It had to be done after the victim's blood was drained."

"That still doesn't get us very far, does it?" Jennings said. "And to hang them up they'd have to already be subdued or unconscious. How did he do that?"

"I don't know," Valerie shook her head. "The preliminary drug screens showed nothing so far, but the more detailed tests will take a couple more days."

"I still think our best hope of narrowing this down is if we can find some kind of a connection between our victims," Garrett said. "If they have something in common, maybe it will lead us to a suspect. Hell, maybe they all dated a psycho machinist."

"Either that or we call a vampire hunter," Jennings answered sarcastically. "I wonder if Buffy has any free time."

Valerie glared at him.

"Thanks, Doc," Garrett said with a guarded expression on his face. "Let us know if anything else shows up."

"I just hope it's not another body," she said quietly.

Jennings waved goodbye as they walked across the parking lot to their cars. He'd go home to his wife and two kids, spending the night trying to get the murders out of his head so he could enjoy his family. It wouldn't be easy.

Garrett went home alone to the apartment he shared with no one. He wouldn't try to forget the murders because he had a lot of thinking to do. It had been a really long time since he'd heard that word, but it would fit the evidence if the killer was something other than a normal human.

He hadn't even thought of it until Jennings said it, but it made sense. It fit. If Jennings was right, even though he'd said it as a joke, all the evidence pointed at one creature that could be responsible.

Vampire.

Garrett sat on his couch, popped the cap off a bottle of beer, and made himself think back twenty years. Back to

Indianapolis, when he was just seventeen and everyone still called him Joey.

Over the years, he'd pushed it farther and farther into the deep parts of his memory. In fact, it'd probably been five years since it had even crossed his mind. Now it leapt forward like it had been waiting for a chance. Waiting to resurface and make him face a reality he didn't want to know about and still couldn't really believe.

Twenty years ago, Joe and a couple of high school buddies felt like celebrating graduation and his eighteenth birthday a little early. They'd gotten fake ID's and decided to hit one of the edgy clubs and see how wild things could get. No one they knew, or more importantly knew their parents, should be at this club. It was known for heavy drinking, wild times, and wilder women.

He'd picked up a waitress, Virginia, that night. Sparks flew and they'd continued to see each other for most of the summer. He'd been practically obsessed with Gina, spending night after night with her at that bar, sneaking back into his parent's house at 3:00 or 4:00 in the morning, until she got really serious one night and said she needed to tell him something.

She claimed she was a vampire. She even said she'd drunk his blood several times and had removed his memory. Now, she wanted to bite him when he knew what was happening because, she said, it could be so sexy.

He didn't believe her. In fact, he thought she was nuts, and he'd started to leave. She showed him fangs and backed him against the wall. He remembered trying to break away from her, but she was unbelievably strong.

Gina kept whispering in his ear that he'd like it and, for some reason, he suddenly stopped struggling. Then she bit him.

At least Joey thought she bit him. Maybe it had been some strange hallucination, or maybe he was drunker than he thought. He did remember screaming, though, as those fangs went in.

Then it felt good. He could feel every muscle, every nerve ending in his body as she drew the blood from his neck. She said it could be sexy? Hell, it was damn close to being better than sex.

She stopped taking his blood and lovingly licked his neck. He was able to move again and started to panic. He yelled at her as she gazed into his eyes and tried to break away from her. He was completely freaked out. Not only from the bite itself, but also from how good it had felt.

She finally let him go, and he ran all the way home. After that night, he'd never spoken to her again. She'd called over and over, but had finally given up.

He'd left for college and refused to think about Gina or that night. He'd convinced himself that she had some serious mental problems and he'd imagined the rest of the whole episode. After all, he was pretty drunk when it happened and couldn't really trust his memory. He was just glad she was out of his life.

The truth, though, was that he remembered very well how it felt when her teeth sank into his neck. He remembered the sensation of her sucking out his blood. When he was honest with himself, he knew that she had bitten him. When he got home after running from her, he'd looked carefully in the mirror. There wasn't even the slightest mark on his neck.

Garrett stood up from the couch and walked over to his front window to think. He'd put all those memories so far back in his head that he'd almost forgotten about it. It'd been so long ago, but he couldn't ignore the possibility that her story might be true.

He gazed down at the street and wondered if another young woman would die tonight. He couldn't ignore what he knew and let that happen. If Gina really was a vampire, then there were others. Real vampires? Prowling the streets of Columbus? Crazy.

His watch said 7:00 pm. It would take a couple hours to get to Indy, see if the club was still there, and try to find out if anyone knew where Gina might be. He could call. No, he needed to see the place.

Parts of his memory were vague and shadowy. If he saw the bar, maybe he'd be able to clear up his scattered thoughts. He might even realize that he'd been imagining most of what he thought he remembered. Whatever reason, something in him made him need to see it again.

"Good God," he sighed. He was really going to do it. He was going to Indy to look for a vampire. He had to.

Garrett walked to the kitchen sink to dump the rest of the beer he'd been working on, grabbed his keys from the counter, and headed down to the garage. He'd need to get gas, and a cup of coffee for the road wouldn't hurt.

Part of him kept asking himself why he was doing this. Odds were great that it would be a huge dead end, and he'd spend the next couple of days telling himself what an ass he'd been to even think about heading back to that bar.

But something inside him kept saying that Gina was telling him the truth. A little part of him kept asking, *What if?* What if it was true? What if it was a vampire that was killing those women? What if he'd been lying to himself the last twenty years?

And what if the bar was gone, leaving no trace of Gina? What would he do? Keep looking somewhere for vampires? Where?

"Shit!" he said out loud to no one as he backed out of the garage. "This is stupid as hell."

But he kept going.

Two and a half hours later, he turned the corner to see that the bar was still there. In fact, it looked better than he expected, better than it had twenty years ago. He found a parking place across the street, and sat there studying what was going on at the entrance.

The building's brick facade hadn't changed, but the entrance had been rebuilt to put the door inside a small alcove and the steps up to it were widened. A new sign above the door proclaimed La Sang Rouge was still the same place.

Seeing the sign made his stomach clench. Why hadn't he remembered that the French name translated to Blood Red? He'd taken French in high school but had never bothered thinking about what that name meant.

The neighborhood was much better than it used to be. New shops, an art gallery, even a couple bistro type restaurants flanked the block around the bar. The old warehouse he was parked in front of was new loft apartments. Looked like La Sang Rouge was now in an area undergoing urban renewal.

A guard stood at the door checking ID's and about ten people waited to get in. It was Friday night. Friday's were always busy at clubs.

Garrett took a deep breath and headed across the street. The wait in line was only a few minutes, and he used the time to check out the customers going through the door. Young, well dressed, looked to have money to spend. At thirty-seven, he smiled to himself realizing that he seemed to be the oldest one there.

The place had changed alright. It used to be a place you could get drunk and maybe hook up. Hell, these people looked like they were still looking to get drunk and hook up, but maybe with a better class of people. Maybe it hadn't changed so much after all. Just the appearance had changed.

Garrett walked in and found an empty stool at the bar. It was still early for clubbing and the place wasn't too busy, yet. The line outside would be around the block by midnight.

Inside La Sang Rouge was all new. Big wooden bar, new tables, new band area and dance floor, and the whole place was decorated in gray, black and red. Blood red. Garrett wondered if the small, private rooms were still behind the band. They probably were.

The guys inside were all wearing a version of the same uniform, expensive jeans or khaki's and an upscale t-shirt or polo shirt. The women wore a much wider variety of slacks and skirts, but all expensive and hot. He realized he was still wearing his jacket and tie from work and started to feel like he had a big sign around his neck saying COP.

When the bartender delivered his beer, Garrett decided he might as well plunge in. The odds of Gina still working here were really slim, but he'd driven for hours to find out, so he might as well ask.

"Any chance a waitress named Virginia still works here?"

"Who's asking?"

Could she really still be here? "I knew her a few years ago when I lived in Indy. Just thought I'd say 'Hi' and see how she's doing."

"What's your name?"

"Joe Garrett."

The guy took a cell out of his pocket and speed dialed. "There's a guy here named Joe Garrett says he used to know you. Will do."

He disconnected. He'd never taken his eyes off Garrett while he talked, but looked slightly more pleasant when he'd hung up. "She'll be right out," he said before turning to another customer.

It probably wasn't going to be her. There were thousands of women named Virginia, and it could be any of them. This was going to turn out to be a dead end and a stupid waste of time.

Then he saw her come through a door in the far wall, and his mouth fell open. She hadn't changed a bit. The same glossy, chestnut hair fell around her shoulders, her light hazel eyes glinted as she smiled at a customer she passed, and her sleeveless little black dress showed off an incredible body and long, sexy legs. Legs that had once wrapped themselves around him.

Virginia hadn't been the first woman he'd had sex with, she'd been the second. And she had taught him things that still made his breath catch when he thought of it.

He knew her twenty years ago, and she was older than him. The woman had to be forty-five now, yet she still looked like the twenty-five-year-old that he once knew. Last time he saw her, she'd been the older woman every seventeen-year-old guy dreams of. Now she looked too young for him.

She smiled as she got close and recognized him. "Joe Garrett," she sighed.

"Hey, Gina. Didn't know if you'd remember me."

"How could I forget?" She gave him a sexy smile making him suddenly feel twenty years younger. "Aden," she said to the bartender, "give me a club soda."

"Still not much of a drinker?" Garrett teased.

"No, but bring yours. We'll go back to my office and talk about the old days. I have a feeling, though, this isn't just a social call."

She'd always been a smart woman. She knew he'd run scared when he left her place that night, and knew that he was here for something more important than saying hello. Hell, she could probably read that COP sign around his neck like it was really there.

They walked to her office which continued the red and black theme with an expensive looking wooden desk and plush carpet. To one side, was a couch and pair of armchairs for conversation. He couldn't help being impressed.

"You've come up in the world," he smiled as they sat on her couch.

"I'm the manager, now. I did the redecorating when the neighborhood started changing and have done really well." She hesitated for a moment. "What can I do for you, Joey?"

He smiled. No one had called him Joey since he'd left for college. Then he looked more serious. "You told me some stuff that last night. I need to know the straight story."

"You've heard the straight story," she said quietly. "I thought you were ready to hear it. I guess I should have given you more time."

He swallowed and looked away from her. That's when he realized that he wanted her to tell him she'd been handing him a load of crap. He wanted her to say it was a game that she'd been playing with him.

"You're a vampire?" he asked quietly without looking at her.

"Yes."

He stood and paced around the room, turning his back to her. "I've spent twenty years trying to forget the stuff you told me. I need the truth, Gina."

"I'm sorry I told you. I figured out that night that some humans are never really ready to hear the truth. I tried to see you again so I could erase the memory, and because I hated losing you. But it's been too long, now. It wouldn't work now."

He looked back at her. "You could have done that?"

"I fed from you six different times while we were together. You don't remember any of that do you?"

"You sucked out my blood six times?" He froze on the spot. He'd had no idea she'd done that.

"Seven, counting that night you left."

"Okay ..." He rubbed his hands over his face. He was here about the murders, not about his own scary shit going through his head. He needed to get a grip. "Gina, I'm a cop now. Homicide detective in Columbus. We've had some murders, and I hoped you could give me some answers."

"You think vampires killed them?"

She sounded surprised. If vampires are real, is it that surprising that they killed people? "It could be."

"They were drained?"

"Throats torn out and no blood. I mean no blood anywhere. Not on them, on their clothes, or on the ground around them."

"Someone must have drained them before tearing out their throats," she said like she was thinking out loud. "That would cover the bite marks."

"You think it was a vampire?" His mind was whirling, yet somehow blank. A vampire? A vampire was really killing women on the streets of Columbus?

"What else could have ripped out their throats without any sign of blood?"

"That's what the ME's been busting her butt to figure out."

"Sit down, Joey." She said patting the couch cushion beside her. "You need to know more than I had a chance to tell you twenty years ago."

Chapter 4

Joe's mind was spinning as he went back to sit next to Gina. Now that he might be getting some answers, he needed to get his brain back to detective mode rather than scared kid mode.

She told him about vampires. How they didn't kill when they fed, how they lived pretty-much among humans, how they used sanctuaries like La Sang Rouge, and about a condition called bloodthirst. Bloodthirsty vampires were the ones that killed.

"So our murderer is a bloodthirsty vampire?" Garrett asked.

"I would say so. But how did you find the bodies?"

"In an alley, on a jogging trail, in a parking lot. All out in the open."

"That's not right," she squinted slightly and shook her head. "A bloodthirsty vampire would dispose of the body so humans wouldn't find it. It sounds like someone wants them to be found."

"Why?"

"That's a good question. It could also be someone very young who hasn't been trained, but he wouldn't bother ripping out their throats to cover the bite marks. Besides, that really doesn't happen anymore."

"Any more?"

"At one time, and I mean hundreds of years ago, vampires were created and left on their own. They killed without any regard for humans, but no one does that any more. We really don't want to kill, and we don't want humans to know about us.

If we change someone, we train them carefully to control their instincts."

"So how do we catch a vampire?"

"You don't." Garrett was surprised at how seriously she said those words. "If you confronted him, he'd kill you, especially if he's bloodthirsty and leaving drained bodies around. Don't even think about going after him."

With all honesty, he thought, he had no interest in facing some vampire who liked killing, but what other choice did he have? "What do you suggest we do?" he asked quietly.

She thought for a moment. "It's interesting that it's Columbus. Did you hear about a warehouse fire recently?"

"A warehouse fire? I think there was one not too long ago, but it was empty and no one was hurt."

Gina smiled. "Over a dozen vampires were killed in there. The building was burned down around them and, once the sun came up, there was nothing left of them but more ashes. It was an unauthorized club where its members could kill humans if they wanted to."

Was she kidding? They were allowed to kill humans?

"Don't look so shocked. There are vampire criminals just like there are human criminals, but they were taken care of. I know who conducted the raid and killed them. Maybe I need to call him and see if anyone got away."

"I'll check him out. What's his name?"

"No," she gently shook her head. "I need to talk to him first. I'll ask him to contact you."

"Gina, this is my case. I need to interview him."

"He may not want you to know about him." He started to protest again, but she cut him off with a raised hand. "I can't reveal another vampire to you. I contact him, or no one does."

"Then ask him to at least call me. I need to hear what he knows."

"He'll probably agree to that. You'll hear from one of us."

"Is that it, then?"

"No. If he can't help you, I will. We can't let someone keep killing like this, and it *is* our problem to deal with. Give me your number."

He gave her a business card and wrote his personal cell number on the back. "Call me any time."

"Won't I be waking up the wife and kids?" she smiled.

"No wife and kids," he said, gazing into her eyes. "Just me."

"Then call me any time, too," she said very quietly.

"I need to go." He stood, ready to leave.

"Back to Columbus tonight?" She leaned back on the couch, stretching her arm across the back, crossing her legs. "You could stay."

"I have to get back." He hesitated as he moved to the door. "Call me, though. We have to stop this guy, and you may be my only hope."

"I'll call." She never moved from the couch as he walked out.

Was she trying to start something again? Or did she think that he wanted to start something? He didn't know and he wasn't interested. He just needed to get another big cup of coffee and start driving back to Columbus.

It was 3:00 in the morning before he saw the signs for I-270 that would take him north to his apartment. But he didn't take it. He stayed on I-70 to head downtown.

Thoughts of vampires and murdered young woman had swirled through his brain during the whole drive from Indy. In fact, he hardly remembered the miles of road he'd crossed.

He couldn't just go home and pretend like he'd be able to sleep. He knew that someone was dying tonight, and needed to do something to try and stop it. What? What could he do that would make any difference? Nothing.

All he could do was try. He had to get to the dark and seedy areas of town and look for any sign that something wasn't right. Any sign that someone might be in trouble. Any sign of vampires.

They had stepped up patrols since the murders started, and every cop out on the street was keeping their eyes wide open, but they didn't know about vampires. They didn't know that a vampire was killing those women.

The idea of some creature sucking the blood out of some helpless woman's neck and leaving her on the street disgusted him. A monster was drinking every drop from them and then ripping out their throats, and Garrett was the only one who knew. He couldn't just go home and ignore it.

His cell rang. Glancing at the caller ID, his heart skipped a beat when he saw that it was Captain Collins.

"Yeah," Garrett said as he answered. "Shit! I'll be right there."

Garrett was only a few miles from the street where the body was found, so he got there quickly. Jennings would probably be another ten to fifteen minutes. Patrol cops surrounded the area with lights flashing.

She was sprawled across the front yard of a dilapidated house on a street that was mostly businesses with a few houses and run down apartment buildings spread out between them. Some of the businesses were in converted houses. The whole neighborhood was old, poor, and in serious need of repair.

The body'd been found by the guy who lived in the house when he was walking home from a bar down the street. He was drunk enough that Garrett knew they wouldn't get any useful information from him. Of course, no information was exactly what they'd gotten from everyone else who'd found one of the bodies.

Crouched over the body to make sure this murder was the same pattern as the others, Garrett felt the hair rise on the back of his neck. The feeling that someone was watching him was overwhelming. Was a vampire watching him?

He'd never had that feeling at one of the other crime scenes, but he'd been talking to Jennings the whole time at those. This time, the other cops were spread out watching the perimeter and looking for possible witnesses. Garrett felt alone and vulnerable.

Was that because of his talk with Valerie, or because he had the feeling that he was being watched? Did the vampire watch them from a distance? He might have been making sure the body was found, might enjoy watching the cops trying, and failing, to find any evidence.

Garrett stood up and looked around at the small crowd that had gathered and at the many buildings surrounding him. A vampire could be in any of the dark windows. The place across the street was abandoned and empty, but it could hold a vampire.

He wanted to go searching. He wanted so much to find the guy, but Gina was pretty emphatic about how dangerous the vampire would be. Besides, if he was watching, he'd see Garrett coming and take off. Jennings arrived while Garrett was still looking around.

"What are you looking for?" Jennings asked sounding tired and cranky.

"Nothing," he shook his head. "Just looking."

"Anything different?"

"Nope. Exactly the same."

"What are we going to do with this, Joe?" Jennings asked as he rubbed his hand through his hair.

"I don't know. I'm still looking in other areas for the same MO, but I just don't know."

* * *

We watched as the cops rolled out that yellow tape, stood around talking, and a woman came in to inspect the body and take it away. We'd tried to stop it, but we'd been too late and there was nothing we could do for the woman.

"Let's go," TJ said. I was more than ready to leave.

We moved silently down the stairs of the abandoned house and out the back door. Once in the yard, we sped out of the neighborhood.

We'd found that woman as we'd been moving silently through the dark streets trying to pick up Parker's trail. We caught the whiff of human blood, and it was more than someone with a small wound. We knew it was the scent of a vampire feeding, and had to check out the situation.

TJ and Quinton wanted me to stay back so the stronger scent of her blood as we got closer wouldn't send me into bloodthirst, but I couldn't. I held my breath and insisted I go with them. Inside, I hoped it was Parker. I hoped we'd find him slumped over his latest victim.

When we got closer, we found the body of the young woman lying on the lawn of a run-down house. There was nothing we could do for her except dispose of her body. Then we heard someone coming down the street.

The scent of the human was almost overwhelmed by alcohol, so we figured he'd just pass by, and was probably too drunk to even notice her. We hid behind some bushes to come back once the man was gone, but had no idea that the man actually lived in that house.

When he stopped and called the police, there was nothing we could do. The sirens were blaring within seconds, so we crossed the street to hide in the abandoned house where we could watch.

A small crowd started to gather as more police arrived on the scene. I knew some people just had to follow the sound of any siren, but was still surprised at how many quickly gathered around the body. Why did they want to see that?

Quinton went down to join the crowd hoping to overhear anything that may give us a hint as to what was going on, while TJ and I stayed hidden in the house. I could see Quinton standing just outside the police tape.

He didn't need to get very close, just close enough for him to listen to what the police discussed. He didn't hear anything that would help us, though. After several minutes, we saw him stroll back across the street. We met him in the back yard so we could move on and continue hunting Parker.

"At least we now know it's not Parker," I said as we slowed to consider what we should do next. We all would have smelled the trace of Parker that remained with the body if it'd been him that killed her.

"Yeah, but who the hell was it?" Quinton asked.

"I know who it was," TJ practically snarled. "I smelled the bastard way before we got there. Donovan. He used to be a friend of Charles, but I haven't seen any sign of him in years."

"You know him?" I gasped. Vampires easily recognized each other by their individual scents. Even though it had been years, TJ still recognized him.

"Yep, and I'll bet he's still working for Charles. The way he's leaving the bodies around, they want to cause trouble with the police. I'm not sure exactly what Charles's new game is, but I'd bet my life he's involved in this and up to something."

"I think he's trying to out us," Quinton said with his eyebrows narrowed into a thoughtful expression.

"What?" I gasped.

TJ looked at him. "You could be right."

Quinton gave us a look that said he now understood what was really going on. "He wants humans terrified of us, and that won't happen until they know we exist and what we're capable of. Maybe the murders are just a first step toward humans finding out about us."

"Then we need to end that first step. Tonight."

"How do we find him?" I asked.

"I'm guessing he's staying at Hidden." TJ looked at me with one eyebrow raised.

"We're staying there!" I was shocked. We were sharing a sanctuary with this guy?

"Yeah, but we need to get him out on the street. Charles may have other followers in there, so we need to take him down without anyone else knowing it was us."

"But we don't really know that he's the one who's been killing all those women," I said.

"Holly, he's bloodthirsty. He's already condemned himself."

My face fell as TJ said that. "Then Parker deserves to die, too?"

"You know that's not what I meant. Donovan chose bloodthirst like Charles. Parker didn't have a choice. He can't help it."

"But what if he isn't the killer?"

"We *know* he killed that woman we found tonight. That's enough."

I couldn't really argue with him. The Assembly and those that supported them had been doing this for centuries. Besides, I agreed that vampires who chose bloodthirst needed to die. That's why I killed Noel without giving it a second thought.

But Parker *was* different. He really couldn't help it, and he tried to stop. He was even trying to stop Charles. We'd kill Donovan. Then we'd find Parker.

Hidden was the Assembly sanctuary in Columbus. It was really nice, but different from Rule the Night. In some ways it reminded me more of Nibble, in Chicago. It was more modern, like Nibble, only the colors and just the feel of the place were different.

All the decorations were in tones of beige with earth toned, patterned cushions on the chairs and modern pictures on the walls. It felt warm and cozy, while Nibble felt cold and hard edged. Rule the Night felt warm, too, only in a very old-world kind of way.

TJ and I waited outside Hidden while Quinton went in to see if Donovan was back yet. We didn't want anyone to see us with him, or see any connection between us and him. If he was inside, we'd wait until he went out tomorrow night. We'd get him before he had a chance to kill again.

While we waited, TJ called Byron and told him about the body and about Donovan being the one that murdered her.

"He'll know how to contact Charles. I can try to get the information from him," TJ told Byron. Then he paused. "Yes, sir. I'll let you know."

I looked up at TJ. "He said Donovan would never tell us anything about Charles, and he doesn't want us to give him the chance to get away or hurt one of us. Byron wants us to kill him quickly, before he even knows he's under attack."

Quinton came back and told us he wasn't in his room, or in the bar, so he must still be out on the street. I just prayed he hadn't decided to kill someone else.

We waited for Donovan a couple of block away from the front door. If we saw him before he got too close, we'd attack and kill him. If he got close enough for the door guard to see him coming, we'd wait.

TJ sniffed constantly to sense Donovan coming and he finally picked up his trail a couple blocks behind us. Perfect. We'd go back, away from the club, to catch him.

"Donovan!" TJ called to him as we got within sight.

"Well, TJ. I thought you stuck with Rule the Night and Byron," he practically sneered. They knew each other, but obviously weren't friends. "What brings you here?"

"Taking care of a little business," TJ answered as he held out his hand as if he was going to shake.

They got closer, and Donovan also reached out his hand to shake, but he looked a little suspicious. TJ moved at the last second, grasped Donovan's head with both hands, and snapped his neck.

Donovan was down and dead before he could blink. I'd never seen anyone move as fast as TJ, and I was sure Donovan had no idea that was coming.

"Well, I guess you didn't need us," Quinton grinned.

"Not against this idiot," TJ answered.

Then we had to get rid of him before anyone saw us. TJ reached down to pick him up, said, "I'll be right back," and sped away in a flash.

"He's good at this, isn't he?" I said.

"He and Byron have a lot of experience working for the Assembly."

"If we could even get close to Parker, I know TJ could grab him. Where could he be?"

My mind was already off Donovan and back to worrying about Parker. I couldn't help it. Parker was the reason I was here. We'd been all over the downtown area that night hoping Parker would pick up my scent, but we'd had no sign of him.

"I don't know, Holly. But we'll find him."

"I was really hoping we'd get him tonight. I just worry about him so much, I don't know how much more I can stand."

"I know," he said and slid his arm around my shoulders. "We'll get him."

"Quinton, do you really think he'll be okay? Will we be able to help him?"

He squeezed my shoulders a little, pulling me against his side. "You know that the odds aren't good, but we'll keep trying," he whispered gently.

I turned to look up at him and realized my face was just inches from his. He stared into my eyes, glanced down at my lips, and then met my eyes again. I had a feeling that he was thinking about kissing me.

His look was so warm and caring. I didn't think I'd mind at all being kissed by Quinton. Except for Parker. We continued staring at each other without saying a word or moving. Quinton had full, pale lips that looked like they'd be really nice to kiss. I felt like I had to say something soon.

"We have a couple hours before dawn," I said hesitantly. "Do you think we should look some more when TJ comes back?"

"Yeah, I think we should," he answered as he moved his arm from my shoulders.

The spell was broken and we moved a step away from each other. I'd never been attracted to Quinton like that before, but had always thought he was really handsome, and he'd always treated me so sweetly.

Somehow, I thought of TJ and Quinton as older. I mean, they actually were a century or so older than me, but does that really matter when you're a vampire? They both looked about twenty-five or so, but so did Byron and most of the vampires I knew.

None of that mattered, though. I loved Parker. He was the one I wanted and would always love. Even if the worst should happen, I wouldn't be ready to jump into someone else's arms.

I thought of the message Parker had left for me. Parker said he wanted me to find someone else to be happy with, but I couldn't see that happening. No, I couldn't see that happening at all.

TJ came back a few minutes later, and we continued searching. As we walked, he told us he weighted down Donovan's body with some rocks and dumped him in the river. At dawn, the sun would shine through the water enough to destroy him, leaving nothing for anyone to ever find.

"Okay, we know it wasn't Parker killing those women, so we need to think again about where he may be," TJ said. "What do you think, Quinton?"

"He said he's after Charles, and Columbus was the last place he saw Charles. We have to finish looking here before we do anything else."

"But what if Charles went back to Chicago and Parker followed him there?" I asked.

"We'll head to Chicago," Quinton said, "but I think we need to concentrate on where he might be spending his days and make sure we haven't missed anywhere here in Columbus. He couldn't go to a sanctuary. He'd need someplace with guaranteed darkness and safety to sleep through the day."

"A basement, an underground parking garage. I haven't been able to narrow down a good place to look," TJ said.

"What about the cemetery where Charles held him?" I said. "I think that's where I'd go."

"That's a good idea," Quinton said and then gazed up at the sky. "We don't have time to search there now, though. It'll be light too soon."

"But that's where we'll start tonight." TJ said. "We'll head out right before dark, and maybe we'll find him still there. I'll call Byron before we sleep and let him know we got Donovan."

We headed back to Hidden and made plans. How I hoped Parker would be there. I hoped, prayed, and tried to keep a good thought as the day passed with me getting very little sleep. I was just too excited about the possibility of seeing Parker. God, I hoped he was there.

Chapter 5

By the time they searched for evidence, filed all the paperwork, and spent a useless hour going over all the details of the murder cases, it was noon when Garrett got home. It might have been Saturday, but they worked any hours when murders were being investigated.

After not sleeping all night, he was dead tired and starving. He never had the chance to get anything for dinner the night before or breakfast that morning. Lunch had been a taco from a food cart on the street.

As hungry as he was, though, he was even more tired. He kicked off his shoes, stripped to his underwear, and climbed into his unmade bed. Food would have to wait until he woke up. Which happened about 5:00 when his cell starting ringing from his pants pocket on the floor.

"Yeah," Garrett said still half asleep, after fumbling to get to his phone.

"Mr. Garrett. Virginia asked me to call you."

Garrett shook his head to wake up. "Yeah ... yeah, this is Joe Garrett. Thanks for calling me so quick."

"I've called to let you know that I think your problem is solved. My men took care of the one that killed that woman last night. I'm pretty confident that he was also responsible for the other killings, so there shouldn't be anymore drained bodies found."

"You're telling me you've already caught him?" Garrett couldn't believe what he was hearing. It had only just happened. How could they have caught the guy that fast?

"Yes."

"How?"

"We have quite a few resources available to us, and I already had some men on the street."

"But how could they have found him? What'd they do with him?"

"Believe me, they found him. And he's dead."

"They killed him?" Even after he'd killed four innocent women, Joe was shocked that they had simply killed him.

"Mr. Garrett, we don't play games with those that kill. He was executed as our laws dictate. He was what you would call a serial killer, and you would have sentenced him to death. We took care of things faster."

"I don't know what to say to you ... what to ask." His mind was reeling. Was this guy just feeding him a line, or had they really caught the vampire who murdered all those women?

"I will give you my number. Call if there are more problems."

He wrote down the number as the guy recited it, and suddenly remembered what he needed to ask. "Hey, what's your name?"

"Byron."

"Are you in Columbus?"

"No. I sincerely hope you don't need my services again. Goodbye, Mr. Garrett."

"Wait a minute ..." But Byron had already hung up.

Just like that and it was over? No more murders? Garrett couldn't let himself believe that until he saw it. He'd talked to

Gina less than twenty-four hours ago, and this guy calls to say everything's taken care of. If it was that easy, why didn't they take care of it after the first murder?

He started to think, but was too hungry to concentrate. Grabbing the phone, he ordered a large pizza with everything and got dressed to wait for the delivery. Should he call Gina? Na, she wouldn't tell him anything about Byron.

No last name, no idea where he was, and no idea how to start looking. All he could do was wait to see if there was a murder again tonight. He really hoped Byron was right and they'd gotten the right guy. Rather, the right vampire.

As he got dressed, his mind worked and he kept coming back to the fact that vampires really existed. He'd tried to deny it for twenty years since Gina told him about herself. There was no denying it now.

Not only were they real, they were against killing and were willing to help the police stop the murders that were happening every night. At least some of them. Others were willing to kill, and Gina had admitted it when she was talking about the one she called Charles and that warehouse fire.

On the other hand, maybe there was more to it than that. Maybe they were all willing to kill. At least as long as they could get away with it.

The problem was that this guy left the bodies out where they could be found. Where human police would get involved and other humans would be aware that someone was stalking the night and killing. How many bodies were never found? How many others just disappeared?

Garrett couldn't let this go. He couldn't just say, *Thanks. It's all good*, and forget about it. He didn't need to find out *who* killed those women, because that guy was dead. At least Byron said he was dead. If the bodies had been disposed of like Gina said a bloodthirsty vampire would do, would Byron have bothered looking for the killer? Probably not. Joe needed to find out.

Did vampires really care if humans were killed as long as it was all kept secret? Thoughts of all the missing people, usually young people, who went missing and were never found flew through his head. How many were killed by vampires? He needed to find out more, more about how vampires existed, where they hid, and what they did with the people they killed that the police had never found.

He suspected that the guy named Byron was the one who could give him those answers. He had to find Byron and get information about him. Maybe the guy had a website, a Facebook account, or maybe he tweeted. They had cell phones, what's to say they didn't use social media? Maybe Garrett could get some hints on the net.

The doorbell rang, which meant the pizza had arrived. *Thank God,* Garrett thought. He was starving.

He threw it on the coffee table, grabbed his laptop, and sat down to start searching while he ate. If necessary, he'd go back to Gina. He'd do whatever he had to. Somehow, he'd find this guy and get some answers to the million questions he had about vampires.

He could have the cell number traced, but that would involve letting the cops in the lab know he was looking for this guy. No, he needed to keep this to himself as long as he could. The best thing was to search on his own.

* * *

Parker and I walked along the street with our arms around each other, talking, laughing, enjoying the quiet night and the star-filled sky. We'd just fed, disposed of two more bodies and felt happy with the world.

He leaned down to lick a smear of blood from the corner of my mouth and kissed me while we walked. Not a care in the world, we relished our power, our hunger, and our freedom to live the way we chose. No one controlled us. We were masters of our world and incredibly happy together.

Footsteps approached behind us. I knew the scent. Parker knew it, too, and we weren't afraid. Why should we be afraid? This was our creator that drew near. Charles created Parker, and I joined him for love. Why should we fear Charles?

"My young ones," Charles said with delight in his voice. "How nice to find you at last."

The biggest man, or rather vampire, I'd ever seen, Charles smiled down at us, and we smiled back. "You've been very busy," he said like he was talking to two small children that had been naughty.

"We've been having a good time," Parker said, with a friendly smile.

"Yes, I imagine you have."

"Would you like to hunt with us?" I asked. I was excited by the thought. Charles could teach us so much. He knew how to torture his victims and prolong their fear and pain. He could make us skillful, horrifying hunters.

"I think not," he said as he reached up and took each of our throats in one of his hands. "You've gone too far. Everyone is looking for you, and you can't be allowed to continue."

He squeezed as he spoke and the pain radiated through my body. I was sure Parker felt the same. Was Charles going to kill us? Charles was our creator! How could he kill us? I tried to beg him to stop, but no sound would come with his hand squeezing harder and harder.

Charles looked at Parker and rotated his wrist. A strangling sound escaped from him right before I heard the crunching of bone and sinew. Parker's head fell to the side, Charles let go of him, and he fell dead to the cement.

I tried to scream, but Charles still held me. His smile was now sinister as he watched Parker fall, and I could see in his eyes how much he enjoyed killing him. I struggled, but could hardly move.

"As for you, Holly..." he said as his grip loosened slightly and he looked back at me, "I think I'll keep you a little while. We could have our own fun, couldn't we?"

His hand slid to the back of my head and he pulled me toward him, kissing me hard. The pressure forced my mouth open and his tongue explored me, plunging in and out of my mouth.

I hit him, kicked him, and tried to pull away, but he was way too strong for me to have any effect on him at all. His other arm went around my waist as he lifted me off the ground, pulling me tighter against him.

"Yes, Holly," he sighed with his mouth a fraction of an inch from mine, "keep struggling. I've dreamed about playing rough with you for quite some time."

I screamed as his lips moved to my neck. I screamed and fought him. I did not want him to bite me. I didn't want him to touch me. I fought against him as hard as I could, but with no effect as I felt his fangs plunging into my neck. So I screamed louder and longer.

I woke up with that scream echoing through the room. I was sweating and panting, fighting against the covers that wrapped tightly around me, reminding me of Charles arms.

Quinton shook me while TJ called my name.

"Holly ... Holly! Wake up. It's just a dream. Wake up!"

I realized it was Quinton and TJ with me, but I still shook uncontrollably, on the edge of panic. This was the worst nightmare, yet.

I pushed the covers away and sat up hugging my knees to my chest and dropping my head onto them. The dream was over, but the fear still held me. Charles killed Parker, and was planning on raping and torturing me.

"We heard your screams from our room, and thought someone was attacking you," TJ breathed deeply and I could hear his heart beating. I'd never seen him scared like that.

"Do you want to tell us about the dream?" Quinton asked.

I shook my head, and finally looked up at them. Just the sound of their voices chased away some of my fear. "It was Charles. I don't want to talk about it." My voice was weak and even I could hear the horror in it.

"We don't often have dreams," Quinton said. "How can we help you?"

"It's okay," I sighed. "I've had them a lot, lately. I just need a minute to get it out of my head."

We were silent for several minutes. I knew they wanted to help me somehow, but had no idea what to do. What could they do? It was all in my mind and I needed to tuck it away, try to forget another dream that outlined everything I feared could happen to Parker and me.

"It's late afternoon," TJ finally said. "We should get ready to go to the cemetery. If you're okay, we'll go get dressed and leave you to do the same."

I was in shorts and a t-shirt, but I hadn't even noticed until then that both of them were in boxers and nothing else. They ran in here half naked to save me. My screams must have been horrible. Who else had heard them?

"I'm sorry, guys. Go ahead. I'll be ready in a minute."

TJ patted my hand that was still wrapped around my knee and tried to smile. Quinton stared down at me with painful eyes. He looked like he wanted to say something, but just turned and walked out. TJ followed him, and I was alone again.

Fragments of my dream were still bouncing around in my head, but I made myself move off the bed toward the shower. It was a quick one. I didn't even bother washing my hair, but I'd woken up in such a panic, my clothes and body were covered in sweat.

Within a few minutes, I was dressed and ready to leave. No make-up, my hair pulled back in a ponytail, and wearing jeans and a plain cotton top, I wasn't looking great, but I was ready.

The knock on the door was Quinton carrying a huge bedspread. My room was one twin, theirs was two queen-sized beds and he'd taken the spread to protect me from the sun. TJ was pulling up the SUV, so I didn't have as far to go in the sunlight.

Hidden was very quiet and felt empty since all the vampires except the daytime guards were still fast asleep. The one at the door nodded when we approached. I didn't know if TJ'd given him some excuse for us to be leaving so early, or if he just didn't bother nosing into the client's business.

No one knew why we were there. They had no idea we were searching for Parker. All they knew was that we were clients passing through Columbus and keeping to ourselves. Not unusual at all in a sanctuary.

They certainly didn't know that we were the ones that had killed Donovan last night. They probably didn't even know that he was dead. It would be a while before his disappearance was noticed and anyone started to wonder.

Quinton draped the bedspread over my head and wrapped his arms around me for us to run to the waiting SUV. It was just seconds before he guided me into the back seat and made sure I was completely covered on the floor. They were both old enough to tolerate a few minutes in the sun, and the SUV windows would protect them as we drove. I wasn't. A second later, we started moving.

They said a few quiet words to each other about the route we'd take. "You okay, Holly?" TJ asked a little louder.

"I'm fine," I said.

We were all quiet for the rest of the trip. Twenty minutes later we slowed and bumped over a rutted road. Or maybe TJ was driving over the grass right up to the mausoleum.

"We're here." TJ said. "The sun's down enough for you to get up, Holly."

I pushed off the bedspread and sat up to see the mausoleum right in front of us. He *had* been driving over the grass.

"Let's go," Quinton said as he opened his front door. He reached for my door as soon as he got out, but I'd already opened it. I was more than ready.

My heart was telling me that we'd find Parker here. He'd still be asleep on the floor of the mausoleum where Charles had tortured him. He'd throw his arms around me and say that he loved me. Everything would work out. We'd take him home, and he'd get better.

But the mausoleum was empty. TJ looked around and couldn't find any hint that anyone had been there since he and Byron had left carrying Parker. The now brown stains of blood, from Byron, Charles and Parker, were still on the floor. The door that Byron broke through had been leaned across the opening, but pieces of it were still scattered across the stone flooring.

We looked around. Nothing had changed. TJ went outside and found the ladder up to the roof still leaning against the building. There was no trace of anyone sleeping there. No trace that anyone had been there at all, except for the workman that had put the door back.

More important, though, there was no lingering scent of Parker. If he'd spent any time here in the last week, we'd have smelled him right away. He hadn't been there.

I sat on the floor and cried.

Why did I keep doing this to myself? Feeling so positive, being so sure everything was going to turn out well, and being sure Parker would soon be in my arms again. And then? Disappointment.

I couldn't stand it. The emotional highs and lows, especially after that nightmare today, were just too much for me and I broke down. I sobbed uncontrollably and shook all over.

TJ and Quinton didn't know what to do. They stood there staring at me, glancing back and forth at each other. I thought of them as being experts at handling any situation, but they weren't experts at handling an emotional, crying woman.

I didn't like being that way. I just really needed something good to happen. After Mom and Dad died, I needed it more than ever. Finding Parker was the only good thing that would make me feel better.

Finally, Quinton put his arms around my shoulders and pulled me up to my feet. Whispering about how everything would work out and how we'd think of somewhere else to look, he held me gently and let me cry on his shoulder. Good old Quinton.

As my tears calmed down a little, I heard TJ call Byron. He told him that we hadn't found Parker at the cemetery but we'd keep hunting the streets. That made me feel a little better. Maybe we'd still find him on the streets somewhere.

I'd set all my hopes on the mausoleum, but that really was a long shot. We were much more likely to find him roaming the streets, or he'd find us through my scent. I'd been sidetracked by the vision of him sleeping there on that floor.

It was more likely that he'd be sleeping in the basement of some abandoned building, hiding, staying out of sight. He'd be attracted by my scent, and come to us. Yeah, we'd find him. Maybe even tonight. We just had to keep looking. *Damn*, I thought, *I'm doing it again.*

"Yeah, she's fine," I heard TJ say. "No problems." Then he said he'd be in touch, and hung up.

"Thank you, TJ," I whispered. He hadn't told Byron that I was a mental wreck. After the nightmare and breaking down like I just did, I wouldn't have blamed him if he'd told Byron that I was hopeless and they were taking me back to Rule the Night.

"We'll find him," he said patting my shoulder and walking out to the car. Did any of them really believe that? Maybe they were wishful thinking, too. Or were they just going along for my sake?

We hit the streets again after driving back to the nasty areas of town where a bloodthirsty vampire would be hunting. We walked all night and kept our eyes, ears, and noses open to any hint of Parker. But we didn't find him.

When the sky was starting to lighten with the coming dawn, we headed back to Hidden to sleep the day away. I didn't want to sleep, though. I was afraid of another nightmare and didn't want to wake up screaming again.

Chapter 6

When Holly left for Columbus with TJ and Quinton, Byron called Chris back in to work the bar, and left Anthony to handle the valet parking. He wasn't comfortable with a human out in the parking lot, and didn't want any of the customers waiting for a drink, so three bartenders solved both issues.

It was Sunday night, which was generally their slowest night, and that Sunday was even slower than usual. Crystal, Luke and Chris had time to re-stock supplies, clean the mirrors behind the bottles, and do the many other basic maintenance jobs that were always waiting.

They talked some, but avoided any mention of Parker, Holly, TJ, Quinton, or Chris's parents. They talked about the customers, what supplies they needed, and anything but what was really on all their minds. None of them could really forget about what might be going on in Columbus. Or what might be going on with Parker, wherever he was.

One of the clients, who'd been staying at Rule the Night for about four nights, sat at the bar and looked around. He'd already fed, there was no card game going on in any of the back rooms, and he was amazed at the difference one day could make. Big difference between Saturday and Sunday.

"Quiet in here tonight," he said to Chris.

"Sundays are usually slow," Chris answered.

"I thought maybe Byron would be around. Is he off somewhere?"

"No, he's in his office."

"I guess he's a pretty busy man. I haven't seen him since I've been here." He looked around the bar again before continuing. "I wouldn't want the responsibility of running a sanctuary."

"Yeah, there's a lot to take care of."

Crystal overheard the conversation, and shook her head. She knew Byron hadn't been out to the bar in over a week. He closed himself up in the office, didn't socialize with anyone, and spent most of the time staring at the paperwork he had spread across his desk.

Every time Crystal went in, he pretended he was working. She knew he wasn't, though, because it sure looked like the same set of papers on his desk to her. Nothing took that long.

She knew she had to do something. Byron was so lost in his own thoughts and guilt that she was seriously worried. The situation with Parker had completely thrown him, and she knew he was constantly worried about Sarita. She couldn't go on ignoring it and letting him deal with it himself.

He needed to talk about what he was feeling, what he was thinking, but never gave anyone the chance to get the conversation going. He sat in that office and refused to talk, then they fell into bed each morning and he made love to her almost desperately. Byron was in so much pain, and she couldn't stand to watch him suffer anymore.

The only time he'd ever relaxed and talked was when he and Holly used to go for walks. If Holly was there, she'd send them out to the dark streets to spend the time together. It would help both of them.

Well, Holly wasn't there. Crystal began to think that maybe she'd do.

"Chris," Crystal said. "I'm going back to see Byron."

"Why don't you take him some club soda?" Luke added. He'd overheard Chris's conversation, too. "You know how he is if someone's concerned about him."

Crystal smiled. "I know how he is. Thanks."

She grabbed the club soda and headed back to the office. He sat there like he usually did since Parker left. Sad, worried, lonely, guilty. It all showed on his face. He glanced up and tried to fake a smile when she walked in.

"Need something?" he asked.

"Yeah." She handed him the club soda and he sat it on his desk without drinking. "I need to spend some time with you, Byron. Will you go for a walk with me?"

"We can talk here."

She walked around his desk, pushed back his chair and sat on his lap. Her hands slid up to hold him around the back of his neck.

"We're not busy at all, and I'd like to go for a walk. Maybe we can feed together, or just talk. Come with me?"

What she really hoped was that walking through the spring night would remind him of Holly. She hoped getting him out there would encourage him to talk about both Holly and Parker.

"I'm pretty busy..."

"No, you're not," she smiled and kissed him lightly. "Come with me."

He put his arms around her waist and kissed her again. A slow, loving kiss that could have continued much longer as far as she was concerned. "I love you, babe, but I know what you're doing."

Crystal smiled at him because she knew that if he called her babe, he was ready to give in. "Then humor me. Let's go for a walk."

He smiled and almost laughed. "Okay," he sighed and gave her another squeeze.

They went out the employee door and told Max, another new guard, that they were leaving.

"I hadn't met Max before tonight," Crystal said as they crossed the parking lot. "How long has he been here?"

"A couple weeks. He's been working the day shift until recently." She knew that 'recently' really meant since TJ and Quinton left. He stopped talking for a minute and then continued. "I used to run this place with just TJ, Quinton, and you alone at the bar. Things have changed."

"Yeah, since..."

"Hey, let's go over by some of the human bars and see if we can find a couple to feed from."

Byron knew Crystal was going to mention Parker or the trouble with Charles, but he didn't want to talk about any of it, so he interrupted her. Feeding could get their minds off everything else. At least for a little while.

Since Parker had been taken by Charles, feeding and making love to Crystal were the only things that allowed him time to stop worrying. Worry about whether Parker was dead or alive, about what Charles was up to, and about his relationship with the Assembly, just to name a few. Then add helplessness as Sarita was slowly dying, and concern about Holly and Chris handling their parents' deaths.

There was so much these days to occupy his mind, and nothing he could really do about any of it. That was the worst part. He was helpless to do anything that would make any difference or solve any of the problems. Being helpless was not a situation he was used to at all.

"Okay." She knew why he interrupted her, too.

They walked in silence for several blocks and came to a place called Chips that was closing. Several people were coming out, but they were in groups and it would be hard to compel that many of them. So they waited around the corner to see if a likely couple would come their way.

Finally, they heard footsteps coming toward them, and they moved out of the business doorway where they were hiding. As they got closer, Crystal was ready to catch the guy's eyes and make him follow her into the nearby alley.

"No," Byron said quietly, squeezing her hand.

He had such a strange look on his face as he glanced over at the man with his arm around the woman. Was he angry? He didn't stop staring hatefully at the half-drunk guy until they were past them.

"Why'd we let them go? Don't you want to feed?"

He took a deep breath and closed his eyes for a second. "That was Holly's uncle. I'd like to beat the crap out of him and drain him. I hit him once after he made a disgusting remark about Holly, but I didn't really hurt him. Here he is, out drunk again right after his brother and sister-in-law were killed in that accident. I don't know if I'd be able to control myself once I punctured his throat."

"Oh," she said in a small voice. What else was there to say?

"Let's forget feeding."

"Sure, we can feed at the bar tomorrow night."

Byron put his arm around her shoulders and she wrapped hers around his waist. She let Byron lead them as they twisted and turned around many different corners. After walking silently, holding on to each other, for about ten minutes, Byron stopped.

They were in front of a school. He led her up the steps and they sat on a bench under an entryway. He looked at her with a serious expression and kept his arm wrapped around her.

"You wanted to talk. This is probably a good place to dredge up old memories."

"Why here?"

"This is where I met Holly. It was raining, and I found out later she'd run away from home. I pretended like I didn't know she was here and ducked in out of the rain. I planned on feeding from her, but she looked so young and naive that I couldn't feed.

"She was pretending to be so sure of herself and brave, and I could smell her fear, yet also felt her anger. All I could think about was how dangerous it was for such a young innocent to be out all alone in the middle of the night. She looked much younger than seventeen, then."

"What did you do?"

"I talked to her a little about nothing, then left when the rain let up, but hung around to make sure she was safe. I followed her home. The front door was wide open and her parents were both passed out in the living room.

"She pretended to be so independent, but I knew she needed someone to protect her. Well, I found her here again the next night, and she'd been crying a lot. I offered her the job helping Sarita and you know the rest."

"You're a good man, Byron," Crystal said gazing up into his eyes.

"I don't know," he said, shaking his head. "I've been thinking a lot about that night lately. If I hadn't decided to help her, none of this would have happened. Charles wouldn't have targeted Parker."

"I think you were already in Charles's sights. He knew you supported the Assembly. Eventually, he would have to face you."

"But Parker wouldn't have been involved."

"And things might have been worse. Charles had already sent Colton and Leslie here, and you were concerned about Parker. They could have gone to his room anytime and might have killed him."

"I don't know." As he spoke he just stared out into the street.

"Byron, any decision we make has an impact on the future. I think Parker and Holly belong together. He'd already noticed her at school."

"That's true."

"I think things happen the way they're supposed to happen. They'll find him. And maybe, with the strength of Holly's love, he'll find a way to beat bloodthirst. Maybe a young one can overcome it with enough help."

"Then I executed all those young ones for no reason centuries ago?"

"They didn't have someone to love them as much as Holly loves Parker. Or as much as you love him."

"I never gave them the chance to tell me who loved them."

"I know. I understand how you feel, but, at the time, you didn't know it might make a difference. We still don't know."

Byron sighed. "I long for time, Crystal. Time to understand everything that's happening and time to do something about it. I have this nagging suspicion that things are happening that I've been left out of. Things beyond me."

"Things with Charles?"

"I don't know. Something with Parker, I think, but I don't really know."

"Have you talked to Constance?"

"That's part of the problem. She doesn't say much and is evasive when I ask her anything. I think she's hiding things from me, and she's never done that. I question whether she trusts me."

"But you've done everything you can. You've told her all you know about Parker and Charles. What more can she expect?"

"I didn't kill Charles when I had the chance in that mausoleum because I wanted to get to Parker. I didn't kill Parker, because I just couldn't bear it. She expected me to do both."

"Well, she's wrong. You've destroyed Charles's closest followers and two different clubs where he tried to promote bloodthirst. You've stayed faithful to the Assembly, and she should be proud of your actions. That's why she didn't take Parker when she came to Rule the Night. It's why she hasn't punished you. She knows you're doing everything you can."

Byron pulled her against his chest and held her tight. "I love you, Crystal," he whispered against her hair. "Let's go back to our room so I can show you how much."

They started heading back toward Rule the Night, but continued talking. Once he started, Byron felt much better telling Crystal how he felt and what he'd been thinking.

"I've been so conflicted since Charles changed Parker," he said quietly while they walked arm in arm. "My loyalty has always been with the Assembly, and you know how long I've known Constance. But Parker's my son. I've only had him for ten years, but I couldn't love him any more if I'd had him for a century. Even so, I made the decision that I would hand him over to Constance."

Crystal gasped when he said that.

"But ..." he said placing his hand along her face and stroking her cheek with his thumb. "I realized that I wouldn't be able to do it. I've been talking to an old friend. He's willing to hide Parker for me. If we can just get him back, I can send Parker to Roland. He's changed and trained many young ones and will take care of him."

"That would be wonderful. Where is he? Could Holly go with him?"

"I won't tell you where he is. I don't want anyone else implicated if the Assembly should find out. TJ and Quinton don't even know about this. I need to be the only one who is answerable to the Assembly."

"And Holly?"

"My first thought was to not involve her either, but I don't think I'd be able to keep her away, and she might be able to help Parker more than any of us. I'll give her the choice."

"Byron, I'm so glad. Parker deserves every chance we can give him."

"You think I've made the right decision? Am I being a hypocrite by not turning him in?"

"No. Parker didn't choose bloodthirst. His change was an attack against you."

Byron's arms tightened around her shoulders. He couldn't believe how much better he felt getting it off his chest. She was right, he needed to talk. Crystal was usually right. How had he lived so long without her?

They got back to Rule the Night, asked the guards if there had been any problems, and went directly downstairs to the suite they shared. The bar was closed, and the daytime guards would be going on duty.

Byron closed the door behind them, and pulled Crystal into his arms to kiss her. His love for her overwhelmed him and he knew he'd be lost without her. How would he survive the situation with Parker if she wasn't here to hold him?

His lips moved down to her neck and he bit her, pulling her blood into his throat. She moaned and pressed her body tighter against his, letting her hands roam over his muscular body.

He picked her up without moving his lips from her throat and laid her on the bed, covering her body with his.

* * *

Hunger! It burned through every part of him, creating pain in both his body and mind. Every time he awoke, it was the same. No, it was worse. Hunger, darkness, silence. The need to feed was overwhelming and the pain of not feeding for so long threatened to destroy him.

Why were they doing this to him? Were they going to let him wallow in his pain until he died? Would they let him slowly starve to death? That's what if felt like.

Whoever had him was starving him to death. It must be Charles. Who else could be so cruel, so good at inflicting pain? Who else had reason to abandon him in this dark, little room and not feed him?

How long had it been since he'd been thrown into the back of that van? He'd thought he'd be taken directly to Charles. Thought that it would all be over that night because they hadn't even searched him, so he still had the gun.

He'd had visions of pulling the gun before Charles had a chance to say anything, and he'd pump one bullet after another into Charles's brain.

Parker knew they'd driven for hours and hours. Maybe it'd even been days. He couldn't remember it clearly anymore. But, when they finally stopped, someone had put him to sleep. He didn't know who or how, but he'd lost consciousness and woken up in this dark room.

This was probably the third time he'd woken up and each time the hunger and pain got worse. Each time, cold eyes starred at him from the darkness, said nothing, but made Parker sleep again.

Someone seemed to be moving close by. The darkness was complete, so he couldn't see anyone, but he heard the soft rustle of clothing and the scent gave them away. A scent he thought he should know, but couldn't place. Maybe someone had come to save him.

"Help me! Please, help me!" he whispered.

"Parker," a feminine voice spoke so close to him, but he still couldn't see a thing. "Good to see you awake."

"I have to feed. It hurts so bad." His voice was course with the pain of such deep, overwhelming hunger.

"I know it hurts, but we can't feed you, yet."

"Then tell Charles to just kill me and get it over with. Don't let me starve to death."

"Charles isn't here, Parker. This is Constance."

"Constance?" He knew she told the truth. That's why the scent was familiar. But why was she here? Was she working with Charles?

"I know it hurts, but it's the only thing that might work."

"Why are you doing this to me?"

He had thought that Constance would kill him quickly and painlessly. Instead, she was slowly starving him to death. Why was she torturing him like this?

"We're trying to save you. It's a new theory that Bartholomew has believed might work for many years, but we never had anyone to try it. We have to let you starve to get Charles's blood out of your system. That should take you back as close to human as possible. Then we'll feed you correctly. Essentially, it should be like changing you again."

"Why's it hurt so bad?"

"Your body has used up all the human blood that you ingested. Now, it's using Charles's blood that he gave you when you were changed. Your body is pulling that blood from your muscles and organs. I'm so sorry it's causing so much pain."

"How long have I been here?"

"Almost a week, but we had to keep you unconscious. You were ranting and screaming, and we couldn't take the chance of you hurting yourself, or of anyone hearing you. We suspect that we have a spy in the Assembly."

"Where's Byron? Where's Holly?"

"At Rule the Night. Besides me, the only one that knows you're here is Bartholomew."

"Then they think I'm dead."

"I'm sorry, Parker, but it's the only way we could do it. There are those who expect me to forgive your bloodthirst because of my long friendship with Byron. I couldn't take the chance of anyone knowing you're here until we know if the process works. You could still die."

"How long will I be here?"

"We don't know. Charles's blood is very strong, but once it's out of your system, we think you'll lose consciousness.

That's when we'll start feeding you. It should be very much like when a human is changed."

"Please, let Holly know I'm here."

"Oh, Parker, I can't do that. Trying to save you is against my own laws. If we fail, no one can ever know we even tried. If we succeed, then it's salvation for anyone whose change doesn't work. That still happens, and we hate that we have to execute those young ones."

"Byron warned me about that when he changed Holly."

"It's true. Sometimes a new vampire can't control it, and they're very much like you. They don't choose bloodthirst, but they can't stop killing. This treatment might be able to save them."

"What should I do?"

"Nothing," she said quietly. "Just rest and try to sleep as much as possible."

"I can't sleep. The pain keeps waking me up."

"That's why we made you sleep, but hopefully it won't be much more than another few days."

"That long?" Parker didn't know if he could stand it another few minutes, let alone days.

"I'm afraid so. A vampire starves very slowly."

"Will it work?"

"We don't know. We hope so."

"Can you put me back to sleep?"

"Yes, but the pain may wake you again."

"Try it. Why is it so dark? Am I blind?"

"I'm sorry. This is the oldest part of the building, kind of a sub-basement. There's no electricity, but I guess I could leave you a candle."

"That'd be good. It's so dark."

"I'll be right back."

Constance left Parker laying there trying to see anything in the darkness. Vampires could see with the faintest amount of light, and he suspected that Constance could see him. Was he losing some vampire senses and characteristics, or was it that Constance was so much stronger than he? Either way didn't matter. He just needed to be able to see something.

The whole thing was insane. Parker wasn't sure if he was really here or dreaming. Light might help give him a sense of reality. Might help him endure through the pain until they could feed him.

Trying to get past the pain, he started thinking about what Constance was doing. She was endangering her own reputation to help him get over bloodthirst. If anyone found out about this, some would want her recalled from the Assembly. That's exactly what Charles would want. He'd want her destroyed and the Assembly to go down with her.

Parker'd been reconciled with the idea of dying. In fact he'd been sure that he'd be dead in a matter of hours once he faced Charles. But this was a whole different thing. Even with all the pain and hunger, it was a glimmer of hope.

Maybe he'd be able to walk into Rule the Night with Constance and show them that he lived. Show them that he'd found control. Maybe he did have a chance.

He'd tried to be so brave when planning to face Charles, but Parker did not want to die. He wanted this to work. He wanted to spend a long life with Holly like they'd planned. He wanted Byron to be proud of him.

Hope. He finally had something that could give him some hope.

"I found one." Constance said as she came back through the door.

Parker heard a shuffling noise beside him, saw a flash of bright light like the striking of a match, and a warm light spread through the room.

"Thank you," Parker said. "That's much better."

Now he could see Constance standing next to him with a warm, but concerned, smile on her face. Seeing her made everything seem more real. He'd only met her once before, but somehow she felt like an old friend. He trusted her, and she was helping him.

"You'll have light if you wake. Now look into my eyes, and I'll put you to sleep," she said quietly.

In a moment Parker slept. Constance looked down at him wishing she could do more to keep him from suffering, but knew she couldn't. He had to bear the pain and discomfort until they knew whether it would work.

She also wished she could tell Byron where Parker was and what she was trying, but that would be taking way too much of a chance. Better that they thought he was already dead than to get false hope. That kind of hope would just hurt them more if she had to tell them that Parker had to be executed after all.

She patted his shoulder and left to talk to Bartholomew.

Chapter 7

I didn't remember any dreams that day after we searched for Parker in the mausoleum and on the streets of Columbus. I didn't think I'd sleep much, but must have been exhausted. I'd slept until it was almost dark.

Quinton called right after I finished my shower. Time to get going on our search, so I told them to come on over while I finished drying my hair.

He got there without TJ, who'd gone up to the bar to see if there was any word about Donovan. I think he was still concerned a little that someone would find out he was dead and how he died.

I guess I should say that he was concerned Charles would find out he killed Donovan. TJ'd already told Byron, who probably told Constance. TJ wanted Charles to wonder what happened, and start looking for him. Anything that would occupy Charles or possibly bring him out into the open would be great to TJ.

Of course, Quinton would love for Charles to show himself in Columbus, too. He was determined to be the one to kill him, and he made sure everyone knew it. Charles had gotten away from him in Chicago, and Quinton was not going to let him get away again. How did Charles keep escaping when so many wanted him dead?

I sat cross-legged on the edge of the bed, while Quinton sat in my one chair, and we waited for TJ.

"How long are we going to keep looking?" I asked after sitting in silence for a while. I was gazing down at my hands and spoke very quietly. I'd wanted to ask the question, but was kind of afraid of the answer.

"I don't know," Quinton answered as quietly as I'd asked. "I'm starting to think he's not here or in Chicago. TJ and I searched Chicago pretty thoroughly and didn't find any sign of him or Charles."

I looked up at him. "Where could he be?"

"He was with Charles quite a while. Maybe he overheard something and knows where Charles was planning on going. He could be almost anywhere."

"I know, but I can't give up, yet. I know you and TJ searched Chicago, but couldn't we go back? Maybe Parker will detect my scent and come to me."

"I haven't given up, either, Holly. TJ will probably go along with returning to Chicago."

"And you know when Crystal and I ran into Noel at Easton? I've been thinking that maybe Charles has a place near there. We've been looking downtown, and Parker could be out near Easton looking for Charles."

Quinton looked at me like he was thinking. "I'd forgotten that. We could check it out tonight. You're good, Holly," he grinned.

"I spend a lot of time thinking about it," I shrugged.

TJ got back without getting any information about Donovan, and we started out to begin searching. He thought going to the Easton area was a good idea, so we headed east.

In my heart, I knew this was a long shot and suspected that they were going along just to make me feel like we were accomplishing something. It was sweet, but I couldn't resist thinking we might find him. Who knew? He could be around Easton looking for Charles's hiding place. But then, he could be anywhere.

* * *

Samuel and Dawson both stood up when Charles walked into the old-fashioned sitting room. Samuel wouldn't be here if he didn't have news, so Constance must have made some decision about Parker.

Charles had felt so good after feeding, but this had the possibility of being very bad news. He wanted time to remember the taste and feel of that young woman that he bled. He wanted a few minutes away from thinking about his plans and schemes, and how none of those plans had been working out.

He was tired of failing. Especially tired of that failure being a result of Byron destroying everything he tried to accomplish, but the last thing he'd do is let anyone else see his fatigue.

"What has Constance decided?" Charles asked without greeting them.

"It's ... not clear," Samuel answered hesitantly.

Charles eyes narrowed and his lips scowled. He couldn't believe Samuel had enough nerve to come here to tell him Constance hadn't yet made a decision. But then, maybe her hesitation could be useful. Useful in getting her thrown off the Assembly.

"Explain," he said coldly.

"She and Bartholomew went to Rule the Night to see Byron's son. They came back and only said that they were still investigating. That was over a week ago. I couldn't get away until now."

"A week?" Charles thought he might explode.

"But there's something going on. I've heard that TJ and Quinton have been away from Rule the Night since Constance visited, and Constance and Bartholomew are being very secretive. It only makes sense that Parker might have escaped, and they are hiding it from the rest of the Assembly while TJ and Quinton have a chance to search for him."

"What makes you think that?"

"I heard there's been some murders in Columbus. It must be Parker. Who else would kill women and leave the bodies to be found? I figure he's completely lost to bloodthirst, and TJ and Quinton have been sent to stop him."

Charles wanted to kill Samuel, but held himself in check. Samuel was his only spy on the Assembly. The only one who kept tabs on what Constance was doing. For now, he needed to live, but the day would come. Someday, Charles would gladly kill him for his stupidity.

"It is *not* Parker killing in Columbus," Charles voice was frigid.

"How do you know ..."

"Shut up! *I know!*" Charles rubbed his hand over his face. "Get back to the Assembly and see if you can manage to keep an eye on Constance and Bartholomew. I want their every move accounted for. I need to *know* what they're doing."

By the time he finished speaking, he was shouting. He felt like everyone working for him was unbelievably stupid. Armand had been the only one who really understood the ultimate goal, and the only one who had the intelligence to figure out other's emotions and motivation.

That stupid little bitch had caused Armand's death. She would pay. She would pay with pain. Long-term, relentless pain. He'd make Holly beg to die before he finished with her.

"But, Charles ..."

"Leave," was all Charles said as he waved a hand dismissing him and started walking toward the basement. He wanted to snap both of their necks.

He had to get in touch with Donovan. Maybe there had been some deaths that couldn't be accounted for. Maybe Parker *was* out there killing, in which case, Donovan needed to find him.

But Donovan's phone went straight to voicemail. Where could he be? There was no excuse for having his phone turned off, and Donovan was better than that. He wouldn't let himself be out of touch. Had something happened to Donovan?

Something was going on. Charles felt it in his soul, and he had no idea what it could be. Donovan had reported in after every draining, and things were going well. Now he doesn't call and his phone is off.

Charles couldn't go to Columbus himself to find Donovan. He was too recognizable, and there were several at that sanctuary that would turn him in to the Assembly. He'd have to send Dawson. Surely, Dawson could handle going to a sanctuary and asking for one of the clients.

Dawson had done nothing but cringe next to the hearth like he wanted to crawl up inside it the whole time Charles talked to Samuel. The man was too meek to be effective, but he should be able to handle that simple of a task.

Charles called him down to the basement to tell him to get to Columbus tonight. He'd probably be glad to get away from Charles for as long as it took him to find Donovan. *Why am I surrounded by such idiots?*

"Do not come back here without finding him. He needs to call me. Do you understand?"

"Of course, Charles," Dawson said.

"It will be close to dawn before you get there, so don't waste any time. Have him contact me before he sleeps. I'll be waiting for his call."

"I understand," Dawson said. "He'll call before dawn."

Dawson left immediately, but Charles had other things to do. Samuel was right that it was very unusual for TJ and Quinton to be away from Rule the Night without good reason. That reason could very well be that they were looking for Parker, and Charles needed to find out if Parker was still with Byron.

The simplest, most direct thing would be to call Byron and see if he could goad him into giving something away. It could even be fun to torment him, let him believe that Charles knew something about Parker's situation. If there *was* a situation with Parker. This could be very entertaining.

It wasn't very often that Byron's cell phone rang with an unknown number showing on the display. A little part of him hoped it could be Parker. Maybe he got a phone somewhere. He'd left his sitting on the desk in his room which, Byron knew, was a clear message that he didn't want to be contacted or found.

"Yes," Byron answered with anticipation in his voice that he couldn't hide.

"Hello, old friend."   Charles's voice was quiet and intentionally held a sinister intent that he was sure Byron would hear.

"What do you want?" Byron said. No more anticipation. His voice showed his fear, and caused Charles to smile. Fear was an excellent emotion in anyone, but especially Byron.

"Want? Nothing. I have everything I want." Charles said lightly like he had no care in the world. He thought he'd take a chance. If Parker was gone and they were looking for him, Byron would now believe that Charles had him.

Byron dropped his head to his hand and squeezed his temples. His worst fear had happened. Charles was calling to let him know he had Parker. "Is he still alive?" Byron practically whispered.

Charles laughed out loud and didn't care that Byron heard it. He'd guessed right. Parker was gone and Byron had no idea where he was. This was too perfect. "I'd like to see you, Byron," Charles said with a friendly voice and completely avoided Byron's question. The words actually meant, *I'd like to kill you, Byron.*

Byron's rage flared. It radiated through him like a bomb exploding in slow motion. "Would I be coming to rescue him again, or to destroy you for killing him?" Byron finally spat out at Charles. "Where are you?" he practically shouted.

Charles smiled to himself, having a wonderful time playing this little game with Byron. Time, though, to end the game. He suddenly saw his chance to accomplish one of his primary goals. Killing Byron. "How can I trust that you'd come alone?" he asked.

"Trust? There is no such thing between us," Byron spat out. "But, if you want me, you'll have to tell me where you are."

"Ah, there you've got me, Byron. You are so right. And I do want you." For the first time in the whole conversation, Charles was now speaking truthfully. "I want you dead. You, along with everyone you care about. Although, Parker's bloodthirst is worse than his death, isn't it?"

"Where are you?" Byron asked again coldly. No emotion showed in his voice now. He was beyond emotion. Byron was now sure Charles had Parker, and he would not rest until Charles was dead.

Charles thought for a second and knew that he wasn't ready to face Byron. He'd bring an army with him, and Charles needed time to put a plan together. And time to find Parker. A vision flashed through his mind of Byron watching helplessly as Parker was tortured and killed, and that brought a smile to his face.

"Oh, I'm in Chicago, but you won't find me. I'll call back to set up a meeting place," Charles said.

"Charles!" Byron bellowed as Charles hung up. But he was gone.

Byron shook from head to toe. His rage made him want to start destroying something, and he almost threw his phone against the wall. But he needed that phone for Charles's return call, and he had to take several minutes to get himself under control and stop the shaking.

He had things to do. Lorna first, then call TJ and Quinton.

TJ answered on the first ring.

"Lorna, Luke and Chris have just left for Columbus. You need to leave for Chicago as soon as they get there, and Holly needs to come back to Adelle with Chris. Take Lorna and Luke with you."

"Have you heard something?" TJ asked.

"Charles called me. Don't upset Holly unnecessarily, but I think he has Parker, or might have already killed him. He's in Chicago, but I don't know where. We need to find him. I'll join you there by morning."

"We'll get back to the sanctuary and wait for Lorna."

The conversation was over. Any other plans would come when they met Byron in Chicago. Holly and Quinton had been hanging on his every word, and TJ would have to tell them. Quinton was no problem, but he knew Holly wouldn't like it.

She didn't. She argued all the way back to Hidden, and continued while they were in her room as she packed her things.

"I still say that I should go with you," Holly said trying to sound very reasonable. "Charles has wanted to get his hands on me since we destroyed his plans at Nibble, and he'd come out of hiding to get me."

"That's exactly why you can't go," Quinton said.

"But you'll be there! All of you! He won't be able to hurt me, and I have to know how Parker is. I have to be there!"

"No matter what you want, you will NOT be in Chicago!" Quinton shouted. "I will not allow it. You are to go back to Rule the Night with Chris, and this argument is ended."

"Oh, you think so?" Holly shouted back. "I am an adult who is capable of making my own decisions. Who do you think you are to tell me what to do?"

"You are a child who doesn't know how to follow orders!"

"I don't believe you! You are so determined to follow Byron's orders, you won't even listen to reason."

"And you ..."

"Stop it! Both of you!" TJ shouted over their voices. "Quinton, go start packing. Now!"

Quinton stormed out of the room, and TJ turned to Holly. He took a deep breath. He knew he had to speak very carefully to calm her down, and calm down himself. "The five of us going to Chicago, are the strongest and most able to defeat Charles. You are too young, Holly. If you're there, we'll need to protect you instead of attacking him. I'm sorry, but you'll slow us down, and make us less effective."

"But ..." Holly tried to interrupt.

"Listen to me." He took both her shoulders and looked into her eyes, speaking calmly. "You are a very resourceful, determined young woman, but you're not trained in battle. The rest of us are. I know you love Parker, and he loves you. I know you want to help. But we have the best chance of defeating Charles if you aren't there. The best chance of saving Parker."

Holly started to cry. "I'll go crazy wondering what's happening."

"I know you will. But I promise you that we'll call as soon as we know anything. I will personally keep you informed. If we find out anything about Parker, I will call you."

"Promise?"

"Yes. I promise. Even if Byron doesn't want me to."

"Okay," she said quietly. Then she got a very determined look in her eyes. "I'll go home with Chris, but you'd better call me! I'll never forgive you if you don't."

TJ hugged her as the tears continued to slowly run down her cheeks, and he held her for a few minutes, letting her cry on his chest. This whole situation was tearing them all apart inside, and needed to be resolved one way or another.

TJ closed his eyes and sighed deeply while she cried. He couldn't wait to get his hands on Charles and knew he wasn't alone in those feelings. They all wanted Charles dead. If only they knew for sure Parker was still alive.

Chapter 8

Parker woke again in darkness. The candle had gone out, so he must have slept for hours. At least the pain had finally calmed down some, but not the hunger. He was so hungry.

Not the kind of undemanding hunger that he'd experienced when he was feeding every night at Rule the Night. Then he hadn't really felt it until he smelled the woman that was led into his room.

This was an unbelievably deep hunger, a hunger that he felt through his whole body. Every bone, every muscle, every organ felt the pangs of it, and it was growing. He hadn't even been so hungry when Charles changed him.

He jerked out of the bed and reached across the room toward where the candle should be sitting on the little table. He found the table, moved his hand up to the candlestick, but found only small remnants of wax. The candle hadn't gone out, it had burned itself out.

He couldn't stand going back to the bed, so he felt his way along the wall with one hand and paced. The only furniture in the room was his bed and the small table, so it wasn't very hard to move around in the dark. The problem was that the room was too small.

Parker wanted to move, to run. To run out into the night and find someone to feed him. He needed to feed or he was going to die. Each time he woke up, the hunger got worse. It was all he could think about, all he could understand, all he wanted.

When he came to the door after following the wall around the room, he decided he'd take care of it himself. All he had to do was find a way out of this place, find some human roaming the streets, and he'd be able to feed.

The door was locked, and he was too weak to break through it. He tried ramming his shoulder against it and tried kicking it. Nothing even budged that door. He knew he wasn't anywhere near strong enough to get through and slamming against it just made him weaker, so he continued following the wall and pacing around the room.

He rubbed his face in his hands and pushed his hair back. He felt the beard stubble on his cheeks, but otherwise, his skin felt dry and tight. His whole body felt tight. He was starving.

Naked except for his boxers, he was so thin, he felt like they might fall off. And so weak. Three turns around the tiny room, and he was tired enough to go back and fall on the bed. He was suddenly so tired he couldn't stay up on his feet anymore, yet every nerve ending on his skin felt charged.

It was a tingling. No, a buzzing, like a million tiny electrical charges moving through him. He realized it wasn't just his skin. His whole body, inside and out, felt the stings. It was the hunger tormenting him. It wanted to be fed.

How long would this go on? He needed to sleep, he needed to feed, and he needed the prickling feeling through him to go away. Why wouldn't Constance come help him? How long could he stand this?

The dark, the loneliness, the weakness, and the dread of dying there in the empty room, were all driving him crazy. He thrashed on the bed and tried again to get up.

"Constance!" he cried out into the dark, but he knew his voice was too weak to get through that door. He yelled again, anyway. "Constance!"

He wanted to get out of there. He wanted to kill Charles. He wanted to hold Holly. He wanted to see Byron. But he couldn't get up, even though his mind wanted nothing more than to break through the door and run out to get what he wanted. He was suddenly too weak to even try getting up.

He felt confused. Why was he trapped in that room? Why had he gotten so weak and tired? His thoughts spun around. He was confused and his memories were unclear, but all thoughts kept landing on the one thing he wanted the most.

More than escaping this crazy place, more than feeding, he wanted Holly. He wanted to see her, to hold her, to kiss her. Where was Holly?

"Holly?" he called with as much strength as his destroyed body could push through his voice. "Where are you, Holly?" he practically whispered.

It was hard to concentrate and hard to even think. He felt like he was dying. No, he knew he was dying. He lay stretched out on that strange bed in that tiny room and started to lose consciousness. His last thought was that, yeah, this was it. He was dying now.

A while later, Constance came in with a new candle to check on him. She tried to wake him, but got no reaction at all. She called Bartholomew.

"It's time to feed him," Bartholomew said looking down at Parker.

"I pray this works," Constance answered. "We've left him here alone and suffering for so long. I keep thinking that his death could have been much faster and easier for him."

"Hopefully, we can return him to Byron. We've taken a chance with him, but it will be worth it if it works."

"Open his lips," Constance said quietly as she moved her wrist to her mouth and bit into her own flesh. Blood began to flow, and she turned it to drip into Parker's mouth.

It pooled on the back of his tongue, and finally, they saw him swallow. That was enough for now. They'd leave him unconscious, giving him barely enough blood to survive. They would bring him back to consciousness slowly. Turn him back into a vampire very slowly, as it should have been done the first time. Within a couple days, he should be conscious and ready to feed from a human donor.

Only a few more days, but she was afraid that he might not survive them. He was so thin and pale, he looked like he was already dead. This had to work. They'd tried for so long to save young ones like Parker. It had to work.

It had been a long time since she'd changed a human, but she knew very well how it would go. The first feeding would be a struggle. He'd fight them and have to be pulled off the human wrist. They'd watch carefully to see how long he struggled.

Then the second human. He'd feed at her neck, and have to find the strength and determination to quit feeding on his own. Then, they'd know.

They'd know if he could control his feeding, or if they'd wasted their time. If he couldn't feed properly, if he was still lost to bloodthirst, they'd have to execute him. Once his fate was decided, then she'd call Byron.

* * *

It seemed no time at all before Lorna, Luke, and Chris arrived at Hidden. After a moment's greeting, Luke and Lorna climbed in the SUV and left with TJ and Quinton, while Chris and I started for Adelle. I couldn't stop thinking about what they may face in Chicago.

I still wanted to be there, but felt like I really would be a hindrance to them. I'd probably just get in the way, because TJ was right about them having to concentrate on protecting me. I was no warrior. I just wanted so desperately to be there.

I wished I was old enough and strong enough to face Charles, but I wasn't. Nothing I could do about that. Their best chance of catching Charles, forcing him to tell them where Parker was, was without me. That's why I was going back to Adelle with Chris. Byron needed his best chance to succeed. We all needed that chance.

"I thought we might have to fight you to get you back to Rule the Night," Chris said after we'd driven for about ten minutes. We hadn't said much before that, but I sure did hug him when they showed up. I'd missed Chris.

"I fought with TJ and Quinton," I said quietly. "TJ convinced me that Byron was right, and I needed to go back with you."

"I'm glad," he answered. "The whole thing scares me, and after the time we had at Charles's secret club, I didn't want you in that kind of situation again. Truthfully, I didn't want to be there either."

"You kinda' got thrown into all this. You didn't even know about vampires until we let you walk into that place with Lorna. That scared the crap out of me, too."

"Lorna and I have been talking about that. I'm the weak human element in all this. At least as long as I'm still human." Chris looked at me with a question in his eyes.

"She wants to change you?" My voice was still quiet, but I know Chris heard the distress in it. I really didn't think I liked the idea of Chris being a vampire.

"No," he shook his head, "I asked her to change me."

"What did she say?"

"She said she wouldn't do it," he shrugged. "I guess the older the vampire, the more sure you are that it'll work. She's old, but has never changed anyone, and she's afraid she's not strong enough, and couldn't stand to come that close to draining me."

"But?" I knew there was more he wanted to say.

"I talked to Byron yesterday, and he said he would do it. But I guess it takes a while, and he wouldn't be able to give me the time until after things were settled with Parker."

My eyes had grown bigger as he talked. How did I feel about Chris being a vampire? I was happy being a vampire. The other vampires in my life were great. But ...

"Tell me what you're thinking, Holly," Chris said. "I need to know how you feel about it."

"I'm thinking that I don't know how I feel. I didn't have the choice, and you know Parker talked Byron into changing me so I wouldn't die. Since then, I've been really happy in this life. I still don't like how easily we kill each other, and that some kill humans. I don't much like the killing at all. But I think that will be behind us once Charles is dead. And ... hell, a lot of humans kill each other, too."

Chris didn't say anything while I rambled on.

"Parker was always asking Byron to change him, but that might have been different if we'd been together and both human. I always wanted kids, too. I know Parker and I would have been so much better at raising kids than Mom and Dad were."

"You can say that again."

"I think," I hesitated a little because I wanted to get my words right. "I think, if you're doing this for Lorna, then you shouldn't do it. If it's because you want it for you, rather Lorna was in the picture or not, then it's okay."

"You'd be for it?" Chris asked.

"No. I can't say I'm for it. But I won't be against it. It's your decision, but don't hurry into it. Give yourself time to really think it through and be sure."

"I think I am sure. I mean, truthfully, I don't have much as a human. No education, I'd never get much of a job," he shrugged and hesitated. "Little sis, I see me starting out like Dad did. I'm afraid I'll end up drinking myself to death like him. This is a way for me to make something of myself. I'd love to be a guard like Lorna, or maybe someday run a club like Byron."

"You could go back to school. There's so much online now, and I know Byron would help you."

"Nah, school was never my thing," he said shaking his head. "I know you liked it, but I suffered every day in school."

"You really hated it, didn't you?"

"Yeah. And besides everything else, there *is* Lorna. We're in love, Holly. Like you and Parker." He grinned at me before saying anything else. "I asked her to marry me."

"You did?"

"But she's too old. You know, no legal identification and stuff, so we couldn't get a license for a legal marriage. We may do our own ceremony, though. Maybe after I'm changed."

"Parker and I planned on a legal marriage, but ..." I couldn't finish that thought. It just hurt too much to consider the possibilities.

Chris looked over at me and saw the tear roll down my cheek. He squeezed my hand and didn't let go of it.

"Byron will bring him back." Chris had such conviction in his voice.

"I know," I said, trying to smile. Trying to be as sure as Chris sounded.

We were quiet for quite a while, both lost in our own thoughts. I watched the lights of other traffic, buildings just off the road, and the little, blinking lights on those cell towers that are all over the place as we moved along the road.

I thought about never again seeing any of the world's scenery in the light of day. It would be a century before I could tolerate more than a few minutes of sunlight, but I was getting to know the stars much better.

"I've thought about the things I miss," I finally said, continuing our conversation. "Mainly the sunshine. I always loved the heat of the sun and the way it would make shadow patterns through the trees. And the glare of it at the pool."

"Yeah, I've liked those things, too," Chris said quietly.

"But I guess I'll miss people the most. I mean, I've thought about watching the people I care about grow old and die. Especially you. Now that Mom and Dad are gone, I'd love to know I wouldn't watch you grow old and die. But I sure don't want you to become a vampire for me.

"It bothered me a lot that, once it was getting obvious that I wasn't getting any older, I'd have to move away to hide it from you. I wouldn't be able to ever see you again. So, I'm really glad I don't have to worry about that since you know what I am."

"I didn't think about moving away and other people getting old," Chris whispered like he was really thinking about it. "But, if I'm a vampire, we'll always have each other. Lorna says there aren't many vampires around with real family from when they were human."

"I bet there aren't. But, Chris, I don't want to convince you either way. I just want you to make sure you think through every part of it. Living on and on through the centuries sounds great, but sometimes I think it could have its drawbacks. Sometimes I think Byron gets tired. You know, tired of the same battles he's been fighting forever. You've got plenty of time to decide. You're only twenty-one and won't be old for quite a while."

Chris gave me one of those grunt laughs. "Lorna's twenty-four. At least she was twenty-four when she was changed. She said I could wait until I'm her age. I'm sure she loves me and wants me around, but I think she's a little afraid of the change."

"Most vampires were changed like me. Attacked and didn't have a choice. I think sometimes they question what they would have chosen. You know, Quinton asked to be changed, maybe you should talk to him."

"He did? That's a good idea. Quinton will be straight with me."

"He's a good guy." I laughed a little. "Except for the fight we had a while ago about me going to Chicago with them. He made me mad as hell."

"What'd he say?"

"That I was a child who couldn't follow orders. He said he wouldn't allow it, like he was in charge or something."

"I'm not surprised," Chris smiled.

"Yeah, he's all about following orders. That military training, you know."

"Not that," Chris shook his head a little. "I think he likes you ... a lot."

"What?"

"Lorna thinks so, too. She thinks he's in love with you."

"Are you kidding? He's never said anything, or done anything ..."

"No, he wouldn't. He knows how you and Parker are. It's not like he'd try to take you away from Parker."

"What should I do? Should I talk to him?"

"Oh, hell no! He'd be embarrassed to death. He'd probably think he had to leave Rule the Night or something."

"But wouldn't he feel better if ..."

"No, no, no!" He shook his head with every word. "You've gotta' keep acting normal like you don't know. I shouldn't have told you. He'd die if he thought you knew."

"Okay, I won't say anything. But I'm glad you told me."

"Yeah, well, pretend I didn't."

That certainly explained the look he gave me when I thought he wanted to kiss me. He did want to. In that moment, I kind of wanted to kiss him, too. But he could never replace Parker. Parker was all I wanted, and all I'd ever want.

We pulled into the employee garage at Rule the Night, and I glanced over to where Parker's bug used to be parked. Gone. Who knew where it was?

Going through the family entrance made me think about that first night that Parker'd brought me into the private areas. How much things had changed. I felt like that was a different little girl back then. Not me at all.

We dumped my stuff in my room and went up to find Crystal who was once more left in charge. She and Anthony were working the bar and were as busy as most nights had gotten lately. She was thrilled to see us.

I didn't know Anthony very well, but he seemed really relieved that we'd come back, too. Maybe they all expected we might secretly drive to Chicago on our own. I guess our prior performance at Nibble influenced that idea.

Chris and I joined Crystal behind the bar, sending Anthony to his usual spot at the front door to help out there. It was nice to be at work because it gave me the chance to forget about Chicago. But, at the same time, I couldn't stop thinking about it for more than a few seconds at a time.

Thoughts of Byron, who had left for Chicago moments after Lorna, Luke and Chris left Adelle to go to Columbus, buzzed through my head. All of them were speeding through the night trying to get to Chicago before dawn.

Charles would be ready for them. He wouldn't expect Byron to come alone, and he wouldn't wait alone. Byron and Charles both wanted the same thing. Each one wanted to kill the other.

All I could hope was that TJ would keep his word and call me as soon as they knew anything. Hopefully, that would be good news and not the thing I dreaded.

Chapter 9

Joe Garrett had been searching for any hint of information about that guy named Byron for a couple of days. He'd immediately found Lord Byron, the 18th century English poet. In fact, he'd found that guy over and over again.

There were towns called Byron all over the U.S. There were music groups, corporations, and individual people, and none of them gave any indication of being associated with the Byron he was looking for.

But Garrett waded through the thousands of hits on the internet, any police records, and even thought to look on some of the history sites. Without a last name, though, he couldn't get anywhere.

As time went on with him working every day and searching the net every night, and without him getting any useful information, he at least had the satisfaction that there weren't any more murders. At least none of the bloodless, vampire variety. There was one guy shot and killed outside a bar, but that was the usual variety, and they already had the shooter in custody.

But there was a pile of paperwork from the murders, and the investigation still went on. Joe was the only one that knew the murderer, the vampire, had been killed and he sure couldn't tell anyone.

So, at work, he pretended to be intent on solving those murders just like all the other detectives and officers were. Eventually things would quiet down and those murder files would go into cold cases. He wondered, though, if Jennings would ever give up trying to solve them.

How had Byron done it so quickly and easily? He'd been really sure they had the guy, and he must have been right. So, either Byron was involved in the killings, or he could be a great asset.

That was the main thing Garrett needed to figure out. Was Byron some great avenger of people killed by vampires, or was he a killer himself? If he was one of the good guys, then his help could be invaluable.

If he was the one killing those women, he could have just moved on to another town and could still be killing. If that was the case, they'd eventually hear about it. Before that happened, Garrett had to know more about Byron. He might eventually have to go after him.

He couldn't just blindly trust that Byron had found and killed the murderer in a few hours. It was more likely that Byron had done the killings himself, knew they were looking for him, and moved on.

Garrett wracked his brain trying to think of a different search. He thought through every word Gina had said about Byron, and what Byron had said to him on the phone, but didn't come up with anything. Anything, except that Gina talked about vampires staying at sanctuaries.

It sounded like they were bars, or clubs, like La Sang Rouge and were all over the country. Maybe they were on the web. Did they have websites? The only one Garrett knew about was La Sang Rouge, so he started searching there.

They had a website. He read through the whole thing, and didn't find anything that would indicate that it had anything to do with vampires, which didn't surprise him at all. They wouldn't exactly announce themselves as a vampire bar.

He also, though, didn't find anything about staying there. Gina said vampires stayed, sometimes for quite a while, at the sanctuaries. He guessed that humans weren't welcome overnight. How would a vampire find one in a new area? Did they have to know them all? That didn't make sense.

Going back to the homepage, he looked for anything that would give him a hint about finding another sanctuary. There, at the very bottom of the page, with the website creator information that most people ignored, was the word *Others*.

From its position, it looked at first like it would be other websites by the same designer, but maybe it was something else. One click showed Joe that it was something else entirely.

That little word was a link to another page that listed states. Clicking on Ohio, Garrett found a list of cities. *God*, he thought, *there are three sanctuaries just in Ohio.* He cringed thinking about how many might be in other states. How many vampires would that be?

They were listed alphabetically, so Garrett figured he might as well start at the top. He clicked on the link for Adelle, Ohio. Rule the Night. Proprietor, Byron.

It was so easy once he thought to search sanctuaries, he couldn't believe he'd just found him. This had to be him. Adelle was a smaller city only an hour or so from Columbus, and it would make sense that Byron could quickly send someone to Columbus to take care of whoever was murdering those women. He might have even gone himself.

He wrote down the address and phone number and sat there staring at the screen, thinking about how to proceed. He could call and ask for Byron, but that wouldn't get him anywhere.

Hell, he already had the guy's cell number. He needed to get some background without Byron knowing he was being investigated.

He needed to go to Adelle, sit at the bar, and observe. Maybe he could get something from the bartender. Maybe some of the customers knew something. Yeah, the vampire customers would know a lot.

But, not tonight. It was already midnight, and Garrett was just too tired to make the drive. He didn't have any need to rush things.

Now that he knew where Byron was, he could take his time and be careful. Tomorrow evening would be fine. Hell, he could go to that Rule the Night place a couple of times a week and get to know some regulars.

The regulars would probably be vampires. Getting to know them, sitting and chatting with vampires, made him cringe, but that might be what he had to do.

Without the nightly murders, he had time to get what information he could about Byron and the other vampires. This would be a long-term project, and he had no idea what he'd do with any information he got.

What *could* he do with the information? The idea of telling Jennings or any of the other officers made him laugh. Anyone would think he was nuts. What he did with it didn't really matter. Garrett just knew that he had to find out everything he could.

Vampires were real, and Garrett had to know what they were up to. Bottom line.

He shut down the laptop and went to bed. He thought a long time about Gina, how she'd fed from him, how she'd tried to tell him, and how he'd hidden the truth from himself for twenty years. No more. The years of lying to himself were over.

* * *

They met right outside of Chicago at one of the many truck stops. It would be daylight soon, and Byron needed to join them in the SUV with the protected windows. He'd leave the sedan that he drove from Adelle in a hotel parking lot.

He'd thought about it all the way from Adelle, but Byron had no idea where Charles might be hiding. He did, though, have an idea how to get the information. Someone at Nibble must know where he was, and that someone might be willing to talk.

Even if they wouldn't, they might let Charles know that Byron was already in town and was looking for him. Charles was way too arrogant to let that go. Knowing Byron was in town would bring Charles out.

TJ pulled into the Nibble parking lot. They went inside to get rooms, and then went to the office area to talk to Beatrice. She was slightly older than Byron and had been appointed as proprietor of Nibble by the Assembly.

None of the guards had ever met her since she'd spent the last couple of centuries in Australia and only came back to the U.S. when she was offered the job at Nibble. Byron, though, had worked with her during the difficult times in the past when the Assembly instituted their rules against bloodthirst.

"Byron," she said as she opened the office door and moved toward him.

They embraced and touched cheeks in a traditional, European greeting before moving apart.

"How wonderful to see you again, Beatrice," Byron said. "You're as lovely as ever."

Petite with dark brown, almost black, hair waving down to rest on her shoulders, she had a gentle smile and light green eyes. The green of her shirt reflected in her eyes. At only 5'3", her body was perfectly proportioned, yet her legs seemed to go on forever in her black slacks. While she looked like a delicate, sweet woman, she was actually incredibly powerful. Byron knew that she could probably break him in half without much problem. The Assembly had chosen her specifically to keep control of Nibble.

"Thank you," she said with a grin. "I hear you're at Rule the Night."

"Yes, I am. And these are some of my most trusted guards. T.J., Quinton, Lorna, and Luke."

They all greeted each other and shook hands. Then the guards stood against the wall near the door while Byron sat down with Beatrice on a small couch.

"I'm sure you've heard of my issues with Charles." Byron said. There was no sense beating around the bush.

"I certainly know how you cleaned up this place, but I'm guessing that if you're here, there's more to tell. Is Charles back in Chicago?"

"He says he is, but I need your help to try to find him."

Byron quickly told her the background. It wasn't easy to tell an old friend that his son was bloodthirsty, but there'd be no way to hide the truth from her.

"Constance is being noncommittal," he said when he finished. He knew Beatrice would wonder. "I'm sure the Assembly is searching for him as diligently as we are, but she hasn't said so."

"What do you need from me?"

"I need your permission to talk to everyone staying at Nibble. I need to know if they're willing to tell me anything about Charles."

"You put me in a difficult position," Beatrice said with a chillier tone to her voice. "I have to assume that you hope finding Charles will lead you to Parker. You know I'd like to help you, but I'll need to check with Constance first, and I'll do what she asks me to do."

"I understand that."

Beatrice looked a little surprised. "You think she'll go along with this?"

"I have no idea," Byron sighed. "She says very little to me these days."

"Maybe she's hoping you'll do your duty without being told."

"I know my duty, Beatrice."

"I hope so. Constance will not be happy if you don't."

"All I'm asking of you is the opportunity to talk to your residents. Nothing else."

"I have to insist that I be present when you talk to them, and if they choose to talk to you privately."

"Agreed."

"The sun has risen, so get some sleep, Byron. If Constance agrees, I'll ask everyone to meet with you at sunset."

"Thank you."

Byron stood and gave her a slight bow. The old-world gesture of respect recognized her as the leader of this sanctuary, and as one older than himself. It was very rarely used anymore, but Byron was letting her know that he wasn't ignoring her position or her power.

The guards did the same as each one turned toward the door. They walked silently to their room.

Nibble didn't have five empty rooms, so they'd offered to set up what they called a dorm-style room. Three twin beds and a set of bunk beds had been moved in and scattered around the walls. That only left room for one dresser, but they did have their own bath and good-sized closet.

"Okay," Luke said as they looked around. "No one has to tell me that I take the top bunk. TJ and Quinton over there, Byron by the door, and Lorna ... you're under me." He waggled his eyebrows at her teasingly.

"You should be so lucky," Lorna answered as she threw her duffle bag on the bottom bunk.

"If you'd rather," TJ said, "I'll take the bottom bunk and you can have the cot."

"Nah, this is fine. I can kick Luke's ass from below if he gets too revolting."

They took turns washing up and changing in the bathroom and all came out in some version of shorts or sweats and a t-shirt. It was already a couple of hours into daylight, and they were all tired.

Byron stretched out on his bed and listened to the deep breathing of his guards. They seemed to have no problem sleeping, but his plan to send Parker to Roland weighed on his mind, and he couldn't stop thinking about the choices he was making.

It was very clear that Beatrice didn't trust him, and Constance surely felt the same way. That's why Constance had barely spoken to him recently and why she wouldn't tell him anything. Maybe Beatrice had already talked to Constance about the situation. She and the rest of the Assembly were waiting to see what he chose.

Would he do his duty that Beatrice spoke of, or would he hide Parker to keep him alive? He knew that it was his duty to execute Parker, or at least turn him over to Constance for execution. No bloodthirsty vampire could be allowed to live.

Byron had done that duty for centuries. There were many in the early days of the Assembly's pronouncement that might have been able to control bloodthirst if they had time. But giving them time meant allowing them to kill.

Right now, Parker could be sleeping after spending a night of killing. He might be on his own, prowling the streets every night, attacking humans and enjoying their fear and pain. He might have joined with Charles, so lost to bloodthirst that he'd given up trying to fight it anymore. He might be dead.

The one thing that was certain was that Parker hadn't followed his plan to find Charles and kill him. Charles was still very much alive, taunting Byron, and forcing him to come find him. Byron was determined to do exactly what Charles expected. Find him, but this time put an end to their battle that had gone on too long.

This time, Byron would kill Charles. If Parker was still alive, he'd take him to Roland to wait out the time it would take to control his bloodthirst. He'd be turning against the Assembly, and turning against all of vampire society, but at least Parker would live.

Parker would be consigned to live for decades, fighting against his own instincts. He'd never be able to live in the open, even after he'd found control, but he would at least still be alive.

Byron would disappear with Parker, Holly would almost surely join them, and he hoped Crystal would choose to follow them into their isolation. Roland would help them find a place to hide, but that shouldn't be too difficult.

Maybe in Alaska, where the interminably long sunshine of summer days discouraged vampires. Or some of the isolated areas of South America, China, or a country like Nepal could support four vampires. It didn't matter right now. It would be decades before Parker would be able to live with them on his own.

The four of them would never again be able to associate with any vampires. They'd have to hide forever, and constantly guard against being found. No one could know where they were or if they still lived. They'd give up the lives they had.

If Holly and Crystal weren't willing to join them, Parker and Byron would go alone. Parker deserved to live.

Parker's parents had been Byron's friends. They knew about vampires because Parker's dad had been his engineer, helping The Assembly build new sanctuaries. Attacked and killed that night by someone Byron had been hunting, he couldn't bear to let their son die, too.

Byron had found the gruesome scene with Parker's mother already dead, and Parker unconscious from being thrown across the sidewalk. He killed their attacker and gave Parker's barely conscious father the choice. He chose to die rather than live as a vampire, but asked Byron to keep their son safe.

That's why Byron had hesitated so long to turn Parker. He couldn't see Parker's father wanting his son to be a vampire. He'd hoped Holly would be the one to make Parker want to stay human, have a human life, and raise children like his parents.

Everything had gone to hell that night that Holly was attacked. Since then, one disaster after another, had led them down this path, but Byron would not let them be led to destruction. Unless Parker was already dead.

If Parker was dead, then Byron had finally failed and none of it really mattered.

Byron had barely slept by the time the sun was ready to set that evening, and the guards started to wake. He got dressed quickly.

"Finish getting ready while I check with Beatrice," he said as he walked toward the door.

"Do you want me with you?" TJ asked.

"No. Be ready when I return."

Byron knew that he teetered on the edge with Constance, and Beatrice would support Constance and kill Byron without a second thought if ordered to do so. Byron would have done the same in other circumstances. But he hadn't crossed the brink yet. Not yet.

He returned to their room within a few minutes.

"Constance agreed to my request, and Beatrice is sending messages to all those in residence to meet us in the common room. They'll be there any minute."

"Then let's get on with it," Luke said. Byron had to smile.

Some might think that Luke didn't get it. That he didn't understand how serious their situation was, or how much danger they could be in. The truth was that Luke simply accepted life for what it was. They had a job to do, so they would do it.

Once they were all gathered, Byron spoke simply, getting to the point without fanfare or unnecessary drama.

"I am looking for Charles," he stated. "He claims to be back in Chicago. If any of you know of his whereabouts, or have seen him, or even have simply heard rumors of where he may be hiding, I would appreciate being told. Does anyone want to speak now?"

No one did. Byron knew how dangerous it could be for anyone to tell him what they knew. If Charles got word of it, he would kill them. So he was not surprised when silence filled the room.

"I will spend the night in Beatrice's office. Please let me know if you have any knowledge of Charles, even if it is simple rumor and you doubt its truth. Thank you."

He turned and walked to the office, but sent the guards out to patrol the streets. TJ wasn't happy leaving Byron to fend for himself, but followed orders.

If they were very lucky, they'd find Charles tonight. If they were lucky beyond anyone's dimmest hope, they'd also find Parker alive. TJ had trouble believing either of those would happen.

Chapter 10

Garrett left home for Adelle about 8:00 the next night. If he wanted to see vampires, he needed to get there well after dark, but he did not want to be the first human to arrive. No way.

He was impressed with the valet parking even though there was a parking lot next to the building, but it seemed full. Could they be that busy already? After leaving his car with the Valet, he strolled up to the guards at the door, showed his ID, and walked inside. They must card everyone. At thirty-seven, he knew he couldn't be mistaken for under aged.

Once inside, Joe noticed the club wasn't even half full at 9:15, so he took a seat at the bar and casually looked around. All kinds of thoughts ran through his head. He remembered what Gina had said. Most of the vampires would be staying at the sanctuary, so their cars wouldn't need to be valet parked. It just made sense for there to be a lot more vampires in the early hours.

Two attractive, young women and one young guy worked the bar. Several waitresses took care of the tables. Music rang out from some hidden speakers, and the stage set with speakers and microphones looked like there'd be live music later. Were all the employees vampires? Garrett had no way of telling.

At least, this time, he'd changed out of work clothes and wore good jeans and a golf shirt, trying to look less like a cop. Maybe he'd be able to figure out how to tell a vampire by sight. Hopefully, he wouldn't have to wait for someone to bite someone else.

The young guy took his order for a draft, smiling pleasantly and asking how he was doing. Everyone else pretty much ignored him, which was fine. He wanted the opportunity to watch, not be watched.

After sipping the beer for almost an hour, he'd noticed more people streaming in. A handful of guys went somewhere behind the bar, and the band started to play. Once they started, some couples started to dance.

All pretty ordinary. All pretty boring. He needed to talk to someone so he could try to get information about the guy named Byron. He signaled one of the female bartenders that he wanted another draft.

"You've got a nice place here," he said trying to get a conversation going.

"Thanks," she said smiling, placing another beer in front of him. "This your first time at Rule the Night?"

"Yeah. I'm surprised to find this big a place in a town the size of Adelle."

"People come from all over. How about you?"

"I live closer to Columbus. I saw your website and thought I'd give it a try."

"Good. I hope you enjoy it."

"Thanks. Hey, the owner around? I'd like to tell him I'm going to let my friends know about this place."

"He's out right now, but I'll tell him you said so."

"Good. Thanks."

She left to get a drink for another guy down the bar. That conversation didn't get him anywhere, and he wondered if Byron was really gone, or if the line about him being out was one they used whenever a stranger asked.

He watched the guy bartender come up to her to quietly say something and wished he was closer so he could hear what they were talking about. They both looked worried. That look, and his cop senses, meant there was something going on that he might want to hear.

Like good employees, they kept working as they talked and slowly moved toward his end of the bar. Garrett picked up something about someone looking tired, and the guy mentioned not hearing anything yet.

Finally, as they both stood filling glasses at the taps, he could hear their words.

"Look at her," the guy said. "She's just going through the motions ... her minds out there somewhere with him."

"I know. They have to find something soon."

"Chicago's a pretty big place to be wandering around looking for someone, Crystal. It could take forever."

"Yeah, but Charles wants Byron to find him."

"True."

The two of them gave each other concerned looks and moved apart to serve the beers to different customers. They hadn't been trying to hide their conversation, but also didn't say anything very revealing. At least it wouldn't have been revealing to anyone who didn't already have some background, like Joe did.

Byron really was out, and it sounded like he was in Chicago looking for someone named Charles. Was it the same Charles that was involved in that warehouse fire Gina had told him about? What, Garrett wondered, could that information get him?

* * *

I'd headed up to work after spending the day with little sleep, and what I did get wasn't restful. The dream included Charles, again, and I cringed every time I thought of his tongue in my mouth and his hands all over my body. Why did I have to be one that could remember dreams?

Crystal and Chris were already behind the bar getting things ready, and customers were starting to stroll through the door. I hoped we were busy tonight, but you never knew in the middle of the week.

I felt like crap and was way beyond tired, but being busy would make the time pass more quickly. Maybe, by morning, I'd be tired enough to sleep without dreaming. Maybe tomorrow I'd get a peaceful sleep. Maybe we'd hear something from Chicago.

"Holly," Crystal said after we'd been open a couple of hours and things had settled down a little. "Are you okay?"

"I'm fine."

"You look so tired." She had a concerned, caring look on her face. "How long has it been since you fed?"

"I don't know. A few days I guess."

"Did you feed in Columbus?"

"No."

"Then it's been almost a week! Holly, that's too long. You have to feed tonight."

"Maybe I'll look for someone later," I told her.

"Holly," Crystal said like she was someone's mother. Not mine. Mine always yelled instead of sounding firm. "Why aren't you feeding?"

"I don't know … It's just … I'm having these dreams."

"What about?"

"Hunting … with Parker. The last couple of days they've included Charles." I shook my head and she knew I didn't want to say more.

"You're dreaming that you're bloodthirsty?"

I just nodded. It was embarrassing to be dreaming every day and remembering all the details.

"Honey, if you avoid feeding and get weak, the hunger will take over, and you *will* be bloodthirsty. You won't be able to control it. You need to take a break *now*. And feed."

"There's no one here, yet."

"There's a good looking guy at the end of the bar. He's a little older than you usually choose, but I was talking to him and he seems nice. Go talk to him, and feed."

It was stupid to avoid feeding, and I knew that a starving vampire could be very dangerous. I don't really know why I'd been putting it off. Yes I did. Feeding reminded me of the dreams.

"You're right. Thanks, Crystal." I walked around the bar and approached the guy sitting all alone.

"Hi, I'm Holly. Mind if I sit here?" I asked as I sat next to him. He was near the end of the bar, but I took the seat at the very end. That way, I'd learned, he'd have to turn toward me when we talked and wouldn't be distracted by what was going on in the rest of the room.

"I'm Joe," he answered with a smile. "You're one of the bartenders, right?"

I noticed right away that he was one of those guys that had a great smile. It lit up his face and made his deep brown eyes almost sparkle. He might not have been the twenty-something I usually targeted, but he was a handsome, friendly looking guy with a body that showed he worked out.

"Yeah, but things have slowed down so I thought I'd take a break."

He looked at me curiously. "How old are you?"

That was a strange question. "Old enough to be a bartender," I lied with a smile.

"You look about eighteen."

I chuckled at his incredibly good guess. "Byron's really strict about ages. You have to be twenty-one to even get in here. How old are you?" I gave him a cute smile as I threw the question back at him.

"Thirty-seven." He answered like it was a deal breaker. Like I'd tell him it was nice to meet him and move on.

"Really? Now you look like you might be pushing thirty, but no more."

"I think I look like the oldest guy in the room. So, who's Byron?"

"The owner."

"How long have you worked for him?"

"Since last October, not long." Saying that made me realize that I'd only known Byron for eight or nine months. So much had changed in that time, it all felt like I'd been there forever. I hardly ever thought about my old, human life. At least not until Mom and Dad died.

"So you don't know him very well."

"Well enough. But what about you? Do you live in Adelle?"

"No, over by Columbus. I was just looking for some place new."

"Well, I hope you like Rule the Night."

"So far. How long's Byron had this place?"

"I really don't know. You seem awfully curious about my boss."

"Well, you don't usually find this nice of a place in a small town like Adelle. I bet most of these people don't live here."

"You're probably right. But I'm glad you came in tonight."

"You trying to pick up an older guy?"

"What? You were sitting here alone, and I thought I'd give you someone to talk to. We're supposed to be nice to the customers."

"Yeah? How nice?"

"What are you getting at?" Every guy I picked up to feed thought they were going to get more than they got, but this guy was being pretty blatant about the whole thing.

"I've seen couples going behind the band into what I assume are private areas. I just thought maybe Byron made more available here than drinking and dancing."

Okay, the guy was calling me a whore. Probably not the first one to think that, but I wasn't interested in arguing with him about it. I had other things on my mind. Now that I was close to him, smelling his very human blood, I began to realize how truly hungry I was. His blood was calling to me, and it was time to end our silly conversation.

"Look at me," I said very reasonably like I was going to explain everything to him. Instead I gazed into his eyes and made a few suggestions. "Would you like me to show you what's in those private areas?"

"Sure," he answered quietly.

I rarely had to enthrall a guy to get him into the room. Normally I only had to use my powers to get them to forget the feeding, but his blood was way too tempting for me to waste time on meaningless conversation. When I finished with this guy, he wouldn't even remember leaving the barstool.

I took his hand and led him behind the band to an empty room and sat him on the couch. My hunger wouldn't let me wait. Crystal had been so right that I'd put this off much longer than I should have. So I sat close, took his face in my hands, and smiled sweetly while I mentally told him he wouldn't remember a thing about what would happen next.

His expression went blank, and I anxiously tilted his head and breathed deeply of the luscious scent of the blood coursing through his vein. My fangs emerged quickly, I licked over his vein once, and bit him. His blood tasted wonderful, and I drank greedily. Why hadn't I realized how hungry I was getting?

It would be so easy to give in to that instinct that told me to keep drinking. Keep drinking until there was nothing left just like I did in the dreams. I would feel so powerful to hear his heart slowing and know that the life was being drained from him with the blood that I drank.

I had never drained a human, but my dreams let me know how I would feel if I did. Armand had told me how powerful I'd feel holding a lifeless human in my arms when it was all over. I would be the perfect predator. I would consume my prey and claim this life that was so helpless in my hands.

I sensed the change that told me I needed to stop. What if I didn't want to? What if I hadn't had enough? Why couldn't I follow my instincts and keep drinking? Keep drinking until I'd drained him. It would feel so good, so intense.

Then something snapped. I don't know if it was the memory of Byron's voice in my head, the horror of actually killing a human, or my own sense of right and wrong, but I could feel it. I had to stop. Now.

I pulled back from his vein, licked the two tiny holes that I'd made on his neck, and watched them heal. *Damn*, I thought, *it would have been way too easy.*

I kept my control over him and told him to come along with me. Leading him back to the bar and sitting him on the same stool, I knew he'd have no idea that he ever left it. Then I released him with the command that he'd not remember anything that had happened.

"Sorry," he said sounding pretty confused. "What were we talking about?"

"The private rooms behind the band."

"Oh, yeah. Aren't you going to invite me back there?"

"Do you want me to?"

"You came over to get something out of me. I figure I'll find out what you want once we get more private."

Something was wrong, here. This guy had been half mad since I'd sat down, and it was almost like he was daring me to do something. I had a feeling that he hadn't come to Rule the Night just for a good time.

"And what did you come in for?" I had to ask. "I have a feeling you had something on *your* mind besides a drink and a pleasant evening."

"What makes you think that?"

"Maybe the beer you've been barely sipping for the last hour, or all the questions about the place and about Byron."

"A guy can't ask questions?"

"And you seem to feel out of place. You're obviously not comfortable here. I mean, who's going to ask a bartender her age except … except a cop. Are you a cop?"

"Does it matter?"

"No. But if you … You're trying to get information on Byron, aren't you?"

"I'm not trying anything. I just got curious."

"Look, there's nothing illegal going on at Rule the Night." *Yeah, well, nothing I can tell you about,* I thought. "Byron runs a nice bar for people who want to spend time with other people ... and maybe meet someone."

"Hey, I didn't mean anything. Like I said, I just got curious about how this guy runs such a nice place. That's all."

"I guess a nice guy just naturally runs a nice place," I shrugged. "But I have to get back to work. Do you want another beer?" I got up from the stool and picked up his empty to dispose of it.

"Nope, I need to head home. Thanks for the conversation." With that he put a $20.00 bill on the bar and walked out.

Going back behind the bar, I watched him go and wondered what that was all about.

"Feel better?" Crystal asked.

"Actually, I do. You were right about feeding. But that guy was kinda' weird."

"Who was weird?" Chris asked as he walked up to us.

"That guy that was at the end of the bar," I answered, talking to both of them. "He was asking a lot about Byron, and I think he was a cop."

"Anything specific?" Crystal asked.

"No. Just general stuff. But he wanted something."

"Then we'll need to keep our ears open," Crystal said. "But there's nothing going on here. Nothing for *him* to find."

"I'll watch out for him if he comes back," Chris said.

"I think we all should," I answered.

* * *

The night wore on with no one coming to Byron to give him information about Charles. He was sure that most people knew nothing, but he was equally sure that there were some that knew where Charles was hiding. He still had followers and he was still recruiting. He had to be.

Since Nibble was the best place to find and recruit travelers, someone that worked with Charles had to be there. That person wouldn't want to turn Charles in, but there was no doubt that Charles would hear about Byron's speech, and Charles would view that as the opportunity to drag Byron into some kind of trap.

Byron waited through the night while the guards went out to patrol the streets. They weren't counting on running into Charles. He wouldn't be that careless. They hoped, though, to run into Parker. If Parker was in Chicago, and alive, he'd be out hunting.

So Byron waited until dawn. The guards returned to Nibble, none of them had seen any sign of either Parker or Charles, and still no one contacted Byron. There was nothing to do but try to sleep and continue looking the following night.

About an hour after sunrise, when Byron still hadn't gotten to sleep, he heard a subtle rustling sound. Then a soft scraping. He sat up and saw a lighter spot on the carpet just inside the door. Even in the almost total darkness, he recognized it as a piece of paper.

He quickly grabbed it and threw open the door to see who left it, but was too late. No one was anywhere around, and obviously didn't want to be found. In the dim light from the hallway, he could read an address.

There was nothing else on the printed page, but Byron had no doubt who the address belonged to. It had to be Charles's location, but whether someone was turning him in, or helping lay a trap, he didn't know. He didn't care. Either way, he would be able to get to Charles tonight and end this once and for all.

He looked around the room at his sleeping guards, and knew that some of them might not survive the night. Each one of them, though, was determined to take care of Charles and wouldn't give up or turn away from what was probably a trap. They were all equally determined.

* * *

That morning, Charles was doing practically the same thing Byron was doing – lying in his bed thinking through his plans, and trying to sleep. He'd called together all his most powerful followers from the whole Chicago area and, even though he knew most of them didn't want to fight Byron, they'd be there as soon as it was dark.

In fact, some had shown up before morning, and the total might be close to twenty that would join the fight tonight. Some of them, like Dawson, would just be fodder. They just weren't strong enough to make a difference against Byron or TJ. But, they'd keep them busy fighting, and Byron wouldn't be able to come at Charles with backup.

Having his address slipped under Byron's door guaranteed that Byron would show up at sunset. Not only would Byron soon be dead, so would his closest guards. Charles smiled thinking about how perfect it was going to be.

Well, close to perfect. The only thing that could make it better would be if he'd been able to find Parker. He would love to see Parker tied to a wall, beaten, sliced and bleeding all over the floor.

As Parker healed, Charles would cut him again and again. Eventually, he'd lose enough blood to weaken, stop healing, and die. It would take a long time for a vampire to die like that, but Charles would enjoy every moment of it.

He'd bring in humans and make Parker watch him feed. Between the pain, the blood loss, and the hunger, Parker would be hysterical, begging to die. If only he'd had the last several weeks to work on Parker before Byron showed up. He'd love to see Byron's face as he realized that Charles had put Parker through that kind of torture.

That wasn't going to happen, though. At least Byron would be dead and maybe Parker would eventually be found. Then he'd capture Holly, too, and torture them both. She deserved the torture more than anyone, after ruining everything he'd worked so hard for. He wanted so badly to get his hands on her.

Then he had a brainstorm. He didn't have to wait. He could get Holly now. Byron and his strongest guards were all in Chicago while Holly was back at Rule the Night practically unprotected.

Byron would go insane when he realized that Holly was here and helpless in Charles's hands. Not only would Byron be driven to try to save her, she might actually draw Parker. Holly, he realized, was the key to everything he wanted. Why hadn't he thought of that sooner?

But it wouldn't be easy to get her to Chicago, and there wasn't much time. He needed her tonight, and she'd have a rough time traveling during the day. Besides, who would she trust enough to let them take her away from Rule the Night?

It was like that cartoon light bulb going on over Charles's head. Samuel! She would leave with him because she would think that he was sent from the Assembly. She'd trust him completely.

Charles picked up the phone and called Samuel. It rang several times before Samuel answered sounding half asleep.

"I need you to take the helicopter to Adelle and bring Holly to me," Charles said without any greeting.

"Tonight?" Samuel asked.

"No. Now! I need her to be here before the sun goes down."

"But she's so young ..."

"Then protect her from the sun! She needs to think she's going to the Assembly. Tell her they have Parker and he wants to see her. Let her think they're ready to execute him if you have to. Tell her any lie you want. Just get her here!"

"Should I call her?"

"No! I don't want her to have time to call Byron, or even think. Show up, wake her, and insist that she has to leave with you immediately. She'll go to Parker without any argument."

"I'll leave as soon as the helicopter's ready. Should be within the hour."

"Good. Wake me when you and Holly arrive."

Charles hung up smiling. This was too perfect, and he could begin her torture right away, before Byron showed up. Holly could watch Byron and his guards die, then she would be his.

He'd spread the word everywhere that he had Holly, and Parker would soon be on his way to save her. Tormenting and torturing the two of them would be more fun than he'd ever hoped for. Too bad Byron would be dead before he knew what happened to his two darling, young vampires.

Charles's thoughts of violence surprisingly relaxed him. Soon, he was sleeping soundly knowing that when he woke, he'd have Holly and the last night of Byron's life would be just beginning.

Chapter 11

Someone was shaking me, but I was sleeping so soundly I couldn't make myself respond. I hadn't slept that well in a really long time, so it must have been the feeding that helped. I didn't have any dreams, either. And now someone was trying to make me wake up while my mind was saying, *Please, let me sleep.*

I struggled to gain consciousness without even thinking about who wanted me awake, but I sure didn't expect a stranger to be standing next to my bed. I squealed like a little girl and cringed against my pillow, hugging the covers to my chest. Not exactly the reaction anyone would expect from a big, bad vampire.

"Who are you?" my voice croaked.

"I'm Samuel. I met you at Nibble when you overthrew Charles."

Okay, he was right. He'd been there with Constance. "Of course. You surprised me. What do you want?"

My voice showed my confusion, but also held a hint of my growing anger. I may have met him before, but that wasn't any reason to sneak into my room and wake me up in the middle of the day. What was up here?

"You're wanted at the Assembly. Immediately."

"What?" Now there was fear in my voice. What had I done?

"Constance sent me," he hesitated and I had the feeling that he was hiding something or didn't know how to say what he really wanted.

This had to be about Parker. Maybe Constance thought that I knew where he was or could at least give her some hints, but I didn't know any of that. I wished that I did. I'd have been with him at that very moment instead of waiting to hear anything from anyone who really did know something.

"Why?"

"Byron's son wants to see you."

"Parker's at the Assembly? Is he okay? What are they going to do?"

"All I know is that we need to get there immediately. I'm sorry it's still daylight, but I'll protect you as we travel."

I jumped out of bed as fast as I could. My heart was thumping as I ran to the bathroom to get dressed and thought about seeing Parker again. I couldn't wait to see him.

Then the reality hit me. They were probably giving him the chance to say goodbye before they executed him. I froze with one leg in my jeans. I'd have to say goodbye to Parker. Did someone else go to Chicago to wake Byron with the same message? Parker would want to say goodbye to him, too.

How could I say goodbye? How could I stand there and wait while Constance executed him? How could I walk away from him knowing that he'd die in a few minutes and we'd never see each other again? How could I survive that?

I had to physically shake myself to get the horrible thoughts out of my head. That moment was not the time to face those thoughts or to start grieving for Parker. I didn't know for sure that they were ready to execute him, but I couldn't think of anything else that The Assembly might do. All I could do was hope with all my soul that it was something else. Anything else.

Making myself finish dressing, I went back out to face Samuel. The cold look on his face didn't give me any hope that this was going to end up being something good.

I picked up my phone from the bedside table to let Crystal know what was happening, but Samuel took it from my hand.

"No phone calls," he said.

"I was just going to let Crystal know where I was. She'll be worried."

"You're not allowed to communicate with anyone. I'll text her from the helicopter."

"Helicopter?"

"We need to get there as quickly as possible."

My vision got blurry as the tears formed in my eyes. Was Constance really in that much of a hurry to kill him? Was he injured and dying? He must be in really rough shape for her to send a helicopter for me during daylight.

We went out through the family entrance. I was a little surprised that Samuel even knew about it, but I guessed the Assembly knew everything that went on at all the sanctuaries.

Once we were in the garage, he told me he had a car right outside.

"As soon as I open the garage door, you'll need to jump into the back of the SUV. You'll be exposed for a couple of seconds, but that shouldn't be a problem."

"No, that'll be fine."

The garage door opened, and he quickly raised the hatch on the back of the car waiting there. He squinted in the sunlight as I raised my hand to cover my eyes. Just those few seconds hurt, so I jumped in and started to cover myself with what I thought was a comforter.

"No," he said flipping aside part of the fabric. "It's a sleeping bag. Get in."

That seemed strange, but there was no time to argue with both of us standing there in the sunshine, so I just crawled in. Soon I was lying there all zipped up into the bag and the car started moving. From the direction he turned out of the alley, I knew we were headed farther out of town.

We drove about ten minutes before I felt the car slowing down. I knew there was a small airport outside of Adelle, but we hadn't gone that far. He could have landed a helicopter almost anywhere, and would want to avoid identifying himself and where he was going which he'd have to do if he landed at the airport. We were probably in one of the many fields around town.

The next thing I knew, someone grabbed my feet while other hands grabbed my shoulders and I was carried to the helicopter. The other set of hands must have been a pilot, but neither of them said anything. Kind of strange that he never asked if I was alright or told me how long the trip would be. He just threw me in there and we took off.

Even muffled through that sleeping bag, the helicopter was so loud that I couldn't hear a word the pilot and Samuel might have said. I spent the whole trip thinking about Parker and what I could possibly say to him. At the same time, I couldn't give up on the idea that maybe I could find a way for us to escape, or somehow talk Constance into letting him live. How could I just say goodbye and watch him die?

The helicopter ride seemed to take forever, but that was probably because I was so isolated, not hearing, seeing, or smelling anything the whole time. Add that to my worry and eagerness to get to Parker, and there was just no way I could accurately judge the time.

We finally landed, and the two guys lifted me back out of the helicopter and into what felt like the back of some kind of SUV. They never said anything to me, not even after I tried to call out to Samuel.

* * *

The phone woke Charles about 3:00. The text message said, "On the ground. Be there in ten." Charles smiled. Samuel had come through.

"Excellent!" Charles said aloud as he read the message.

The timing would be perfect. Holly would be tied and bloody by the time Byron arrived, and then the real fun would begin. Byron would be dead, Holly would be enduring deep, debilitating pain, and maybe Parker would be found and join in the fun with Holly. With any luck, this would be the night that he destroyed them all.

* * *

It was hot in that sleeping bag, and I was getting a little claustrophobic. I knew I could have gotten the zipper down by slipping my finger through the top of it. In fact, I was strong enough to just rip through the thing. But knowing it was still daylight kept me sitting tight.

Why didn't they at least tell me where we were or how long it might be? They could have said, "Okay in there?" Beside, if I could have calmed down enough to stop fretting about Parker, I would have been better off, but I couldn't.

I was sure I was being taken to see him one last time and was going crazy with wondering how long it would be before the Assembly executed him. Even though I wanted to get to him as soon as possible, I knew in my heart that the sooner I arrived, the shorter Parker's life would be.

I was so torn up emotionally, I didn't know what to think or what to feel. It could be only a matter of minutes before Parker was executed, and I would have to stand there and say goodbye. Would they make me watch as they snapped his neck? I wouldn't do it. No matter what, I couldn't watch.

Finally, we stopped and I was again pulled out of the car. Up a couple of stairs, and then down many more stairs, I was laid down again. But not unzipped.

"Samuel!" I called out as loud as I could. "Let me out!"

"Gladly," a voice said quietly. A voice I recognized.

My mind was spinning as the zipper slowly traveled down the bag and light started leaking in. Was Charles back with the Assembly? No. The truth came to me like a flash of lightening. Samuel had kidnapped me for Charles.

Byron once said that Constance suspected Charles had a co-conspirator on the Assembly. Now I knew it was Samuel. One of the three that came to clean up what was left of Nibble, Samuel was like the third in command. He was in on all their plans. Constance listened to him.

Within seconds, Charles was standing over me with that evil grin that I hated and knew too well.

"And here we are, together again," Charles said as he reached down and grabbed my upper arms, lifting me and squeezing way too tight.

"Where are we?" I asked.

"My current home. Not as nice as Nibble, but perfectly functional." He continued grinning down at me and didn't let up the pressure on my arms.

"And Byron?"

"Oh, he'll be here soon. Aren't you going to ask about Parker? Or do you already know where he is?"

"If I knew where Parker was, I'd be with him. And I wouldn't be telling you." I was angry and let it show clearly in my voice.

He slapped me. His hand let go of my arm and swung out at my face so fast that I never even saw him move, but I sure felt it. My whole cheek burned, my left eye watered, and my lip must have been split because I could taste my own blood. His hand was so big that the whole side of my face took that blow.

The slap threw me sideways, but I didn't fall because Charles still gripped one of my arms. I couldn't help groaning at the pain, but then I brought my gaze back to stare into his. I was mad as hell, but didn't want him to know that I was also scared to death.

"You'll tell me everything you know, sweetheart. Trust me on that."

Then he squeezed harder on my arm and practically dragged me over to the wall. My arms were quickly pulled up over my head and fastened to cuffs and chains hanging on the wall. Then my legs were bound to cuffs at the floor. I tried to struggle, but Charles was just too strong.

All I could think about were those people locked up in the basement at Nibble. He had the same kind of restraints here, and it was my turn.

"Time to feed, dear," Charles sneered. "I'll join you again shortly."

Once he was gone, I had time to think. Charles had found a way to kidnap me from Rule the Night without anyone having any idea that I was gone. That was bad. Really bad. Unless I did something to get away, I probably wouldn't live much longer. In fact, why hadn't he killed me already? I knew he wanted to.

He had some disgusting reason for keeping me alive, at least for a while. He probably wanted to use me to keep Byron from killing him. Or maybe he thought I'd attract Parker. Of course, I had no guarantee that he didn't already have Parker, or hadn't already killed him, but I had the feeling he didn't know any more about Parker than the rest of us knew. He got so mad when I said I wouldn't tell him anything.

Quicker than I expected, Charles came back. He had a giggling young woman with him. I wondered where he'd found her.

"Bondage will cost you extra, sugar," she said with a coy smile when she saw me chained to the wall.

Charles smiled back and slid his hand along the side of her neck like he was caressing her. I knew that hand would soon move to her throat and squeeze the breath out of her. I think he liked the look of fear in a woman's eyes when she couldn't breathe. I wasn't about to stand there and watch that happen.

"Hey, lady," I said sweetly.

As soon as she looked at me, my eyes locked on hers and I used all my strength to push my will into her. I wanted her unconscious so she didn't have to face being tortured by Charles.

She passed out and slid to the floor right out of Charles grip, and he left her there while he turned to me. He knew what I'd done. The look of hatred on his face as he walked toward me made my stomach rise into my throat.

"You don't want her to suffer? You don't want her to feel the pain of my feeding?" His tone of voice was vile, like yelling with the volume on quiet. It sounded so evil. "Maybe you'd rather take the pain for her."

His fist flew into my stomach without any warning. All my breath rushed out and I doubled over as far as the chains would allow. The pain was so bad, I thought I might pass out, but then it got worse.

Grabbing my upper arms again, he stretched me upward against the wall. As my stomach muscles clenched to bend me over, he stretched me up. My feet were off the ground, but I couldn't bring my knees up because of the chains on my ankles.

While I winced in pain and cried out, he laughed. My head was down, tears ran from my eyes, and my whole body was tense as it tried to bend me over to relieve some of the horrible, cramping pain.

"Was it worth it sweetheart?" he asked while I was barely aware enough to hear him. "Was it worth trading places with that stupid whore?"

He squeezed my arms even harder until I thought he might actually break them. The chains cut into my ankles as he stretched me higher against the wall, and it seemed like there wasn't anyplace that didn't hurt.

He held me there until I finally opened my eyes. The way he held me, I was almost face to face with him, and his glare showed his evil intent. He held me there until I thought I couldn't stand it another second. Then he dropped me.

It was such a surprise that my legs buckled under me and I fell toward the floor, but was stopped suddenly as my arms reached the end of the chains holding them, and I squealed again.

I scrambled to get my feet back under me to relieve the pressure on my wrists as the cuffs dug in. It hurt so bad. It was no exaggeration when Luke said Charles was a master at inflicting pain.

He laughed at me as he walked back to the woman stretched out on the cold cement floor. Picking her up with one arm, he carried her close to me. I knew he wanted to make sure I watched.

"You'll enjoy this," he grinned as he bent over her and bit into her neck.

The smell of her blood rushed into me. Charles stopped drinking and raised his head to look at me. He made sure I saw the blood on his lips, his fangs, and running down her neck.

He was trying to get me to lose control and struggle to get to the woman. I wasn't about to give in. I had to fight the hunger. I had to show him that he couldn't send me into bloodthirst.

I looked away from that luscious blood, stopped breathing and kept telling myself that the hunger was not the one in charge. I could barely resist the desire to drink. He was way too good at this temptation game we were playing.

Charles dropped her back to the floor and came toward me. I could see the blood on his lips and fangs and couldn't help smelling it as he smiled. He grasped my chin in his hand and leaned toward me, and I suddenly had a horrible vision from my dreams.

Squeezing my face and forcing my mouth open, he plastered his lips against mine in a repulsive kiss. The taste of the woman's blood attacked every muscle and nerve in my body. I licked the blood from his lips and fangs just like I had licked it from Parker's mouth in my dreams.

He was winning. I wanted that blood. I wanted to feed from her. If he had put her vein to my lips, I would have drunk greedily. I might have drained her.

Charles knew he had won when he moved away from me and picked the woman up again. He didn't give her to me, though. He stood just inches from my farthest reach and drained her while I struggled and roared my need for that blood.

Her lifeless body hung backward over one of his arms and he smiled at me, again tempting me with the view of her blood on his lips.

He dropped her and slowly moved closer to me. I backed against the wall as much as I could, but he kept walking until his body was pressed tightly to mine. He lifted me by my arms again until my feet were dangling in the air like the last time, and smiled.

"You really are a lovely, young woman, Holly. Too bad you're such a bitch." Then he kissed me again, sending the taste of that blood through me once more.

He let go of my arms, but I stayed off the floor by the pressure of his body. Then his hands were all over me, and I forgot the taste of that blood and started to struggle. I tried to kick and squirm as much as I could, but the chains wouldn't let me move much.

With him keeping me lifted off the floor, the wrist chains were loose enough that my hands could reach his head, so I grabbed his hair and pulled his face away from mine. I tried to gouge out his eyes with my thumbs, I was so mad and determined to get away from him. He yelled from the pain and took a step back, letting me fall and struggle to get my feet under me again.

Then he started hitting me. My face, my head, my body were all attacked so fast I couldn't do anything to even begin protecting myself. He kicked my legs out from under me, and I thought my wrists were torn to pieces it hurt so much as I fell.

Charles never said a word while he was beating me, but finally he grabbed my throat and lifted me so my feet were back off the floor.

"You need to learn some manners," he snarled. "My plan was to kill you in front of Byron, but maybe a few lessons in how to treat me would be better. You think he'd enjoy watching that?"

I spit in his face. I decided when he was kissing and groping me that I'd rather make him mad enough to kill me than let him rape me. No way was that rape going to happen in front of Byron.

He stepped away and backhanded me one more time. My face was so torn up, bleeding, and hurting by this time, I didn't really know what difference one more punch would make.

"You will pay for all this, little girl. You will pay," he declared as he picked up the woman he'd drained and started to walk away. He stopped and turned to face me. "I can keep you helpless, but alive, for a very long time. Think about how much fun that will be." Then he walked up the basement stairs and closed the door at the top.

God, I'd never seen him so mad. He might be ready to kill me before Byron even got here. That would probably be best. Parker was probably already gone, and I might as well join him. Yeah, it would be better if he killed me sooner so Byron didn't have to watch.

I started to take stock of myself. I hurt everywhere. Blood was running down my arms from my wrists. They'd been torn up more than once and one of them hurt so bad, I was sure it was broken again.

My face had to be a bloody mess. I could feel the blood traveling down my neck and could see it soaking into my blouse. My nose was definitely broken, but hopefully it would heal straight. I was worried about my nose healing? Hell, I'd be dead before that happened.

My left knee hurt more than any other spot. Charles had probably broken it, too, when he kicked me. I was bloody all over, had at least two broken bones, and God only knew how many bruises. I felt like one big bruise from head to toe.

At least he hadn't cut me. That would probably come next. He'd want me to lose blood faster so I'd get weaker and not be able to fight him anymore. That's what he'd done with Parker. But Parker had been only days old. I was stronger than that and would keep fighting him with everything I had.

If I could get my hands on his head again, maybe I could break his neck. He'd have to be really relaxed, though, and I'd have to catch him completely off guard. Oh, God! I might have to have sex with him to get the chance to kill him, but I really didn't think I could do it.

I hated him. Hated him so much, I didn't think I could ever convince him that I'd given in. I just wasn't that good of an actress. I had to come up with some way to get him close, but off his guard. I had to think, but I didn't know how much time I had.

According to Charles, Byron was on his way here. I didn't know where I was, but I bet Byron knew I was waiting for him and hoping he'd rescue me. No. Byron had no way to know I wasn't safely asleep in my room.

Crystal wouldn't even discover I was gone until it was dark and she went to my room to look for me. I wasn't sure of the time, but I knew it wasn't dark yet. Byron would be coming here to kill Charles and he had no idea that I'd been taken captive. No one had any idea.

Chapter 12

"Where have you been all day?" Constance asked Samuel as he answered his door. "I've been looking for you."

"Nowhere special." Samuel practically stuttered as he answered. Constance knew right then that he was hiding something and she wanted to know what he'd been up to.

"Where?"

"Since when does an Assembly member have to account for his every move?" Samuel answered, but not with as much confidence as his words would imply.

"Since he takes the helicopter to disappear in the daylight and won't answer a simple question."

Constance sensed Samuel's efforts to conceal his feelings from her, which made her more determined to get an answer to her question. "I was with a woman," he finally answered.

"I can smell that lie on you, Samuel. No one lies to me. Where have you been?"

"My private life is none of your business," Samuel spat out letting his anger show.

"No? I think it is. Especially when you're sneaking around and hiding your actions from me." Constance moved closer to him, gazing into his eyes. "This is the third time you've been missing without an explanation, and I *will* know what you're up to."

As she spoke, she gathered her power and commanded him to tell her the truth. Constance was one of the oldest and most powerful vampires still in existence, but few realized how powerful she really was.

It was almost impossible for a vampire to compel another unless he or she was centuries older and incredibly stronger. Constance had that strength, but rarely found a need to use it. There were also subtleties to enthralling another vampire that Constance had always been very good at.

But Samuel was incredibly powerful himself, and Constance had to use every bit of skill she could throw at him. She eased into his mind, moving around the blocks he set up, and forced her way into his thoughts. It was worth using that power to find out once and for all what Samuel was up to and what he was honestly thinking.

Samuel cringed as he felt her influence. He tried to fight it, or block it, but couldn't keep her from reaching into his mind to find the information she wanted. After a few seconds, his whole body trembled with the effort.

"Where were you, Samuel?" Constance whispered. The effort of controlling him was straining her also.

He didn't want to answer her, but couldn't resist. "Chicago. With Charles." His voice was strained, rough, and his lips barely moved.

Constance wanted to scream when she heard that. She'd long suspected that Charles had a partner in the Assembly, but assumed that it was one of the minor trainees, or possibly one of their servants. Not a member of the Central Committee itself.

"What were you doing?"

Samuel started to shake more violently as he struggled to mentally fight her and his grimace showed the mental pain he endured to try avoiding her question. But it was no use. He couldn't resist her and fell to his knees.

"I told Holly the Assembly wanted her. About Parker." A gagging sound came from his throat as he continued trying to resist. "I took her to Charles."

"Where?"

"Chicago. Dawson's home." He could barely get the words out as he strained.

"Did he kill her?"

"Kept her. Wants Byron to see her suffer."

So Byron must have gotten information from someone at Nibble. It was most likely information from someone working with Charles and would be a trap. But Byron was smart enough to know that, also.

"You have been such a disappointment, Samuel. I had great hopes for you when I first accepted you into the Central Committee, but you have betrayed us. All of us."

Samuel cringed as he knelt in front of her, his head dropped practically to the floor. He knew what was coming and could do nothing to stop it.

"Look at me," Constance said after a moment of silence.

Samuel strained to fight it, but weakened and raised his head up to look again in her eyes. She reached out and clasped his head with both hands, twisted quickly, and let him drop to the floor. *So many dead because of bloodthirst,* she thought.

It was the scourge of vampire society, but it was also a basic need in all of them. They had to do everything they could to eradicate bloodthirst or the humans would realize what was killing them and start to hunt and destroy every vampire they could find. They had to kill each other to keep humans from killing them all.

It was a struggle because bloodthirst was a vampire's natural state. Asking them to give it up was like asking all humans to be vegetarians. Some found it easy. Some found it impossible. Some simply chose not to do it.

She went to Bartholomew. Even though he'd known for some time that they had a spy among them, he was shocked to hear that Samuel had been working with Charles. With the information Constance had gotten from him, they both knew what they needed to do.

Constance woke Parker from his deep sleep. "We have a situation we need to explain to you," she said very seriously.

* * *

It took Joe a while to realize that Holly had bitten him. She'd drunk his blood and erased his memory of it. That could be the only explanation.

He was back in Columbus, sitting in his apartment, thinking about what he'd learned at Rule the Night. His first thought was that he'd really learned nothing. Then he started going through everything he'd seen and everything that was said, and realized he couldn't remember some stuff.

He was missing time in his memory. He'd been talking to Holly. A second later, he couldn't remember what they'd been talking about. What happened in that time? How big was that hole in his memory?

During that time, his beer had gotten warmer, his neck a little stiff, and he'd been confused by the fact that he couldn't remember his last words. As a detective, he was very good at concentrating on a conversation, listening to whoever was answering his questions, and watching how someone reacted.

Holly's reaction made him feel suspicious. She'd been casually talking, trying to get close to him, and suddenly she changed and seemed ready to get rid of him. Missing time?

Joe had been trying to figure out which of them might be vampires and which ones were human, but he didn't have any doubt anymore. The only thing that could explain his missing time, was that Holly had done something to him. She was a vampire and had removed his memory, but had she bitten him?

He should have realized that everyone working at Rule the Night was most likely a vampire. But, damn, she'd been slick. He couldn't remember anything from the time that was missing.

He went to the bathroom and inspected his neck very carefully. Not a mark. Nothing. When he pressed, though, he felt a little tenderness. It was nothing he'd normally pay any attention to, but it was there.

How could he have been so stupid?

Joe's anger was growing as he thought about how he'd let himself be used. He couldn't just walk away without knowing what was really going on. Who was the bad guy here? Byron or Charles?

He had to get more information, but all he really knew was that Byron was looking for some guy named Charles in Chicago. That wasn't much to go on, but maybe the sanctuary in Chicago could give him a hint.

He went back to the internet and found the one he wanted. Called Nibble, it was run by a woman named Beatrice. He almost missed the tiny word *Notice* at the bottom of the page, but immediately clicked the link.

Charles removed. Beatrice appointed by the Assembly.

Wasn't that interesting? It had to be the same Charles that Byron was looking for, and the information would obviously be important to vampires thinking about staying in Chicago. And what was the Assembly?

What kind of secret was behind those simple words? Did the vampires really need to know that Charles was gone? There seemed to be much more to that statement than the basic message. Maybe Gina would give him some answers. He didn't know what, but Byron and Charles were at the center of something.

"Calling at 4:00 in the morning?" Gina said when she came to the phone. "Up all night?"

"I need some information, Gina," he said without any greeting. "Why was Charles removed from Nibble?"

"Where would you have heard such a thing?"

He hesitated for a second. "I went to Rule the Night to find Byron and overheard that he was looking for a guy named Charles in Chicago. The Nibble website says Charles was removed." He didn't see any reason to hide anything from her. What was the point?

"You've been busy."

"Yeah, I have been. Tell me about Charles."

She sighed deeply and seemed to be thinking for a minute. "I'm only telling you this so you'll understand that we don't approve of killing. We fight it constantly." Then she paused again before continuing. "Charles is the worst kind of bloodthirsty vampire. He kills, not because he can't help it, but because he thinks it's fun. He ran Nibble for those who secretly shared his point of view. They were raided, but Charles escaped and is still being hunted. The message on the website lets other vampires know that Nibble is now being run by Assembly rules."

"What's the Assembly?"

"A counsel of vampires that established our modern society and enforces the rules. They are very powerful."

"And Byron's planning on catching Charles for the Assembly?" Joe asked.

"Byron's planning on killing him," she stated without any emotion. "They are bitter enemies."

"You think Charles is back at Nibble?"

"No. But everyone's sure he had followers in Chicago that were never caught. He'd be able to find help there. Someone to hide him and help him gain power again."

"Thanks, Gina."

"Joe," she said before he could hang up. "Don't think about finding Charles. He likes to kill women, but you would die without him giving you a second thought. He is ruthless and thrives on torturing his victims. It'd be best if you forgot you ever heard his name."

"I'll be careful," Joe answered.

"No! You can't be careful enough if you face Charles. Empty your gun into him, and he'll simply drain you so your blood can help him heal. Stay out of it and let Byron take care of him."

"Was he behind killing those women?"

"He's not the one who did it, but I sure wouldn't be surprised if he was involved."

"Then if others are killed, it's Charles I need to go after."

"Joe, don't. I'm not exaggerating his strength or his ruthlessness."

"And I'm not heading off for Chicago. I just wanted to know."

"Now you know, so stay out of it. Let us take care of our own problems. It could have been dangerous even for you to go to Rule the Night."

"Yeah, well ... I think the lady bartender bit me."

"Oh God, Joe. Did she flirt and act like she was trying to pick you up?"

"You've got it. And I think there's some missing time."

"She probably fed from you. That's how we do it. If you don't want to be bitten, stay in your own world."

"Don't want to piss you off or anything, Gina, but remember it was you who dragged me into your world."

"Only because I wanted you to stay with me," she said quietly. "Some of us have human lovers that we care a great deal about, and I thought you cared about me, too."

Joe didn't expect that. She cared about him? "I was scared," he answered. "Shit, I was still seventeen ... just out of high school."

"I know. But you're not 17 anymore."

Joe didn't know what to say. She was the best thing he ever had in his life. And not just the sex. The sex was unbelievable, but she seemed to respect him. Did she really care?

"When you came in La Sang Rouge, I thought maybe you wanted to see me again. I was glad you came," Gina continued.

"I'll tell you, Gina," Joe practically whispered. "I'm still not clear on what I'm feeling."

"Think about it, Joe. You'd be welcome at La Sang Rouge any time."

"Goodnight, Gina."

"Goodnight, Joe."

He hung up and stared into space. She wanted him back. At seventeen, Joe thought he was in love. Thought Gina was the perfect woman for him. It was the vampire stuff that sent him running.

Was that because he was so young and hadn't ever felt anything for anyone like what he felt for Gina? Over the years he'd almost convinced himself that she was crazy and just putting him on about being a vampire.

When she told him the truth, he'd been scared to death and had run for his life. He guessed that he always knew it was real, but wouldn't accept that. Maybe what he felt for Gina was real, too.

He'd been with many different women since Gina, and some of them were pretty great. He'd even thought seriously about proposing to Maggie but never went through with it, and she'd left. When it came right down to it, none of them had been Gina.

I need some sleep, he thought. He was exhausted, hadn't slept well for weeks, and couldn't get the whole vampire thing out of his head. And Gina. He didn't know what to think about Gina. A warm shower, a double shot of scotch, and blinds pulled to keep out the rising sun, didn't help at all.

The darkness didn't mean a thing, the shower just made him hot, and the scotch kept him thinking about how much he wanted to know what was happening in that bar in Chicago. No way could he stay on his bed staring at the ceiling.

Getting dressed and heading out to the car, his intention was to simply go into the station and do some of the paperwork that always needed to be done. Subconsciously, though, he wanted to head for Chicago.

He knew nothing would happen until dark, so there'd be plenty of time to get there and maybe even take a nap in the car.

Whatever. He couldn't resist the nagging in his brain that made him head northwest.

As the sun was setting that night, Joe sat in front of Nibble wondering why on earth he'd given in to the urge to show up there. He'd driven all day, slept for a couple hours in a hotel parking lot, and pumped way too much coffee into his stomach.

Finding the address on GPS, he now sat in front of Nibble waiting for something to happen. Gina had said that Charles wouldn't be there, but it was the only place he knew of to find any vampires.

As it got dark, Joe watched five people walk out, four guys and one woman. A couple of the guys looked like they could handle themselves really well, and the woman would be able to keep up with them without much of a problem. Then he realized he recognized one of them.

The scowl on the face of one of the big guys was the same expression Joe had seen at the last murder scene. This guy had stood out as Joe scanned the crowd. He was too big, too intense, too composed to just be another drunk heading home from a bar. Joe realized he'd been staring at a vampire that night.

The same guy that had been in Columbus showing up here was way too much coincidence for his detective mind to accept. One of the other guys must be Byron. He was probably the biggest one that looked like he was some kind of enforcer.

Joe let them get a couple blocks away before he got out of the car to follow them. He'd have to be careful. Vampires would know he was there if he got too close, but he knew how to keep a low profile.

He'd keep close enough to make sure he had them in sight and maybe cut around a block or two so they wouldn't notice him. But he was determined not to lose them. They had to be heading to Charles, and Joe was determined to be there with them.

* * *

I kept hearing Charles walking around upstairs. Like all vampires, I could also sense that it was starting to get dark. Many vampire abilities grew as a young one got a little older and a little stronger, and it was fairly recently that I could sense the absence of the sun and the coming of night. We didn't need a clock or a view out a window to know it was safe for us to venture out.

Now, though, I heard more footsteps above me. Besides that, the scent of several strange vampires wafted through the building. I couldn't tell how many, but quite a few were gathering to Charles.

He'd said that Byron would be there soon, which meant only one thing. Charles had set a trap for Byron, and all those vampires above me were prepared to counter Byron's attack. Not just counter the attack, Charles planned to kill Byron and everyone involved with him.

I wondered if Byron had any idea that he was walking into a trap. TJ, Quinton, Lorna, and Luke would be with him, and I wondered if they had any idea. I prayed they wouldn't be walking blindly into this place expecting to find Charles alone. The five of them could be pretty formidable, but not against all the vampires I was sensing.

I'd had such brave thoughts a while ago about facing Charles and dying. Not anymore. This night could be the end of us all. What would Crystal and Chris do if none of us ever came back?

Tears started running down my bloody, beaten face. I wasn't crying for myself. I was crying for the loss of everyone else. Almost everyone I loved and was close to was about to be killed. I was mostly crying for Chris.

Without Lorna, I didn't know what Chris would do. He'd just lost our parents, and I didn't want him to have to bury Lorna and me, too. Crystal would probably be running Rule the Night, and she'd keep Chris on, but he'd probably stay human. Maybe he wouldn't want to stay at Rule the Night if the rest of us were gone. I didn't know, but I couldn't stand the thought of Chris having to face losing everyone he loved.

Interrupting my thoughts of dread and loss, Charles came down the stairs and approached me with a nasty smug look on his face. I just glared at him.

"I see you're healing nicely," he said as he took my chin in his hands and turned my face from one side to the other. "You must have fed recently."

I didn't want to talk to him at all, but needed to get some idea of what all the noise was that I kept hearing. "What's going on upstairs?" I asked.

He smiled. "Several of my friends are waiting to welcome Byron."

"Don't you mean waiting to kill him?"

"He won't die until I'm done with him," he grinned evilly. He let go of my chin to stroke my cheek. "But I'm not sure when I'll be done with you. I'd thought to kill you in front of him, but it might be more fun to keep you around for awhile. Let him die knowing my plans for you and knowing he can't do a thing to help you."

The look on his face told me I'd be some kind of half dead, sex slave. I'd kill myself first.

"You've set a trap for him, haven't you?"

"Of course I have, but Byron probably knows that. What he doesn't know is how many still come when I call. He'll be amazed how quickly his guards die."

I cringed at the thought of all of them dying.

"Poor Holly!" he said pretending shocked concern. "You're close to all of them, aren't you? You've lost Parker, and now you're about to lose all the rest. Such a shame."

"Stop it!" I screamed at him. "Just shut up!"

I expected him to hit me, but, instead, he laughed in my face. Then he leaned down and kissed me again. I hated those lips, that tongue. I thought about hitting him, kicking him, but I couldn't move enough. Besides, he'd probably enjoy it. I hated him more than I could imagine hating anything.

While still thinking about how much I'd like to really hurt him, he slid an arm around my waist and pulled me against him. His lips suddenly moved to my neck and he bit me. It hurt. When he started taking some of my blood, I didn't get that sexy, warm, together feeling I'd had with Parker. It just kept hurting.

He continued drinking and squeezing me against him when I realized what was pressing into my stomach. He had an erection. I'd thought that being raped by Uncle Steve was the most disgusting thing that could happen. I was wrong. Charles would be the most sickening thing imaginable.

"Stop!" I growled while he continued to drink. It took him a minute, but he finally pulled his face away from my neck.

He leaned his head back with his eyes closed and his mouth a little open like it was some kind of sexual ecstasy. I almost gagged.

"God, Holly, you taste amazing," he groaned. My blood was still on his fangs and lips, and I wanted him to get his hands off me.

"Go to hell," I said. I'd never said that and meant it more.

If my hands had been free, I would've tried to break his neck right then and there, but he had pulled me away from the wall, keeping the chains on my arms and legs tight. So tight I couldn't move at all. He never licked the wounds to heal them, and I could feel the blood running down my neck. I didn't care, though. The last thing I wanted was for him to lick me.

"I'd love to spend more time with you," he sighed. He was still squeezing me hard against his body, but I refused to think about him moving against my stomach. "Unfortunately, the party upstairs should be starting any time. As you hear the screams and smell the spilled blood, remember that it is your friends dying. They won't last long once they show up, but then you and Byron will get to enjoy some quality time with me."

"I hope you die," I sneered. Then I spit at him again. That got him to step back a little.

Wiping his face on his sleeve, his eyes were filled with all the hate and evilness I knew he had in him. "I'll see you soon, dear. And the pain you've felt so far? It was nothing compared to what I have planned."

Chapter 13

Joe followed the vampires through the streets as carefully as he could while still keeping them in sight. Luckily, the five of them were easy to spot among all the regular humans wandering around. Those five would be easy to spot anywhere.

Not just their size, but their attitudes, the way they moved and almost commanded the street. They were like warriors heading into battle. Just watching them, Joe started to understand what Gina meant when she said he wouldn't have a chance against vampires.

So he kept his distance. He didn't want to be seen, or smelled. Gina told him how good a vampire's sense of smell was, but these guys didn't know him and wouldn't be able to identify him. If they smelled the same human along their route, though, they'd figure out they were being followed pretty quickly.

After about a mile, the big guy Joe thought was Byron slowed down and stepped into an empty lot. The neighborhood was filled with abandoned, run-down houses, empty lots, and storefront bars. Not a place to let your guard down, but Joe was sure the vampires weren't worried. They would be strong and fast enough to get out of any situation with humans. Joe, however, kept his eyes open for any hint of trouble.

He didn't dare get close enough to hear what they were saying, but after a few minutes of shaking heads and discussion one of the smaller guy continued on alone. A scout. It would be a scramble to keep him in sight without letting the other four see him.

Joe watched to make sure he didn't turn any corners, then jogged over a block, up the parallel street for a couple blocks, and then strolled back to the original street. He slowed down and acted like any stray human who was on his way somewhere.

It worked. The vampire was now two blocks ahead of him, and still going in the same direction. Then he stopped in front of a house, and Joe had to cross the street and pretend to change his path. Joe hid behind a house across the street and watched what the vampire was doing.

All he did was stare at the dark house. There were no lights on and it looked to Joe as if no one was home. He turned his head and his nostrils flared. Was he sniffing the place?

After several minutes, he turned and headed back toward the other vampires who were probably waiting in the empty lot.

Joe didn't know what to do. He could follow the guy back to the others, but then what? This was obviously the house where they expected to find Charles, but he didn't seem to be home. Byron would probably decide to wait for him down the street. Would he be able to smell him all the way from that lot?

There were too many questions here, and the biggest one in Joe's mind involved what went on in this house. Charles could be killing people again, and Joe had to know.

Once the vampire that scouted the place was out of sight, he moved to the back of the house next door, and sneaked into Charles's back yard. He wanted to look in, listen for any sounds, maybe get in the back door.

He could hear Gina's words in his head, *Empty your gun into him, and he'll simply drain you so your blood can help him heal.* That was a scary thought, but, hell, he'd come this far. The house was obviously empty, so why not see if he could get any real information?

* * *

Charles and his followers sat silently in the living room. All lights were out and all blinds were drawn. When Byron showed up, and the fight started, he didn't want any humans to see what was happening and try to interfere. Cops showing up would just complicate things.

He knew Byron had been standing outside moments before, sniffing out how many of them waited inside. He'd been alone, but would undoubtedly be back with some powerful vampires at his back. How powerful and how many, Charles had no idea.

But there were twelve of them inside, and Byron hadn't had time to gather too many for his attack. Charles figured that Byron's plan would be to move swiftly and target Charles himself while just getting through everyone else in the room.

A new scent wafted through the house, and Charles glanced over at Dawson.

"Human," Dawson whispered as he started to get up. "I'll take care of him."

Charles shook his head to stop him, and headed for the back door himself. The scent was human, and Charles had a sudden, enticing plan for the stranger that was sneaking around the back yard. Probably some petty thief or drug addict looking for something to steal, he could add an entertaining element to Holly's torture.

Moving silently through the unused kitchen, Charles detected the human right outside, but he didn't want him to scream or make any other noise that could attract other humans.

He waited for the stranger to move away from the door and into the yard.

The scent moved toward the side of the house, and Charles opened the door silently. He was at the guy's back and had his hand across his mouth within a second. That guy never even heard him coming, but struggled violently. Charles could tell this man was in good shape and not lost to drugs or alcohol, but that wouldn't help him at all. In fact, it might mean he'd be more fun.

Charles spun him around to glare in his eyes, and the guy relaxed. No more struggles, no more attempts to yell out.

"Come with me," Charles whispered. He led him into the house and down the basement stairs.

"Look what I brought you, Holly," Charles said quietly.

Holly had smelled them coming and refused to look at Charles or the human man she knew was with him. "Go away," she said while gazing down at the floor.

"So stubborn," Charles said. "You'll eventually want him. Maybe sooner than you think." With that, Charles raised Joe's wrist to his mouth and bit him to start blood dripping onto the floor. "Huh," Charles said sounding genuinely surprised. "He actually tastes good. No drugs, no alcohol. I believe I found you a healthy one."

Then Charles laughed while he led the guy to the wall next to Holly and chained his arms and legs. Holly couldn't resist looking as the blood seeped down his arm. Charles wanted her to hunger for his blood and be close enough that she might struggle to feed from the guy.

"I won't drink from him, Charles. I'd rather die than play your bloodthirst games. You're wasting your time." Holly held her breath while she returned to staring at the floor. So far, she hadn't let herself smell the man's blood and didn't want to take any chances with her fragile control.

"You'll be hungry eventually," Charles said as he moved toward Holly and grabbed her jaw to make her look up at him. "You're not old enough to resist his blood once the scent fills the room, and he will bleed a lot more once I've dealt with Byron." He leaned forward until his lips were within a breath of touching hers again. "Give into it, Holly," he whispered with the movement making his lips brushing hers. "You'll enjoy it."

Holly glared at him.

"I'll see the two of you later," Charles smiled as he turned and went back up the stairs.

Once Charles was gone, Holly looked over at the man chained next to her. His head was down and he was obviously still enthralled. His blood was quickly drying on his wrist and wasn't as tempting anymore.

"Hey," she said quietly. He raised his face to her, and Holly gasped. His blank stare showed that he didn't recognize her in the dim light, but she sure knew him.

"What are you doing here?" she stuttered.

He just smiled. Holly had to snap him out of it, so she stared into his eyes and forced her powers to overcome Charles's influence. The guy blinked a couple of times.

"You!" he said accusingly. "What've you done to me?"

"How do you know Charles?"

"I don't know Charles! How'd you get me in here?"

"Have you noticed that we're *both* chained to this wall?" Holly didn't care how sarcastic she sounded. "Charles brought you down here. Where'd you meet Charles?"

Joe started to look like he was figuring things out. "I was following Byron. One of his guys led me here but went back to the other vampires. I tried looking in some windows ... and somehow ended up here."

"You know about vampires?"

"Yeah."

"You're a cop?"

"You knew that at the bar."

"It was easy. You act like a cop."

"You bit me at Rule the Night, didn't you?"

"Yes."

"You bit me again!" he practically shouted when he realized there was dried blood on his arm.

Holly was tired, scared and royally pissed off. This guy kept thinking all his problems where her fault. Wrong! If he hadn't been trying to follow Byron, he'd have no problems.

"*Charles* bit you," she sneered, "you idiot! He's trying to force me to lose control and suck you dry. But that's not until he's killed Byron and tortured and raped me. Eventually, he'll kill me, too, but not until you've had a ring-side-seat to his disgusting games. So stop blaming me for everything!" She was shouting through every word and Joe finally recognized that she was obviously not in great shape herself.

There was a long pause in the conversation while Joe stared at her. "So what do we do now?" he asked.

"Hope Byron wins," she snapped out and looked away from Joe.

"So Charles grabbed you, too," Joe finally said.

"He had me kidnapped from Rule the Night so he could make Byron watch me die," Holly continued with the same half-yelling tone. "He's had some other ideas since." With that, her voice was quieter and she didn't try to hide her disgust and a little fear.

"What is with this guy? What does he want? What's he got against Byron?"

"It's complicated," Holly sighed. "You know about the Assembly?"

"Yeah. And I know Charles is bloodthirsty which puts him on the Assembly's most wanted list."

"How did you learn all this?"

"I have a ... friend. She's filled me in on some things."

"Well ... Charles wants us to go back to the old ways. He wants us to drain humans every time we feed, and he's been plotting against the Assembly for decades."

"Is Byron part of the Assembly?"

"No, but he's been one of their enforcers for centuries and he broke up Charles' sanctuary. Then Charles kidnapped Byron's son and changed him into a vampire. A bloodthirsty vampire."

"Byron's son wasn't a vampire?"

"No. Vampires can't have kids. Parker was adopted. He was human when Byron got him." Tears welled up in Holly's eyes as she talked about Parker.

"He adopted a human? So where is he?"

The tears rolled down her cheeks. "I don't know. Charles probably killed him," her voice skipped as she said it.

"I'm sorry. You care about Parker."

"I love him," Holly whispered through her tears. She took a deep breath to try to calm herself and stop thinking about Parker so she could speak again. "Charles hates all of us because we've ruined his plans. He wants us dead, but he gets off on torture. He won't kill any of us quickly."

They were silent again for several minutes. Joe didn't know what to say about the whole thing. He didn't even know what to think. But he wasn't about to just wait for Charles to come back to kill them.

"We need some kind of a plan, Holly. Do you think we can get out of here? Is there any way we can help Byron?"

"I could make you ignore the pain if you think you could get a hand to slip through those cuffs," Holly said sarcastically, "but I think all the bones would end up crushed."

Joe looked at her. "Cute," he said with a sneer.

"Sorry, but I've been trying to figure something out for a while. He lifted me off my feet to kiss me." Joe could tell from her face and voice that she didn't want to think about it. "If he did that again, there might be enough slack for me to break his neck. But I may not be strong enough."

"He didn't take my gun. If I can get to it ..." Joe stood on his tip toes to give himself some slack in the chains around his wrists and tried to reach into his shoulder holster under his jacket. He couldn't get anywhere near the gun.

"I think our best chance is to be rescued," Holly said, shaking her head, thinking they might be out of options. "What if you stretch your chest as far as you can toward me. Maybe I can get a hand on the gun."

Joe stretched, sticking out his chest to get the gun closer to Holly. His jacket fell open, and she reached toward him. The pain from his wrists and ankles was clear as he grimaced and pushed toward Holly.

"Almost," she whispered and felt the cuffs cutting into her own wrists.

"Don't drop it," he groaned as she barely gripped the end of the stock between her index and middle fingers. She had it, but only her vampire strength made it possible for her to pull it free. If she'd just had human strength, it wouldn't have worked.

Holly curled her fingers slightly and bent her wrist up, causing the gun to slide out. Once it was free of the holster, she flipped it, catching it in her full grip. It was a great feeling to actually have the means to kill Charles, and she smiled as she relaxed and adjusted the gun so she could get her finger on the trigger.

Joe held out his hand to her obviously thinking that she was going to turn it over to him. "Give it to me," he said when she didn't.

"No," she shook her head, no doubt in her voice or face. "I'm going to shoot him."

"No way. You're not trained to use a gun."

"And you're a cop. You're trained in how to avoid shooting and will hold the gun on him like he's human. I'm going to shoot him in the face as soon as he hits the bottom step."

"What?"

"He's a vampire. He won't die unless you blow his brains out of his head. I'm not taking any chances with you hesitating."

"Believe me, I'll shoot."

"Look, vampires are too fast. When you raise that gun, he'll be on you before you can pull the trigger. Besides, I've waited a long time to kill Charles, and I'm going to kill him."

"Don't be stupid," Joe sighed. "We can shoot through the chains and be out of here. We could get help or go find Byron."

"That would take four shots for each of us. As soon as Charles hears the first shot, he'll be down here in about two seconds and we'll be dead. At least you will be. He may still keep me, so I'm not taking any chances. I'm going to kill him." The determination in her voice and the cold glare in her eyes let

Joe know that there was no way she would be handing him that gun.

Joe sighed but didn't say anything else. He couldn't force her and he couldn't convince her. She was determined to take this guy out, and part of Joe understood that. Vengeance and the need to rid the world of someone who'd hurt so many could be overwhelming.

"Charles beat you, didn't he?"

"Who else?" Holly practically snarled.

"It looks old. How long has he had you?"

"A few hours. We heal quickly. Especially with fresh blood, and I'd just fed from you."

"Not comfortable thinking of myself as fresh blood," Joe winced.

"Sorry, but that's the way it is. We need blood to survive, but otherwise most of us wouldn't hurt a human for anything. It's Charles and a few others like him who think it's all fun and games to torture and kill people."

"So Byron's really the good guy in all this? He doesn't kill people?"

"Byron wouldn't kill anyone. At least not a human. He's tried to stop bloodthirst for a couple centuries, so, yeah, he really is one of the good guys. One of the best."

"Tell me about Parker."

Holly looked at Joe thinking that she understood why he wanted to know more of the story of why Charles had to die. He deserved to know some details of the fight he'd fallen into. He deserved to know what he was probably going to die for. She took a deep breath, hoping she could talk about Parker without crying.

"I lost control and attacked Parker when he cut himself and I smelled his blood. I almost killed him, and Byron had to send me away." Her words were hesitant, but she plunged through. Joe was impressed with her strength as the story continued.

With each atrocity, Joe watched Holly's face change. She took on a cold, hard expression that reflected her feelings for Charles. After hearing what Charles had done to Parker, Joe was sure the poor guy was dead, but he sure wasn't going to tell Holly that.

"Charles escaped twice?" Joe asked when Holly finished. "Is he that good, or that lucky?"

"Kind of both. He had an illegal sanctuary in Columbus, but wasn't there when we attacked. He was torturing Parker at the time." Holly swallowed hard and Joe could see she fought against tears. "We killed everyone else and burned the place."

"The warehouse? Gina ... my vampire friend ... said that was you guys."

"Yeah. We got Parker back, but he couldn't learn control. It was horrible. Parker gave up and ran away to find Charles and kill him."

"He didn't make it?"

"We don't know what happened to him. By Assembly rules, Byron should have executed Parker, but he couldn't do that. Parker left us a message that he was going to kill Charles and turn himself into the Assembly." Holly's voice caught again, and Joe finally heard a quiet sob.

"I'm sorry. You do love Parker, don't you?"

"With all my heart. But Parker's probably dead." Holly paused in her story. That last statement had been hard for her to say. "I'm guessing he found Charles, and Charles killed him."

"Shit, Holly. I hope you splatter his brains all over this damn room."

"So do I," she said, finally able to look in Joe's eyes again.

Chapter 14

"Is he there?" TJ asked Byron as they met in the empty lot.

"He's not alone. I didn't take the time to count, but there's probably about a dozen. The lights are out, blinds drawn. He's set his trap for us."

"What's the plan?" Quinton asked.

Before he could answer, Byron's phone rang. Caller ID said it was Crystal, and Byron's throat constricted. She wouldn't call unless it was an emergency.

"What's happened?" Byron said.

"We think the Assembly has Holly."

"What?"

"She wasn't in her room when I went in to wake her, and there was a scent of a strange vampire. Anthony says it was Samuel. It doesn't look like she took anything with her, there aren't any cars missing, and we've searched the streets."

"Then they must have Parker, too." Byron practically whispered.

"I thought you might want to call Constance yourself." Crystal answered.

"Thanks, Crystal. If the Assembly wanted her, you couldn't have stopped them."

"But I wish they'd come to us instead of sneaking in while we slept."

"I do too."

Byron immediately called Constance's number, but had no idea what to say to her. They probably executed Parker and found out that Holly was planning to hide him. They were within their rights to execute her, and then come for him.

Constance didn't answer. Neither did Bartholomew.

"Looks like the Assembly took Holly," Byron explained to his guards. They all stood stock still except Luke who grimaced and rubbed his hair back off his face.

"Which means they probably have Parker and will come for me next. If any of you need to leave before we attack Charles, please go now. I won't hold it against you, but, be warned. If you stay, Constance may see it as your support for me trying to find and hide Parker."

"None of us are going anywhere except down that road to take out that bastard once and for all," Luke said quietly as he pointed in the direction of Charles's hiding place. "Constance can think whatever the hell she wants."

"So, let's get on with it," Lorna added.

"Are you sure about this?" Byron asked one more time.

They all five nodded. "Tell us what you want us to do," TJ said with no emotion.

Byron sighed. He knew he was lucky to have the loyalty of the four vampires surrounding him, but felt like he was using them. Some or all of them might die. He wanted to order them to leave, but knew he had no chance alone. Charles had to die, and they had to find out what happened to Parker. They had to do this.

"It's simple," Byron said matching TJ's attitude. "He knows we're close, so there's no point in stealth. We take off from here and all attack through the front door. I don't care if some run out the back. Charles will stay because he wants me. I'll lead through the door because I want him. Kill everyone."

"Let me go through the door first," TJ said. "I'll distract them, and you can go directly for Charles."

"No. The most important thing is for Charles to die. I want each of you backing me up in case I fail. Get any weapons in hand, say any prayer you choose, and we'll be ready," he paused looking each of them in the eyes. "Let's go."

They all took off running, covering the distance to Charles's house in seconds. Bursting through the door, Byron glimpsed several vampires he knew, but pushed thoughts of them from his mind. He twisted the necks of two before they had a chance to defend themselves.

A gunshot echoed through the house followed quickly by another, but no one had time to detect where they came from. Byron and each of his guards were attacked from all sides, but as fierce as the battle was, Byron's eyes kept scanning the room for Charles. Once again, Charles was nowhere to be seen as he let others fight to protect him.

Just after Byron entered the house, a black Mercedes pulled up in front of Charles' hiding place. Although the house was closed up, dark and quiet to any human ears, the three in the Mercedes could smell the blood from inside and heard the grunts and blows from the battle.

"Holly!" Parker gasped.

The scent of her blood mixed with all the other vampires in the building, but Parker knew that she was there. Her scent permeated his brain and called to him.

"Where is she?" Constance asked.

"I don't know," he said, practically stuttering with his need to get to her. "She's close."

"We need to move," Bartholomew stated as they hurtled out of the car.

They dashed into the house and immediately began pulling vampires off Byron and his guards. They snapped their necks, let them fall, while trying to protect Parker.

Parker had only one thing on his mind. He followed his connection to Holly while throwing a kick to break the legs of a vampire that was trying to attack him. Nothing was going to stop him from finding her. He didn't even take the time to scan the room to determine if Byron and the others were surviving the battle. Once he caught Holly's scent, she was all that mattered.

* * *

"If you're going to shoot him, we have to get him down here," Joe said quietly. "You could call him."

Holly thought for a minute. "Brace yourself," she said quietly as she adjusted the gun in her hand so it was pointing directly at the doorway.

She let out a deadly howl that Joe thought might deafen him. "Chaaarles!" she screamed. "I have to feed! Don't leave me like this. Please! Let me feed!"

Then she screamed again. "Pleeease! The hunger! Anything you want! I'll do anything! Let me feed!"

They heard the unhurried, deliberate steps coming down to them. Holly knew Charles was purposely walking at a snail's pace to torture her. *Good*, she thought, *he'll be slow and relaxed when he hits the door.*

She screamed one more time and continued to moan.

He appeared at the door and actually stopped, probably thinking he'd take a moment to enjoy her torment.

There were scrambling sounds coming from upstairs, but Holly ignored them and kept up with the bloodthirsty act.

Charles hesitated for a minute, listening to the sounds upstairs, but then turned and faced Holly and Joe.

Holly fired at the center of his forehead, but she didn't count on his incredible speed. Charles flinched to the side and blood spurted from his head as the bullet deeply grazed him. That bullet didn't stop him, so she fired again.

The second shot went into his chest, and blood spread quickly across his shirt. Before she could fire a third time, Charles was on her.

She felt her wrist snap as Charles twisted the gun from her hand and threw it to the floor. Then he started beating her.

Holly thought the last beating was horrible, but it was nothing compared to the blows he threw at her this time. His hands and feet hit her so fast, she barely registered the pain from one before the next one fell. She felt her left leg snap below the knee and she hung from the chains by her wrists because her legs wouldn't hold her anymore.

She tried to scream out her pain, but his hand was around her throat before any sound left her. While that hand squeezed, his other hand continued to connect with every part of her body.

She heard Joe yelling at him to stop and realized that Charles quit hitting her only long enough to reach out and strike him. Joe was unconscious in a second, and Charles continued his assault on Holly.

Somewhere in her confused mind, she heard the sounds of fighting, and caught the smell of vampire blood being spilled. Those thoughts quickly disappeared as the worst pain of all radiated through her.

He'd begun to cut her with a slice across her stomach. Her blood gushed through her shirt and down her legs as Charles slowed down to slice the length of her arms and across her upper chest. He was out of control. She knew all his thoughts of slow torture had disappeared as his anger and hate flared.

This was it. She knew that she'd lost and would die. She began to hope it would be soon. Charles was really good at letting someone slowly bleed to death while keeping them barely alive. The cuts hurt like hell, but she knew they weren't too deep and wouldn't cause her to bleed too quickly. Even in his blind hatred, he was still playing with her.

His temper was getting the best of him, but the sick pleasure of beating someone to death was taking control. Finally letting go of her throat, he kept battering her face and head, causing it to snap back and forth as the blows fell on her.

Holly's only reality, now, was pain. Pain everywhere, but she was thankfully losing consciousness. Charles was so mad he was out of control, and she knew she would die now after all. Maybe she'd get to be with Parker again once she died. But poor Chris. One more blow violently snapped her neck to the left, and that was it.

The last thing her barely-functioning brain registered was the scent of Parker, and she smiled inside, but her bloody, damaged lips wouldn't move. She was dying and would be with Parker. Holly hung helplessly from her wrists as Charles kept beating her bloody, motionless body.

* * *

Parker thought his brain might explode when he caught the scent of Holly's fresh blood coming from the basement. She was here, with Charles, and she was bleeding. Bleeding a lot. He burst through the door of the kitchen and found a vampire standing at another door.

180

This vampire looked like he was guarding something and was old and powerful. But Parker could see the fear on his face and smell it in his blood. He stared at Parker like he wasn't quite sure what he should do next. But Parker wasn't about to let anything stop him from getting to Holly.

"Move," Parker snarled.

"No one's supposed to go into the basement," Dawson said. He'd been with Charles when Parker was changed and wondered how out of control his bloodthirst and insanity had grown since he'd gotten away. He knew Parker could be deadly.

"Move before I kill you."

"I can't ..."

"Move!" Parker yelled as his anger and desperation to find Holly flared. He backhanded Dawson so forcefully, he flew across the kitchen and slammed into the empty cupboards. Parker was on him in a second, and snapped his neck.

Parker leapt down the basement stairs hitting only one step in the middle. Holly's blood swirled through his brain as the scent grew stronger, and Parker burst through an unmarked door.

Charles was beating Holly's unconscious body, and Parker lost any control he might have still had. He dove at Charles. Screeching out a feral cry, he grabbed Charles from behind, knocked him to the cement floor, and landed on top of him.

Parker began beating Charles with every ounce of strength his anger, hate, and Constance's blood coursing through his veins could give him. Charles was caught out of control, unaware, and weakened from his own blood loss.

He'd been so lost to the beating he inflicted on Holly, he hadn't heard or smelled Parker approaching. The blood that had been constantly streaming from the gunshots in his scalp and chest had weakened him, especially since the exertion of the beating had kept it flowing freely and hampered his healing.

Still, Charles should have been able to handle such a young one. Something had changed in Parker, but even with a stronger, more determined Parker, Charles threw him off, sending him flying across the room and into the wall.

A split second later, Charles was on Parker, pummeling him with blow after blow. He felt like things were finally going his way. He'd killed Holly, would quickly kill Parker, and then would head upstairs to bring Byron down to survey the spoils of their ongoing war.

Parker wasn't about to given up. As Charles's blows fell, he reached up to try pushing him away, and found the long gash that the bullet had carved in Charles chest. He plunged his fingers inside and ripped it wide open. Blood and guts spurted out and Charles screamed as the pain radiated through his torn flesh.

As Charles stop punching, he felt Parker's hands on either side of his neck. Before the reality could register in Charles's mind, Parker twisted his head, and Charles felt and heard the bones of his upper spine crack.

He was unable to move, but not dead. Parker knew his grip hadn't been right. It hadn't been positioned carefully enough to completely snap the spinal cord of someone as strong as Charles.

Parker looked around and crawled across the room to the discarded gun that Charles had torn from Holly's hand, and walked back to stand over Charles.

"Now you die, asshole," Parker sneered. "And you can spend an eternity in hell remembering that it was me that killed you."

Parker pulled the trigger sending the bullet into Charles forehead. Then he shot three more times obliterating Charles's face and leaving nothing but an unrecognizable, bloody mass.

Parker dropped the gun to the floor and stood breathing deeply for a minute. He couldn't bear the thought of looking at Holly's mangled body hanging against the wall. The glimpse he'd caught when he came through the door had almost killed him. All he could think, though, was that he needed to hold her.

He walked over and lifted her weight off the chains, reached up to pull them out of the wall, and lowered Holly to the floor. He sat next to her and did the same to the chains that held her ankles.

Sitting on the floor, Parker pulled Holly into his arms and held her on his lap like a baby. He never wanted to let go of her. Charles's death was almost meaningless. What did it matter now that Holly was gone?

He reached to stroke her cheek, but couldn't find a spot that wasn't bruised, cut, and covered with blood. Charles had bloodied most of her body. The only spot of her shirt that wasn't cut or torn was right over her heart. It was covered in blood from the slice across her chest, but that's where Parker gently rested his hand.

Parker sat there trying to see her beautiful face through all the damage and tears streamed from his eyes.

Had he felt a movement?

He froze and concentrated on his hand that rested over her heart. It was beating. Faintly, slowly, but it was beating.

His mind focused on the human that was still unconscious on the wall next to her. Unconscious or dead? Parker sniffed and could smell the blood still running through the veins of that man. He was alive.

Gently resting Holly on the floor, he jumped to his feet and tore out the chains that held the human. Dragging him over to Holly, he broke the metal cuff from the man's wrist and gently opened her mouth with one hand while biting the man's wrist.

Blood slowly dripped through Holly's lips, but she didn't respond. He didn't even see her swallow. But he had to keep trying. The blood would seep down her throat, wouldn't it?

He moved one hand back over Holly's heart. It still beat, and Parker would keep giving her blood until she swallowed, or her heart stopped.

"Please," he whispered. "Keep beating. Please come back to me, Holly."

Fighting for his life while keeping his eyes open for Charles, Byron knew the battle had changed even before he caught sight of Constance. He only had time to notice her and the two other vampires with her. They were quickly killing Charles's followers which meant Byron could concentrate on finding Charles.

He heard three more gunshots, but his brain was filled with nothing but the need to find Charles. Byron hurried through the kitchen door, saw the dead Dawson on the floor, and headed for the basement where he knew Charles must be hiding. What he saw when he got to the bottom of the stairs stopped him in his tracks. The windowless room was lit by one bulb hanging from the ceiling, and it illuminated a sight that couldn't be real.

Blood was everywhere. A faceless Charles lay dead, Holly was horribly beaten and unconscious with blood from a human dripping into her mouth. And Parker. It was Parker that held the man's wrist with Holly in his arms.

With all the carnage in front of him and the memory of what had gone on upstairs, Byron could only focus on Parker. He was alive.

It took a few minutes of staring for Byron's brain to register that Parker was feeding Holly. He was watching the human blood drip into Holly's mouth, and not reacting. His voice sounded calm and in control as he whispered to Holly, begging her to survive.

"Parker," Byron said quietly. The word was somewhere between a statement and a question to see if what he saw was real.

Parker looked up at Byron. "He almost killed her. Help me."

Byron moved swiftly. He knelt next to Parker and took Holly's head in his hands. He tilted her chin up to change the angle of her throat, allowing the blood to finally slip down. He reached for her wrist to check her pulse but stopped when he realized how mangled and broken they both were.

Finding the spot below her ear he stilled to feel how strongly her heart was beating. It was weak, slow, and sounded like it might stop any minute.

"We have to stop some of her bleeding," Byron said.

He tore the back of the human's shirt and used part of it to bind her stomach tightly, hoping to slow the bleeding from her worst wound. Then he wiped some of the blood from her arms and inspected those shallower wounds for any sign of healing. He did the same to her face.

He touched Parker's shoulder. "Her body is trying to heal her. She needs more blood, but this human has given all he can. I'll get TJ to find another."

He ran upstairs and was back in seconds followed by Constance. She carried towels and a tub of water.

"We have to clean her wounds to find the ones we need to help heal," she said as she began washing her.

Constance started by washing some of the blood from her face, then moved to her stomach and chest, removing the bandage Byron had made from Joe's shirt. "Oh," she sighed sadly. "This is deep."

Surprisingly though, she pulled the wound farther apart and the blood that Byron had tried to stop, flowed heavily out of her.

"What are you doing?" Parker cried as he pulled Holly closer to his chest.

"I'm going to help her," Constance said calmly. She bit her own wrist and let her blood drip deep into Holly's wound.

She slowly moved her wrist above the length of the gash and they watched as Holly's bleeding slowed and finally stopped. Constance squeezed the sides of the wound together and waited for the knitting to begin.

When she could tell that the sides would hold together, she bit her wrist again, dripped the blood into her own hand, and smeared it across the cuts on Holly's chest and arms.

Constance bit herself a third time and let it drip into her palm until it was ready to overflow. Quickly licking herself to heal the three bites, she dipped one of the towels into her palm and used it to wipe Holly's face.

"Byron," she said.

He immediately bit his own wrist and held it over Constance's palm until it filled again with his blood. Constance used it to wipe Holly's wrists, ankles, and once again over her face.

"That's all we can do until TJ returns," she said as she stared down at Holly.

"She'll be okay?" Parker asked.

"I don't know, dear," Constance answered. "We've taken care of the surface. There are probably several broken bones and I'm sure internal organs are damaged and bleeding. We'll feed her again and take her to Nibble. Then we'll wait."

Chapter 15

Joe heard the voices around him, but it still took a minute before he was really awake. It took an effort to open his eyes, but he was finally able to see the three people that surrounded Holly. Sprawled across the floor behind the one guy, was a body without a face. *Charles, I hope*, Joe thought to himself.

"Did he kill her?" Joe whispered because his throat wouldn't work normally.

"Are you alright?" the woman asked.

"I guess. What about Holly?"

"She's alive," the lady answered. "Look at me, and I'll explain what happened."

"No!" Joe said as he quickly closed his eyes and turned his head. "I don't want anyone erasing my memory. I know about vampires. I know everything Charles did and about Byron and Parker. The last thing I remember was Charles beating Holly after she shot him. I tried to reach toward him, and he hit me like a cannon ball. What happened?"

"How do you know all this?" Byron asked with the same surprise that was on the Constance's face. Parker still looked at Holly.

"Holly told me. Are you Byron?"

"Yes," Byron said hesitantly.

"I'm Joe Garrett, the guy Gina told you to call."

"How on Earth?" Byron gasped through the shock on his face. "I think you have some things to tell us, Mr. Garrett."

"Joe. Call me Joe."

TJ burst onto the scene with a peacefully smiling human and surveyed the room. He had a million questions flying through his head about who killed Charles, why Constance was here, and especially about Parker. Byron said that Parker was with Holly, but could it really be? All questions waited, though, because the most important thing was getting some blood into Holly.

He walked the guy over to sit on the floor and join the circle that surrounded her. Holly looked like hell, and TJ could hardly bare to look at her. Poor Holly.

Byron had told him the bare facts that Holly was near death, Parker was feeding her, and Charles was dead. There was a lot more going on here than that. Looking at how Holly'd been beaten, what TJ really wanted was the chance to kill Charles all over again.

TJ immediately bit the human's wrist and let the blood drip into Holly's mouth that Parker held open.

"She needs blood to get better?" Joe asked, and TJ glared at him. "I would've given her some."

They looked mildly surprised, but it was Parker that answered without moving his eyes from Holly's face. "She's already had yours. She needs more."

Joe finally noticed his wrist. "Then would whoever did this, lick it so it heals?"

Parker finally turned his gaze toward Joe. "Who the hell are you?"

"You must be Parker."

"Yeah," Parker glared.

"Holly really loves you. She thought you were dead."

Parker's glare softened and Joe thought for a minute he was going to cry. "I love her, too," he said quietly.

Parker reached down, grabbed Joe's wrist rather roughly, and raised it to his mouth. He licked twice, removing the partially dried blood, and watched the wound heal.

"I thought you were bloodthirsty. Wouldn't that make you want to drain me?"

"Not anymore," Parker growled and looked back at Holly in time to see her swallow. "She's taking it," he gasped.

"Yes, she is," Constance answered. "When she's finished feeding, we'll get her out of here and settled at Nibble. I'll call Beatrice on the way, and she'll send in some of her people to clean up this place."

TJ started walking the enthralled human back upstairs while the rest of them stood. Parker leaned over to pick up Holly. He cradled her in his arms as he gazed into her face. The cuts and bruises were finally beginning to heal, but she still looked so gruesome. She was covered with smears of her own blood as well as what Constance and Byron had used to help her heal.

"I'll clean her up when we get there," Parker said quietly as he started walking from the room. No one knew if he was talking to them or to himself.

"What about me?" Joe asked as he struggled to his feet. Parker ignored him as he concentrated on carrying Holly as gently as possible.

"Good question, Joe," Constance answered, looking at him like she was analyzing a science experiment.

"Look, I know all about you guys, and have known for years. I'm a friend of Gina's at La Sang Rouge. I just need someplace to rest before I head home."

"Then I guess you should come with us," Constance said with a now blank expression. "I'll want to talk more with you."

Four hours later, Parker sat on the bed next to Holly. She was still unconscious, but looked comfortable and continued to heal. He had washed every drop of blood from her body and slipped on a sleep shirt so she was covered when others came in to see her.

Everyone else was busy with cleaning up Dawson's house, which they would simply burn to the ground. They'd also fed to heal numerous minor wounds that all of them had suffered.

They'd flown in Dr. Jamison from Adelle to set Holly's leg and both her wrists. He said her nose, one cheek, and her left jaw were also broken, but they would all heal on their own. There were also numerous broken and cracked ribs, but she was breathing easily and obviously hadn't punctured her lungs. He was most concerned about a skull fracture, but didn't see any signs of serious damage.

Her bruised internal organs worried him, but there was no evidence of pooling blood, and vampires would naturally heal an amazing amount of damage. Besides, surgery was the only way to fix internal bleeding, and Jamison had no idea if anyone had ever done surgery on a vampire. What he did know, was that the beating she'd taken would have easily killed a human, but Holly was healing.

Those deep slices were holding together and knitting well without stitches because Constance applied her own blood and some from Byron. Without taking her to a hospital, there was nothing else he could do.

Dr. Jamison had also looked over Joe, but he was surprisingly unwounded except for bruises, a black eye, and a cracked cheek from Charles's fist. Joe just needed to get some human food in him and rest for the day. Some pain killers helped him sleep.

By that time, all anyone could do was wait for Holly to wake, so Parker sat and stared at her. He refused to leave or sleep until she could speak to him and smile. He didn't care how long it took.

Constance hadn't left Nibble either, because she refused to go back to the Assembly without Parker. He needed to feed soon, and wasn't ready to be on his own. While his training had gone well, it wasn't complete, and she wasn't about to take any chances when they were so close to success.

"I didn't even feel the hunger when I bit that guy to feed Holly," Parker argued when Constance came in her room again to try to convince him to leave.

"That's because all your instincts were centered around saving her. You've only fed twice on your own, and been exposed to a lot of human blood. We have to make sure you can pull away again when you need to."

"Give me another hour. Please! She has to wake soon, and I can't leave without telling her I'm okay. You heard Joe, she was sure I was dead."

"Okay, another hour. But if you feel hungry at all, we have to go."

"Thanks, Constance. Hey, thank you for everything. I can do it. I'll have to do it to stay with Holly, and I will."

Constance smiled. "I'll be back in one hour."

Parker looked at the healing scrapes and cuts on Holly's face, and dropped his eyes to the casts that Dr. Jamison had put on both her wrists. He knew there was a bigger cast on her left leg, under the covers, but didn't want to think about all her injuries. He rested his hand on her fingers, careful not to move her hand and hurt her. He just stared at those still-swollen fingers and waited for what seemed to be forever.

"Please talk to me, Holly," he whispered as his head dropped to his chest. "I don't have much time left."

"Parker," Holly sighed like her voice barely worked. "I knew we'd be together."

"Holly," Parker gasped as his head snapped up to gaze at her. Tears pooled in his eyes.

"Don't be sad," Holly sighed again. "When Charles killed me, I knew it meant I'd see you again. That's all that counts."

"Holly, babe, we're not dead. We're both okay. Charles is dead. We're both okay." He smiled and nodded his head trying to convince her that they were both alive.

"We're alive?"

"Yes. And you're healing. We'll have the rest of our lives to be together. Just the two of us."

She tried to reach for him, but winced in pain. Parker leaned down and barely touched her lips in a tender kiss.

"How?" she asked with her damaged voice. "How did we get here? Who saved me from Charles? Where's Joe?" All the questions came streaming out like one long word as she glanced around the room.

"I killed Charles," Parker said with a lot of satisfaction in his voice. "Byron, Constance, TJ, Dr. Jamison, and even Joe helped you heal. He's resting, and he's okay. You'll hear the whole story when you're stronger. Just remember that you're getting better, now, and we'll be together as soon as possible."

Constance quietly opened the door. "It's time, Parker," she said.

"She's awake," Parker answered smiling at Constance.

Constance's smile lit the room as her eyes met Holly's. "You're going to be fine," she sighed after she approached the bed and looked down at Holly. "So is Parker."

Parker couldn't take his eyes off Holly and continued to gently stroke her fingers. Unless he was touching her, he had trouble knowing everything was real.

Holly smiled as a single tear ran down her cheek. "How, Parker? How did you get better?"

"Constance did it. She let me starve until most of Charles's blood was out of me and then fed me herself. It's like I was changed again. By Constance."

"Which is why I have to take him away from you, dear. His training isn't complete. I'll bring him back as soon as I'm sure he's ready to feed on his own."

"Parker," Holly said with questions and longing in her voice. She could barely stand the idea of him walking away as soon as she'd gotten him back.

"It's okay, Holly. I'll finish my training while you heal. Then we'll have our lives together. I promise," he emphasized. "Nothing will keep me away from you. I'll control it. Promise."

"I'll miss you," she whispered.

"Me too. But this time you'll know where I am and that I'm coming back as soon as I can. I'll call you everyday. Hell, five times a day," he smiled. "It's all over, babe, and we'll be together."

Parker leaned in to kiss her again, but let his lips barely touch hers. They were still so bruised and cracked, he was afraid of hurting her.

"I'll tell Byron you're awake," he said quietly with his lips just inches from hers. "You should probably feed again, then all you need to do is rest. Try to sleep while you wait for Byron."

"Okay. I love you."

"I love you so much. I'll be back as soon as I can."

"Heal well," Constance said as she reached for Parker's arm and led him from the room. She knew he'd never get up and leave on his own.

Holly watched Parker and Constance leave. Her mind swirled, trying to reconcile what she remembered with the little Parker had told her. It felt like someone had waved a magic wand and made everything work out, but there had to be much more to the story.

Holly was just too tired to think anymore. She had flashes in her head of Charles touching her, kissing her, and beating her. And flashes of Parker holding her. But, within a few seconds, she couldn't think anymore and felt herself fading into sleep.

* * *

Parker and I walked along the quiet street holding each other. He had an arm around my shoulders and the other arm across my waist. I had both arms around his waist, squeezing tight. We were as physically close as we could be while walking.

He smiled down at me, and I noticed the spot of blood next to his mouth. Smiling back, I stretched up to lick it away, and he caught my lips in a kiss. A kiss that slowly grew more passionate, until we both smelled the human nearby.

Our passion and desire for each other was wonderful, but the need to taste that human's blood was overwhelming. We had to follow the scent to find him.

Holding hands while we hunted, we both knew that we were getting close. We followed his blood into another dark alley and saw him standing on a plastic crate, leaning over, picking through a dumpster.

"Find anything?" Parker quietly asked the guy.

"None of your business." His speech was slurred and he smelled of alcohol and unwashed clothes. Alcohol did such nasty things to human minds and bodies.

"Oh, I think it is," Parker answered.

"You two get out of here. Go on! I found this stuff. You go find your own dumpster." He waved a broken bottle at us in some futile attempt to threaten us. Imagine thinking anything he could do would be a threat to us.

Parker and I both laughed, and the guy got madder. "I said GET OUT", he yelled and actually got off the crate and took a step toward us brandishing that stupid broken bottle.

We were still about ten yards from him, but Parker crossed that distance in the flash of an eye. He took the bottle out of the bum's hand and wrapped his own hand around the guys' throat. I thought his eyes would pop out of his head when he saw Parker's fangs.

What did these human's think when they saw that? Did they think it was some kind of hallucination from their drunken brains, or were they sober enough to realize that vampires were real and they were about to die as their blood was sucked out of their bodies?

"You smell like shit," Parker sneered. "But your blood will taste good."

I was right next to Parker and licking my lips and fangs as I stared at the half-drunk guy that would be our next meal.

"After you, sweetheart," Parker smiled at me and moved his hand so I could get to his neck.

I grabbed his hair, pulling his head back, as I stared into those terrified eyes and showed him my fangs with a hideous smile. I bit into his vein and began to suck greedily. Parker bit the other side of his neck.

Our chins were pressed hard together as we both drank, and the sound of his scream made his blood taste even better. We let him scream as his blood raced down our throats until he started to lose consciousness.

Parker and I each grabbed one of his arms to keep him on his feet until he was nothing but dead weight. And we kept drinking. He wasn't dead, yet.

His blood flowed more slowly no matter how hard we sucked until his heart started skipping beats. Then it stopped. We drank what little more we could, until he was drained dry.

We still held him up when our heads turned to each other and we lapped the blood from each other's lips, teeth, and tongues. This was the moment when we felt most alive, most powerful.

When we broke the gruesome kiss, Parker lifted the man by grasping both arms and threw him into the dumpster.

"It'll be easier for him to reach his treasures, now," Parker laughed, and I laughed along with him.

We held each other again as we continued strolling down the street, but didn't make it very far before Parker pulled me into the entrance of another alley.

"I want you, Holly," Parker said. We held each other and he backed me up against the scratchy bricks of some building.

His lips kissed me deeply and his hands roamed over my body. I had my eyes closed kissing him back and feeling the desire in his touch. My desire flared just as hotly as I stroked his back and ran one hand through his hair.

"You will be mine, little girl," he said.

My eyes flew open as I realized that the voice I heard was not Parker. It was Charles. His hands tightened until the pain once again radiated through my body. The pressure of his mouth against mine felt like my jaw would break and my skull would be crushed against the bricks behind me.

I struggled, tried to kick or hit him, but my wrists and ankles were back in those chains. I screamed into his mouth – a gagging, strangled scream that went nowhere.

Charles pulled back and laughed. "There's no one to help you. No one to save you. You're mine until I decide I'm tired of you. Then you die."

I screamed and called out, "No! Nooo!" Then screamed again as I listened to Charles's hateful laugh.

"Holly! Wake up, sweetheart. You're safe now. Wake up."

I opened my eyes to see Byron looking down at me with sadness and concern. I realized my arms were stretched above my head as if the chains still held them.

"Byron," I sighed.

"Just a nightmare, sweetheart. Everything's okay now."

He gently took my elbows to move my hands down to my sides. Instead, I used the leverage of his strength to pull myself up slightly to wrap my arms around him.

"Oh, Byron," I said as I buried my head against his chest and sobbed.

He wrapped his arms around me and stroked my hair. It really was over. I slowly started to realize that we were all going to be okay.

"Is he really dead?" I asked through my tears without moving my head from his chest.

"Yes, he's really dead," Byron said while stroking my hair. "Parker saved you. Your blood called him to you, or we wouldn't even have known you were there. You would have been so proud of him. He fed you by biting Joe's wrist. He watched the blood run into your mouth. He had complete control, and saved you."

"So he's really okay?" I raised my head to look into his eyes. Byron wouldn't lie to me. He wouldn't hide the truth from me. "Really?"

"Yes! He's really okay," Byron said gazing into my eyes. "Constance wants to watch him feed for a little longer, but he's not bloodthirsty anymore. She's being very, very cautious because she wants to use the cure for others. He should be back with us within a week."

I dropped my head back to his chest and sobbed again with relief. Seeing Parker here with me seemed like the dream I was waking from. Hearing him tell me that we were going to be together, that he was fine, that Charles was dead, seemed like the illusion, but it wasn't. All I'd hoped for and waited for was finally true.

Chapter 16

Byron let me cry some more. He knew I had to let go of all the emotion I'd been holding inside me for so long, and crying my eyes out was a good start. As he stroked my hair, I felt like the weight of the world was lifting from my shoulders.

I was still mourning for Mom and Dad and would continue to do that for a long time. We still had the situation with Sarita getting older and sicker, and I was still concerned about whether or not Chris would choose to become a vampire. But shaking off the worry of what happened to Parker and the threat of Charles trying to destroy all of us was going a long way toward healing me.

I think Byron held me for about a half hour before I eventually ran out of tears and was ready to talk again.

"I'm sorry, Byron," I finally said, lifting my head to look at him. "I didn't mean to keep you here so long or soak your shirt with my tears. You don't have to stay any longer."

"You don't need to be sorry, and I'm going to stay until you feed and fall asleep."

"I am a little hungry," I smiled.

He smiled back and pulled his phone out of his pocket. "TJ, Holly's ready to feed." He straightened my pillow and blankets before moving away from me. "You need to rest while we're waiting. Then I think you'll sleep for quite a while."

"Yeah. Tell me about Parker."

"I found him in the basement when I was looking for Charles. He was holding you, letting the blood drip from Joe's wrist into your mouth. I couldn't believe it. Most much older vampires couldn't have done that. He asked me to help him save you," Byron's smile lit his whole face as he told me about Parker. "All he could think about was saving you."

"I thought I was dead," I whimpered.

"It was close, sweetheart." He looked so sad when he said that. "Constance used her own blood to drip into your deepest wounds to start them healing. You were just too weak to do it yourself. TJ brought a human and Parker watched him bite his wrist and watched the blood dripping into you. He even licked Joe's wrist to heal it. I was so proud of him."

I could tell from Byron's face how proud he was. But there was also something there that said he was surprised and relieved. No wonder. Parker's turn-around was almost beyond belief.

"Constance really thinks he'll be okay?"

I'm sure I sounded like I kept asking the same question again, and again, but I had to know. I'd been so scared for Parker for so long, that I needed to be reassured. I had to keep asking to make sure the answer wasn't just my own wishful thinking.

"Yes, she does. She said she wants to use this method with young ones that can't find their control, so she has to finish with Parker. She has to be able to convince others that it will work."

"Then he's okay," I said more to myself that to Byron. "He's okay," I sighed with relief looking back at Byron.

"Yes. He's okay," he nodded.

I reached over to take Byron's hand, but my cast kept me from gripping anything. "When do the casts come off? They itch."

"Dr. Jamison's going to fly back tonight. He thinks you'll be ready to get them off by the time he gets here."

"Good. Have you told Crystal and Chris what happened? Is Chris alright?"

"Yes, I've talked to them, and sent Lorna back to help Crystal."

"So TJ, Quinton, and Luke are staying at Nibble with us?"

Byron's face fell. His joy had turned suddenly into deep sadness. "TJ and Luke are here. We lost Quinton."

I made some sound between a gasp and a subtle scream, and Byron held my fingers that were sticking out of the casts.

"I didn't want to tell you, yet, but I couldn't hide it from you. Three of Charles's followers attacked Quinton, and one of them broke his neck. Luke was seriously injured, but he's healing."

"Oh, Byron," I sighed, and tears slipped from my eyes again. "Quinton was so wonderful and he took such good care of me."

Byron had stopped looking at me and gazed down at our clasped hands. He stroked my fingers, comforting himself as much as me.

"We had a ceremony this morning and gave him to the sun. We praised his courage and faithfulness. It was especially meaningful since Constance and Bartholomew were there."

"Gave him to the sun?"

"We don't bury our loved ones. We leave the bodies out at sunrise. Our bodies can't fight the sun at all when we're dead, so it's like being cremated. We let the ashes go back to the earth."

"I think that's nice. God, I'll miss him so much."

Byron nodded and stroked my cheek. Another person to mourn. "Quinton was always so strong and determined. He treated me like I was his little sister, like Chris does. Rule the Night will seem empty without him."

Someone knocked gently on the door. "Come in, TJ," Byron said.

TJ led an enthralled human into the room and gave me a huge smile that made me smile back, even though I was really too sad to keep it on my face long. He recognized the pain in my eyes, but leaned down to gently hug me anyway.

"What's wrong? Are you in pain?" he asked.

"I just told her about Quinton," Byron answered.

TJ suddenly looked devastated. "It was a great loss," he said quietly.

"I can't believe he's gone," I said.

"We all feel that," Byron said quietly. I don't think TJ knew what to say. I understood that.

"Holly, you need to feed and sleep," Byron said. "We'll talk more when you're stronger."

"Okay. I'll take his wrist. I'm too tired to sit up to take his neck."

After feeding, I slept. I have no idea what time it was when TJ and Byron fed me, but the next thing I knew, someone was waking me. I jumped and squealed a little, with a sudden vision of Samuel trying to take me to Charles again. It was Dr. Jamison.

"I'm sorry, Holly, I didn't mean to scare you."

"That's okay. I was just really sound asleep."

"I think your casts should be ready to come off," he smiled.

"Oh, thank you," I sighed.

He got this little thing that looked like some kind of rotary cutter, plugged it in, and started on my closest wrist. The vibrations from it felt weird, but the cast was quickly coming apart.

"I don't want you to use this much for another day. Don't lift anything heavy, or twist it around. There was more than one bone broken in there, so we don't want to take any chances. Let's see you move it a little."

I flexed my wrist, flexed my fingers, and Dr. Jamison felt it and turned it. He even did the twisting that he told me not to do.

"Looks good," he smiled.

Then we did the same kind of stuff with my other wrist and my knee. I was more relieved than I expected to be when he said everything looked good. I think the broken bones scared me. It was easy to see cuts and bruises healing, but who knew what was going on inside?

"I'm thrilled with the way you're healing," the doc said after looking over all my bruises and cuts, "but I need to see you walk on that knee."

He took my arms and helped me scoot over to sit on the edge of the bed. "Put weight on that leg slowly," he said, supporting me around the waist while I stood. "Any pain at all?"

"No, it feels fine," the surprise was in my voice.

"Byron said you got blood from him and Constance. That's awfully strong stuff."

"I didn't drink it. I don't think I drank it."

"No, you didn't, but it was put directly into your wounds. It seeped in and helped the inside heal, too. Anyone would want to have some of what Constance has in those veins," he smiled.

"Can humans drink vampire blood?"

I really didn't think they could, but wasn't sure. And Dr. Jamison was one hundred percent human. He'd taken care of Parker and Sarita for years, and was sometimes called in for vampire care. That had been twice now for me.

"No. Something in it doesn't agree with humans, and they can get a violent reaction unless they're already essentially drained of their own blood. Usually an accidental drop or two doesn't hurt, but otherwise it can be pretty dangerous."

"Wouldn't it be great if vampire blood could be adapted to heal humans? It could be like a miracle cure for a lot of things."

"I don't know of a way anything like that could be done. You wouldn't catch me being the first one to try it," he grinned.

He seemed uncomfortable discussing it. Had he thought of it before? Had he experimented with it? He probably wouldn't take that chance, but it was an interesting idea.

During that discussion, he'd been walking me around the room. The knee felt fine, my wrists felt strong, I knew my swollen face was getting back to normal, but I was as tired as I'd ever been in my life.

"That's enough," I sighed. Dr. Jamison led me back to the bed. "Why am I so tired?"

"Every bit of your body's energy has gone into healing you. I'm guessing you feel like you haven't fed in a week.

"Close," I smiled.

"I'll tell Byron to feed you right away, then I'll want you to feed again in the morning. By tomorrow night, you should be close to normal."

"That sounds great," I sighed as I rested back on my pillow and pulled up the covers. "Where is Byron?"

"When I got here, he was still sleeping. He was helping Beatrice clean up some things, and I don't think he rested until late this afternoon."

"Poor Byron. What time is it?"

"7:45. Just getting dark."

"I don't want you to wake him to feed me," I said.

"The setting sun will wake him any time now. It can wait for then."

"Good. Thanks, Dr. Jamison. I really appreciate you flying up here to take care of me."

"It's no problem," he said shaking his head. "Holly," he hesitated, "could I ask you some questions while we have a moment alone?"

"Sure." I had no idea what this may be about.

"Have you been happy since your change? Is it worth it?"

Was Dr. Jamison thinking of becoming a vampire? He was involved with Alice, one of the Rule the Night waitresses. They'd been together for a long time.

"Yes, I've been happy. But you were told I was attacked and didn't have a choice, weren't you?"

"Yes."

"I don't know what I would have done if I'd been able to choose. Parker and I might have decided to stay human. But Parker always wanted to change, and I probably would have become a vampire with him. It's hard to know what we might have chosen."

"I'll be forty on my next birthday and I've been in love with Alice for years. She's never pushed me, but I know she fears me getting old and dying. At one time, I thought it would be okay, but, lately, I've been afraid of it, too.

"Because of what's happening to Sarita?"

"Does that sound selfish? I've been watching her get worse by the day, and I don't want Alice to have to watch something like that happen to me. I guess I'm old enough now to realize that all the terrible things that I've seen happen to other people could easily happen to me."

"Chris is thinking about it, too," I said quietly. "Maybe it would help both of you if you talked to him."

"Thank you, Holly. I think I'll do that," he said. Then he got his usual doctor's voice back. "And you rest and try to sleep while you're waiting for Byron. I'll check on you when you're back at Rule the Night."

"Thanks. I'll see you there."

But I wasn't very sleepy anymore, just physically tired. Dr. Jamison had certainly given me something to think about. But what I thought mostly about wasn't Dr. Jamison. It was Chris.

With Mom and Dad now gone, I didn't see any reason he'd choose to stay human. With the two people he loved the most, Lorna and me, being vampires, why wouldn't Chris want to be a vampire, too?

With all my stray thoughts, I barely heard the phone vibrating against the dresser across the room. I had no idea where my phone was. I didn't even remember if I'd taken it with me when I left Rule the Night with Samuel.

Well, some phone was ringing, so I got out of bed carefully, and hurried over to it as fast as I could. I didn't know the number on the caller ID, so I answered with a simple, "Hello?"

"I did it, Holly. I stopped drinking, all on my own. I healed her wounds and erased her memory, all without Constance or Bartholomew even there."

"Oh, Parker! That's wonderful!" I almost squealed. "Was it hard?" I said more seriously.

"Kinda," he sighed. "My hunger told me to keep going, but I thought of you. I knew that I had to stop or never see you again."

"The first time I did it, I thought about how disappointed you and Byron would be if I didn't stop."

"Constance said it's natural to want to keep going, but we all find something that makes it worth stopping."

"Oh Parker," I said again as I started crying. All the tears! There was just so much emotional stuff going on, it seemed my eyes were ready to throw out the tears at any time.

"Don't cry, babe," Parker said quietly. I think my tears where sparking his emotions, too.

"I'm just so relieved and so happy for you. Happy for us. When will Constance let you come home?"

"She says another feeding or two. I wish it was now."

"So do I. Here comes Byron." I ran over and opened the door before he got the chance to knock. I'm sure he didn't expect me to be out of bed.

"It's Parker!" I told him with joy in my voice. The tears were suddenly gone. "He did it. He stopped."

The look on Byron's face made me think that he may cry any second. "May I talk to him?"

I handed him the phone with a smile. His relief might have been even bigger than mine. While I was afraid Parker may never be cured, I think Byron, deep in his heart, had been *convinced* that Parker would never be cured.

They talked for several minutes. I think Parker was giving him a blow-by-blow account because Byron kept nodding and saying things like, "Uh, huh". When he was finished, he said, "I'm so proud of you. I'll see you soon." Then he gave the phone back so I could say goodbye.

"Constance is waiting to talk to me, so I'd better go," Parker said. "I'll call you back later. Okay?"

"Of course it's okay! Dr. Jamison said that I'd be feeling almost normal once I fed tonight, so you'd better call."

"Goodbye, sweetheart. I love you," he whispered.

Ellen Fritz

"I love you, too."

Chapter 17

After feeding, talking to Parker for over an hour in the middle of the night, and sleeping soundly and peacefully the whole next day, I woke up feeling great. On top of that, I didn't dream and no one woke me up unexpectedly.

I took a long, hot shower, washed my hair, and took time to dry it so I could leave it down around my shoulders. I hoped to meet Beatrice and all the others that helped us since I was brought in so wounded, and wanted to thank them and make a good impression.

I also wanted to look around Nibble to see the changes that had been made. That place held such awful memories for me, I thought it would be good to see it in another light. Maybe that would help me get Charles out of my mind once and for all, although I didn't know if he'd ever be completely gone.

Byron came in to check on me. He was thrilled to see me up, clean and dressed. I had put on the simple green, sleeveless dress that Beatrice had sent down for me. I got the feeling that someone had gone shopping to get that dress as well as the underwear and sandals. The clothes I'd been wearing were nowhere in sight. I hoped someone burned them.

"You look lovely, Holly," Byron said as he hugged me. "And relaxed. It's been too long since I've seen that."

"Thank you. It's been too long for both of us," I said as I hugged him back. "Who do I thank for the clothes?"

He smiled. "With a little cell phone help, Crystal and I managed to take care of it."

"Cell phone help?"

"I was in the store describing stuff, and Crystal told me what to buy," he shrugged.

I had to laugh. "You two are amazing."

Together, Byron and I walked out to see the place, which, of course, he'd already seen. We'd only gotten as far as the common room when I stopped and stared at that small door that led to Charles's human prison and torture chamber.

I would have bricked up the door and filled the rooms with dirt. It was where he tortured and killed innocent humans. Who knew how many? In my mind it represented all the hatefulness and evil that Charles had been capable of.

"I want you to see it, Holly," Byron said as he reached for the doorknob. He knew I wouldn't want to, but we both realized you have to face the hard things to put them behind you.

The hallway was all painted a soft cream color and there was a pretty collection of pictures on the walls. The first time I sneaked down that corridor, it was dirty gray and empty. The once bare cement floor now had a soft beige carpet and overhead lights made the place look almost cheerful.

The room where victims were chained to the wall now contained a bar, a comfy-looking couch, and several chairs. Gone was the dim lighting, the dirty, blood-spattered floor and walls. Most important, there was no sign of the chains and cuffs that once hung from the walls.

We walked through that room into the space that had once held the big boxes of supplies. I'd hidden there while Charles and Armand brought a client in to torture one of the human prisoners. All those supplies once concealed the cell. Now it had game tables and chairs. Pool, poker, even foosball. No sign of where the cell had once been.

I was glad to see the secret back entrance had a big EXIT sign on it and wasn't a secret anymore. The whole thing looked and felt like a different place. Thank God.

We finished the tour and headed up the stairs. I felt better already knowing that horrible place was gone. TJ joined us when we got to the bar. I had the feeling he'd been waiting for us to appear, and he gave me a big hug again.

Seeing the bar made me think of the time Luke and I had spent there, and the hours Quinton had hung around pretending to flirt with me. That all seemed so long ago, and now Quinton was gone. He was such a good guy and deserved to live a long, happy life. Thinking of his death made me feel my hate for Charles again. Just one of the many reasons I would hate him for as long as I lived.

Luke walked out from the office with a huge smile and gave me the warmest hug of all. "Man, it's good to see you, Holly," he sighed.

"You too," I said. "Byron said you were injured. Are you okay, now?"

"Oh, sure," he winked. "One of Charles's goons stabbed me in the back, but you can't keep me down long."

I smiled, but it faded quickly. "Byron told me about Quinton. Were you able to go to the ceremony?"

"Yeah," he sighed. "It was hard. The two of us had gotten to be pretty good buddies."

"I know," was all I could say, so I just hugged him again.

The rest of Nibble had been repainted, mostly refurnished, and all the employees were different. I didn't know any of them, but they sure knew me.

Everyone greeted me, said it was good to see that I was better, and some actually thanked me for my part in the clean-up of Nibble. It was amazing.

Beatrice surprised me. She was petite and lovely, but cold. She said all the right "Nice to meet you" type words, but seemed pretty unfriendly.

"She's very unhappy here," Byron said when we left her office. "She'll go back to Australia soon, now that Charles is dead, and the Assembly will put someone else here."

"Then why did she come?"

"Because Constance asked her. They needed someone strong enough to face Charles if necessary, and she's more than strong enough."

"She doesn't look it."

"Appearances can be deceiving," he grinned.

"I guess," was all I could say.

"We'll be going back tonight, so let's go for a walk while we have the chance."

"Tonight? Shouldn't we be leaving to get there before sunrise?"

"Constance is sending the helicopter for us, and it won't be here until 1:00 or 2:00."

"Helicopter," I sighed. "Not my favorite way to travel."

"It'll be better this time," he assured me.

"Have you talked to Constance? I thought Parker would call me by now."

"No. I haven't talked to her tonight, but I'm sure he'll call as soon as he can. It's Parker I wanted to talk to you about on our walk."

"Why? Did something go wrong?"

"No! No, nothing's gone wrong. I'm sorry. It would have been more accurate to say that I wanted to talk about me."

"What is it?"

We started down the sidewalk with Byron holding my elbow like the old-world gentleman he really was. "I know you had doubts about me. About what I decided to do about Parker's bloodthirst. I want you to know that I never could have executed Parker or turned him over to the Assembly. I'd arranged for a friend overseas to take both of us. All four of us if you and Crystal were willing to go. We would have stayed there forever."

"Seriously?"

"The arrangements were all made. I hadn't told anyone but Crystal. Holly, I couldn't let you think that I would ever hurt Parker."

"I was afraid you would," I said quietly, staring up into his eyes. "I'm sorry. I should have known better." I shook my head. "I should have known."

"I'm sorry I couldn't tell you sooner. I couldn't take the chance that anyone else would be implicated. I even kept it from TJ. When Parker ran away..." Byron shook his head and looked like he was actually in pain. "I thought I'd waited too long. I couldn't see any way that he'd survive and come back to us."

I wrapped my arm around his waist, and he slipped his arm around my shoulders. We walked silently for quite a while.

I could feel another level of my anxiety peel away. I had tried not to think about it, but I *was* worried that Byron would give Parker to The Assembly for execution. That had been a deep fear that I wouldn't let myself face.

We continued walking and talking quietly about nothing important. The night was warm, and the sky was full of stars. I could gaze up at the sky and see us walking in Adelle. It felt so good.

When we got back to Nibble, we hung around the bar and waited for word from Constance about the helicopter. Parker called, though, and my time went much faster while we talked.

It reminded me of all the time we spent on the phone when I was afraid of losing control with the human Parker, but much more personal and intimate. I told him I couldn't wait for us to be together again. He said he could already feel me in his arms.

I wondered what the helicopter was doing that made us wait so long for it to get to Chicago, but finally, Constance called to say that a driver was on his way from the helipad. I wondered where the helipad was. I didn't even know we had one. Or rather, the Assembly had one.

The trip home was uneventful, and the lights of the cities were amazing to see from far above. I could see the line of headlights moving along the freeways. Even in the middle of the night, there were so many. The curve of Lake Michigan as we first left was magical. I couldn't take my eyes off all the darkness over the water and the million little city lights that surrounded it.

We landed somewhere outside of Adelle, and Lorna, Chris and Crystal met us with a ride back to Rule the Night.

I don't think I ever hugged Chris so hard.

"You really okay?" he asked more than once.

"I feel great except that I still get a little tired. I really am fine."

"I was so worried," he said while still hugging me.

"I know." My visions of Chris being left alone haunted me, but that was one more worry that I could leave behind.

Byron walked over to kiss Crystal. I could see by the look on his face that he'd never want to be separated from her again, and I smiled.

Byron teased Crystal about leaving the bar with inexperienced employees. "So who is in charge?" he asked.

"Who cares?" she teased back before wrapping her arms around him.

All the way home, Chris held my hand, patted my knee, or held me around my shoulders. It was really touching that he'd been so worried. I really loved my big brother, and it was good to be reminded that he loved me, too.

The bar was closed by the time we got there, which worked out really well. The employees gathered around us, hugged, said how relieved they were, all the things I needed to hear. Looking at their smiling faces, though, part of me expected to see Quinton. But he was gone, and a wave of sadness moved through me.

I got tired pretty quickly and was ready to head to bed early. Byron wanted to know if I needed to feed, but I wasn't hungry at all and just wanted to get some sleep.

Just before dawn, Byron, Crystal, Chris, and Lorna, all walked me downstairs while TJ and Luke continued talking to the other guards.

"I think you can take care of yourself from here," Byron smiled once we got to the door of my room. "Sleep well, and we'll see you tonight."

"See you later, everyone," I sighed looking forward to crawling into my own bed and sleeping through the whole day. First, though, I thought I'd call Parker.

I turned on the light, and someone was standing at my dresser looking at the perfume and jewelry displayed there. My mouth fell open and my brain went blank for a second as I tried to clear out what I thought I was seeing. Was this real?

"I'm home," Parker said quietly as I stared at his huge smile, and the reality finally sank in.

I threw myself at him and squealed and laughed and jumped up and down like a little girl. He kissed me, squeezed me against him, and kept whispering, "I love you," against my lips.

"You're here! You're really here!" I kept repeating.

"I wanted to surprise you," he said when we finally broke apart to look at each other.

"The best surprise, ever," I whispered as I gazed into his eyes.

"How are you feeling?" he asked with some concern in his eyes.

"Back to normal except for getting a little tired."

"Tired? Hopefully not too tired. I have plans for you this morning." He gave me a sexy grin and nuzzled my neck.

I sighed. He felt so good. His lips on my neck, holding our bodies together from head to foot, the scent of him. It all felt so good, so right.

"I suddenly have all kinds of energy," I whispered into his hair.

As his lips met mine, he swung his arm under my knees, picked me up, and started carrying me toward the bed. His lips never moved an inch from mine.

"Last time I held you like this," he said as he broke our kiss and stopped next to the bed, "you were unconscious. I'm going to carry you to bed every morning until we both forget that night. Deal?"

"Oh, yeah," I sighed.

He laid me on the bed and crawled in on top of me, even though we were still fully clothed. That didn't last long. We made love quickly but passionately because we'd both missed each other so much. Then we held each other and talked.

We went through everything that had happened to both of us because it had been so long, and there was still so much each of us didn't know. We talked about how we each felt during our ordeals, about how afraid we were, and about how much we had been afraid that we'd never see each other again.

We cried, we laughed, and we made love again. This time slowly, tenderly.

We finally slept holding each other and planning on never letting go again.

Parker was back. He was cured of bloodthirst. He was in my arms. Everything was back to normal, and it all felt too good to be true.

Chapter 18

Joe stayed at Nibble that night that Charles was finally killed and through the next day. He slept a lot, some human brought him food, and he finally got up to shower just before the sun was setting. The knock on his door made him figure that they were ready to kick him out, but that was okay, because he was ready to leave.

"Oh. Hi," he said with surprise as he opened the door.

"May I talk to you for a minute?" Constance asked.

"Sure. Come on in. I figured you left."

"Soon. I thought I should settle things with you myself."

Joe invited her in. He gave her the one chair in the small room and sat tensely on the edge of the bed.

"Are you going to erase my memory?" It didn't take any special skills to hear that Joe didn't want his memory gone.

"I haven't decided. How old are your memories?"

"Twenty years. I tried to forget it most of that time, but I've recently learned a lot more."

"I talked to Gina," Constance said. "She thinks you can be trusted, and she thinks it may be useful having a detective aware of us."

Joe nodded, but he obviously had something else on his mind. "She told me bloodthirsty vampires dispose of the bodies where they'll never be found. That bothers me. How many do you think?"

"Not as many as you may imagine. Bloodthirst is almost eradicated, and with the death of Charles and his followers, there can't be many left. Far more people disappear because of human crime than vampire crime."

"Yeah, that makes sense."

"Gina also said that you were pretty stunned when she first told you."

"I was seventeen, a kid. I think I can handle it now."

"You *think* you can handle it. I expected you to be trying to convince me that I didn't need to remove your memory. You're not convincing me."

"I'm trying to be honest here. I can promise you, though, that I'll never tell anyone. Hell, who would believe me?"

"Good point. Others finding out about us is a concern. So you'll just go on with your life and keep this secret to yourself?"

"I'll keep your secret, but it's the going on with my life I'm not clear about. I've realized that I haven't been very happy. Not thrilled with my job, but worse with my personal life. I guess I need to talk to Gina."

"I thought you'd want to hurry back to Columbus tonight for work."

"I called in and took a week's vacation."

"I'm willing to let you keep your memories, Joe. I couldn't erase them all, anyway. Tell Gina to let me know what you decide."

"I will. Thanks."

Joe left right after Constance. His car was still parked outside Nibble, right where he left it. He sat in the driver's seat staring at the dark streets that surrounded him. He didn't know what he was going to say to Gina. He had a lot to tell her, and still had a million questions.

He felt like he should be more comfortable with the whole vampire thing since he'd met so many of them. Besides, they had all treated him well, except Charles. He was the bad guy through everything, but Joe still knew humans who had done much worse things to other humans.

"Ah, hell!" he said as he finally started his car and headed for the freeway. The truth was, on top of everything, he was still interested in Gina. He'd spent twenty years subconsciously comparing every woman he met to Gina, and none of them had come close to being as special as she was. "Maybe because she's a vampire, ya think?" he asked himself.

But, no. It wasn't just the vampire thing. She was strong, caring, funny, and always fun to be around. Not to mention that she was gorgeous. Gina was everything that Joe wanted, and he'd found her when he was seventeen.

She'd been serious enough to tell him the truth about vampires. She wouldn't have done that if she thought he'd be gone in a few weeks. She was telling him so they could move on to a long-lasting relationship.

He felt like he'd wasted all those years. All those years looking for the right woman to share his life, and she'd been there all along. But did she still want him? Was she interested in what was now an older man who would just keep getting older?

Joe always had the standard vision of wife and kids. Growing old together, playing with grandchildren. Was Gina worth giving up that dream?

That's what he needed to figure out. Could they still be as happy together as it once seemed they would be? Was being happy with Gina worth giving up every other vision he'd had of the future? He needed to give himself some time to get to know her again.

As soon as he walked into La Sang Rouge, he saw Gina talking to a table of customers. And she saw him.

She made an excuse to the customers and walked over saying, "Hi, Joe. Come on back to my office." He followed her.

"Your poor face," she said gently stroking the still visible bruises once they got behind her closed door.

"Couple of the others really had the crap beat out of them, but they're all healed," he grinned. "I take longer."

"I'm sorry you ended up in the middle of all that."

"No problem," he shrugged. "But I don't have an explanation for the guys at work. If it's okay, I thought maybe I'd stay here in Indy for a couple days."

"That sounds lovely," she whispered.

"I have a lot of stuff to talk to you about," he said.

She sighed, moving closer to him, "I'm really glad you came."

* * *

Parker and I walked through the dark streets with our arms around each other. Light clouds covered the moon and stars, making the shadows even deeper than usual. We could see much, much more than any human, though.

We hardly talked as we moved silently through the night. Humans would have called it the middle of the night, but it was our favorite time. We loved the quiet, the solitude.

The scent of several humans drifted to us from the path up ahead, and swirled through our senses. There was one scent in particular that caught our attention, and we smiled. He was only about a block away, and I knew he hadn't seen us, but we knew exactly where he was. I wondered, though, why he was out walking alone so late.

"Chris," Parker yelled ahead to get his attention.

"Hey, guys," he called and hurried toward us, but I could hear the sadness in his voice.

"What's wrong?" I asked him as we got close enough to speak quietly.

"I decided to walk past the house, just to check it. Everything looked good there, and I thought about Uncle Steve. He's in an apartment with some woman, and I thought I'd go see him and kinda say goodbye. It was stupid, but ... Anyway, I found him coming out of Chips, drunk as hell, acting like an ass."

"His usual Friday night," I said sadly.

"You'd think what happened to Dad and Mom would keep him out of the bars, wouldn't you? I don't get it."

"I know. I've never gotten it, either."

"Come on, man," Parker said as he reached around Chris's shoulders. "Walk with us for a while."

"Are you scared about tomorrow?" I asked after the three of us had walked silently for about a block.

"Not scared. Nervous, though."

"That's understandable," I answered.

"Byron's been really straight with me, and I know all the stuff that can go wrong. I just wish it was done."

"I hate that we won't be able to see you much for a while. But Lorna will be there."

"Yeah," he grinned. "I guess what really worries me is that I might panic while he's draining me and change my mind. Doesn't it feel like you're dying?"

"Holly and I both thought we were dying," Parker said. "You'll know different. I don't think you'll panic."

"I hope not," Chris shrugged.

We'd all been home and getting back to normal for almost three weeks and Chris didn't want to wait any longer. He'd spent a lot of time talking to Byron and hearing all the details of his change. He was sure.

I'd have been so scared if it was me. Even though everything should go smoothly, there was always the outside chance that Chris could die. I wouldn't let myself think about that.

When we got back to Rule the Night, Chris went on down the hall to the room he shared with Lorna. He'd moved out of his apartment when all the trouble started and Byron thought it was too dangerous for him to stay alone. He never even considered moving back when we were all safe, again. He and Lorna both knew that he was where he belonged.

I'd moved into Parker's suite, our suite, the day after he got home. It was designed for the two of us and we'd been unbelievably happy there. The half of the closet that had been so empty, waiting for my clothes, wasn't empty anymore.

The next evening Parker and I went to Lorna and Chris's room. Byron had been there for a while already, talking one more time about what would happen and making sure Chris was ready.

He was ready, and more determined than ever. I think I was more nervous than he was. I knew he was sure about becoming a vampire, but I was anxious anyway. I just couldn't help it.

"Chris has something to ask," Byron said when we were about ready to leave.

"What's that, man?" Parker asked. We all knew we couldn't be there while Byron came so close to draining him, or when he was feeding from his first humans. It would just be taking too big of a chance for us to smell all that human blood.

"I'd like you two to take some of my blood before Byron ... finishes it."

"Why?" I asked.

"I've fed both of you before when you needed it," he answered, "and it meant a lot to me that I could do that for you. Mainly, though, I just want you to be a part of this. It's a big thing, and I want my family involved."

"I'd be glad to," Parker said. "I feel like you're asking me to be your best man or something," he smiled.

"I'll do it, too." There I was fighting to keep the tears out of my eyes again. Asking us to be part of draining him was huge. I was proud to be a part of his change, but really glad I wouldn't be around to see the finish when he was so close to death.

"The rest of us should leave so you can say what you want privately," Byron said as he started to direct us out into the hall. "Who wants to go first?"

"I will," Parker said. "I think Holly should be last." He smiled at me and squeezed my hand.

* * *

We all left Parker and Chris alone. When my turn came, I would love the few minutes of time alone with him.

"Sit down, man," Parker said as he pulled two chairs together. "Want me to take your wrist?"

"That's cool," Chris said.

"It doesn't surprise me that you asked Holly to do this, but thanks for including me."

"I never had a brother. I guess I feel like I do, now."

"Me, too," Parker grinned. "And I keep thinking about how many years we have ahead of us to be a family, and you know how we feel about Lorna. The four of us will be together for a long time."

"That's the way I see it."

"Then let's get this done," Parker smiled.

He enthralled Chris to take the pain, leaned over his wrist and fed. When he was done and had healed Chris's wounds, he gave him a huge hug. "See you in a while, big brother," he grinned.

* * *

Parker came out smiling and it was my turn. I walked up to Chris and gave him a huge hug and kiss on the cheek before I said anything.

"You aren't going to cry, are you?" he asked with a smile once we let go of each other.

"I never know, anymore," I smiled back. "Sometimes it just happens."

"I love you, little sis," he said looking into my eyes. Yeah, a few tears pooled in my eyes.

"I love you, too. You're the best brother anyone could ever have."

"No, Holly, I'm not. If I'd been in the house, Uncle Steve would never ..."

"Don't say that. There have been times when both of us needed to look out for ourselves, and you had to leave. I remember how tough Dad was on you. Those fights were getting worse all the time, and he was going to end up beating the shit out of you one of those times when he was so drunk. You had to get out."

"Yeah, to Gretchen," he shook his head. "An old woman with a thing for seventeen year old boys."

"She wasn't that old. How old do you think Lorna is?"

We both laughed. "Come on. Bite me so we can get on with the rest of our long, long lives."

"I'm gonna' take your neck because I want to hold you. Look in my eyes and it *won't* be sexy like it is with Lorna."

I blocked his pain, leaving a pleasant feeling of well-being he'd get from the bite. He stretched his neck over to give me access. I smelled the blood running through his vein and bit him. I knew that this would be the last time that I smelled or tasted his human blood. I'd miss him being human, but looked forward to having centuries of him being around.

I only took a little, and licked his wounds. Chris smiled at me when I finished, and kissed me again on the cheek. "I guess it's time for Byron," he said.

"What about Lorna?"

"She took some earlier," he grinned. I should have known.

"We'll come see you in a while, but you'll be out. Byron will make you the best vampire he can. I think he'll be even more careful with you than he was with me."

"He knows you'll kill him if he isn't."

"Damn right," I grinned. I knew the next time I saw him, he'd be well on his way to being a vampire.

We went to the door, and let Byron in. We'd all go to work while Byron drained him and fed him. Lorna didn't try to hide the fact that she couldn't watch him being almost drained and coming so close to death. I didn't like that thought either, and couldn't stand just sitting around somewhere waiting. Besides, the bar was even busier these days, and customers kept streaming in.

* * *

"Why don't you sit on the bed, and I'll be able to lay you down when you get weak," Byron said once they were alone.

Chris moved to the bed. He'd already changed to light sweats and a tee shirt so he'd be comfortable. "If I start to panic, or something, and want you to stop, don't stop."

"I'm going to control the pain and make you relax. You won't panic."

"Then I'm ready."

Byron sat down and turned Chris so they almost faced each other. He enthralled him, felt his fangs push through his gums and bit into Chris's vein.

* * *

After Chris's change, we'd all gotten settled into our usual routines. Crystal, Chris and I worked the bar. It was safer having such a new vampire inside where everyone could keep an eye on him. Not that Chris wasn't doing wonderfully, but why take a chance?

Besides, Chris had realized he really liked being a bartender while substituting for us, and he did a great job. It was fun working with them every night, and I found that he was as good with the customers as Luke had been. Especially the ladies.

Luke went on guard duty, taking Quinton's place. Most of the time, he was more serious than he used to be. I think it was out of respect for Quinton. TJ was still in charge of the guards, with Lorna as his second in command. They all three pretended to be the bad guys with the customers, but we knew how sweet and gentle they really were.

Parker decided he liked the valet parking, only he was now the one in charge. With the increase in business, he now had two vampires working for him, and thinking of hiring a third.

It bothered Parker a lot that he'd missed finishing high school because of Charles, so he was getting ready to start online classes like I'd done. Of course, Byron hadn't given up on both of us getting college degrees. With everything online, who knew? We may decide to do that someday.

At that moment, though, I was watching Chris smile at a really cute redhead as he walked her out of a room behind the band and back to one of the tables. He was doing so well. Byron said he didn't fight them much at all, even less than me, when he had his first taste of human blood. This girl was the third one that he'd fed from alone.

We were all so happy those weeks, but still worried every day about Sarita. Anna, who had been doing Sarita's cleaning job, was now her full-time nurse. Doctor Jamison discovered that she'd started nursing training before losing herself in drugs which led to prostitution, and life in that cage with Charles's craziness. Byron was happy to offer her the job. Sarita loved her, and Anna was thrilled to be doing the job she had once planned for her future.

But, other than knowing there was nothing anyone could do for Sarita, it looked like we were at the beginning of that happily-ever-after that Parker and I had planned. What I would always remember as the worst year of my life, had finally turned out to be the beginning of the joy that would last for centuries to come.

Then I saw TJ walking Constance and Bartholomew through the bar just as we were ready to close, and spotted Byron come out of the half-hidden door to meet them. I knew that something was up. Something serious. Something that had the potential to take all that contented joy I'd been feeling and sling it in the trash.

Chapter 19

All the customers were gone, and the clients were mostly settled in their rooms. It was almost 3:30 in the morning and we were all nervous wrecks. Byron had been in his office with Constance and Bartholomew since 2:00, and none of us had heard a word about what was going on. Even TJ was being left out.

My mind kept stirring around the horrible stuff that could be happening. We'd all had enough of horrible stuff. As we went through our duties to close the bar, we kept looking at each other with those *What could it be?* looks that had no answer.

Of course, it could be something good. There was always that possibility. Maybe Constance was asking Byron to serve on the Assembly. Maybe they were planning on expanding or even moving Rule the Night to keep up with our increased business. Maybe anything, and that was the problem.

Finally, TJ's phone rang. He listened for a few seconds, and looked over at the rest of us. Parker, Chris, Crystal, Lorna, Luke, Anthony and me had all been hanging around the bar. TJ'd been sitting alone at one of the tables near the hidden door. I guess he didn't want to conjecture and worry with the rest of us. He'd keep his thoughts in his own head. That was just TJ.

"Byron wants all of us to meet in his room," he said as he walked toward the bar. "You, too, Anthony."

When Quinton died, Anthony had become a night guard. It was a promotion for Anthony, but I think he still felt a little out of place with all of us who were so close to Byron and had been so involved with overthrowing Charles. We all knew each other so much better than Anthony.

Constance, Bartholomew and Byron were already there when we got to Byron's suite. I was so worried walking in there that I think I was slightly shaking all over. Parker kept his arm around my waist which helped a lot.

"It's good to see all of you again, and I'm sorry to have to bring you this news," Constance said once we were all settled, "but I thought it would be best if everyone got the information from me."

Okay, I thought, *It's bad. It's really bad.*

"We've found out that Charles was not the leader as we supposed, but was second in command of an organization trying to bring back the old ways." I gasped. Most of the others were able to keep their reactions inside and silent. "The leader operates out of New York, but we haven't been able to identify him, yet. We do have some suspects and will continue investigating them. The Assembly and Rule the Night have been threatened in a text message. It said that Charles would be avenged."

"Was the message traceable?" Parker asked.

"No. It was one of those disposable phones. It could have been anyone, anywhere."

"Then what do you need us to do?" TJ asked in his usual calm, controlled style.

Constance looked at Byron, indicating that he should tell us.

"We've put together a plan, but I would rather not involve all of you. Constance feels I must give you the choice," Byron said with that tone in his voice that said he wasn't happy. "In the next few days, we'll be removing all the clients and replacing them with members of the Assembly and those who Constance is sure of. We can't do anything about the human customers, but we don't see that they'll be attacked."

"So Rule the Night will be the bait," TJ said.

"Unfortunately," Bartholomew answered. "But you are the ones who destroyed Charles, and that puts you in a delicate position. We think this is about more than simple revenge. The leader is most likely afraid that others will move to follow Byron and the rest of you, so he wants you out of the way before he continues his other plans."

"Once the clients are gone," Parker asked, "the rest of us just sit and wait to be attacked?"

"And try to look like you have no idea you may be targeted," Bartholomew said.

During this conversation, Byron couldn't take his eyes off Parker. I knew he'd want Parker to leave with the clients, but Parker had wanted to fight bloodthirst since his parents were killed. Add that to what Charles had done to the two of us, and Parker would insist on being in the middle of it. Byron and I both knew that.

"Parker," Byron said quietly, but seriously, "I want you, Holly, and Chris to leave. You killed Charles. You will be the one he wants, and the three of you are simply too young to face this kind of fight."

Parker looked back at Byron, and I looked at Parker. I wanted to leave. I was so tired of being scared, and I so didn't want to face the risk of losing Parker or Chris. I was sure, though, that Parker would stay, and I knew that I'd stay with him.

"They killed my parents," Parker said quietly. "Tried to kill Holly, me and you. You saved me and protected me when I was a child, but I'm not a child anymore. I can't walk away, Byron, and I think you understand that."

Byron never took his eyes off Parker. He nodded, giving in because he had no choice, but not happy about it. "I understand. What about Holly?"

"I'm not going anywhere." My voice was determined as I glanced between Byron and Parker.

"I want you to go, Holly," Parker said. "I need to know you're safe."

"I'm staying." No way was he talking me out of this.

"Everyone here will be protecting me. If you're here, they'll have to protect you, too. I'll be safer if you leave."

"You'll be safer if the two of us are fighting side-by-side." My voice was still calm and determined even though I was screaming inside. I didn't want to stay, but I wouldn't leave Parker.

"Holly, please," he sighed.

"I'm not being separated from you again," I said, showing a little more emotion.

"Wait a minute," Chris jumped in. "Is everyone just assuming that I'm walking away? I'm not leaving Lorna, or Holly, or any of you! I killed like four or five vampires at that place in Columbus when I was still human. Give us guns. We'll take care of anyone we need to."

"The three of you need to listen ..." Byron started to say.

Constance interrupted gently, reaching over to touch his knee. "Byron, I think they've made their decisions."

I think they'd both known all along that we wouldn't leave, but Byron kept hoping that he'd talk us into it. If it had been just me, he wouldn't have had to talk much.

"I need you two," Byron said looking at TJ and Lorna, "to stay with them. The five of you are to be attached at the hip, you understand?"

"Yes, sir," TJ and Lorna both answered. Neither of them looked happy. They wanted us to leave, too, but I knew TJ would've been protecting Parker and me no matter what. Lorna, I was sure, had no intentions of getting more than a few inches from Chris.

We talked about the plans for hours, but couldn't really pin anything down. We didn't know what this New York vampire would try to do, so everything was conjecture and 'what if'.

The one thing we knew was that we'd get all the clients moved out in the next few days with lies about a detailed remodeling job. Byron would tell everyone that he was expanding, and needed an empty space to get the job done quickly. Once they were gone, vampires from the Assembly would start joining us.

Other than anticipating an attack, that's all we could do. It was strange to me that so many vampires wanted to come to Rule the Night because they thought it would be one of the safest places around the country and because they trusted Byron, yet we had become some kind of 'ground-zero' and had to move them out to keep them safe.

By the time the sun rose, I was tired and even more nervous. I'd been spending weeks getting past all the crap with Charles and trying to convince myself that everything was okay. But everything wasn't okay.

There were times when something would remind me. Usually something stupid and unrelated, but I'd suddenly get visions of my dreams, or of Charles beating and kissing me, or of that horrible video of Parker killing that woman. Once in a while I saw someone walk in that I thought was Quinton. I wasn't over it, yet. Not in my mind, anyway.

Now, someone else out there was planning how to kill all of us. Someone we didn't even know. He was, at that moment, probably making his own plans to strike Rule the Night.

I was a nervous wreck, and felt myself losing it. I really didn't know if I could deal with it again, but there was no way I was leaving Parker and Chris there without me. Leaving them, not knowing what on earth was happening, would be so much worse than facing this new threat from some unknown bad guy, so I'd have to find a way to deal with it.

Parker pulled me into his arms as soon as we stepped into our suite. He held me so tight.

"Holly, I want you to leave with Constance," he whispered into my neck.

"No way," I said trying to sound brave and sure. I pulled back from him a little to look into his eyes. "Not unless you and Chris go with me. In fact, I'd love it if we all left. We could all just disappear and wait for Constance to take care of finding that guy in New York." I knew Parker could hear the pleading in my voice.

"Oh, Babe," Parker sighed. "I know you're scared, but Constance won't know who he is until he tries something with us. You know Byron won't leave."

"But he should, because we've all been through enough. We fought Charles for months! Why can't someone else fight this guy?"

"Because he's coming for us."

"Let's talk to Byron," I almost begged. "You know he wants us to leave, and I'm sure he'd rather not have Crystal here, either. Maybe he'll give in and we can all go to California or

Europe ... anywhere! Some place far away were no one can find us."

"And we'd have to check into a sanctuary without knowing who was there that might make a phone call to this guy in New York. The vampire community really isn't that big. Someone would know Byron and a lot of people would know Lorna. Word of our whereabouts would get out."

"There has to be somewhere we could go!" I practically shouted. I don't know why I was so terrified, but it was all coming out at Parker.

"And let bloodthirst go on?"

"No! Just let someone else fight them this time. We're not the only ones that don't want humans dying."

"Oh, sweetheart," Parker said as he pulled me close again.

"Please, Parker," I said into his neck. "Let's just talk to Byron. He's been fighting bloodthirst for so long, maybe he'd be happy to let someone else take over."

"I don't like the idea of just walking away. They killed my parents, Holly. And you ... God, what Charles did to you. I don't know if I can ignore that."

"But we're just too young," I practically whined.

"Holly," he sighed. "You're really determined in this, aren't you?"

"Yes. This all just feels so wrong. I ...I can't let us be separated again to spend our nights worrying about each other." A chocking sob escaped from my lips, but I was determined not to cry. I couldn't stand it if he gave in because of my tears. He needed to listen to reason. I took a deep breath. "I think we all at least need to discuss it."

"Okay," he sighed. "We'll talk to Byron tonight. Will that work for you?"

"Yes! Oh, Parker, yes. That's all I want. We need to at least talk about it."

He gave me a gentle squeeze, but I practically jumped him, clasping him around the neck like I'd never let go, and kissing him so hard, I could feel his fangs on my tongue. I scraped that tongue along his fang so he could taste my blood, and he sucked on it while groaning deep in his throat.

"Carry me, Parker," I sighed.

He lifted me in his strong arms and continued kissing me as he walked toward the bed. Parker knelt on the bed and I knelt in front of him.

"I love you so much, Holly. No matter what Byron decides, I'll keep us safe." He was staring into my eyes and said those words with so much conviction.

"I know you will. No matter what, we'll be fine as long as we're together. We can't be separated again."

We moved from our knees to the bed, and I sighed as he took me in his arms again. Being with him, feeling his body against mine, enjoying our hands touching and stroking each other, made all my fear disappear. I knew that we'd get through it together, no matter what.

The sound of the explosion seemed to happen in a dream, but I hadn't been dreaming. Parker was shaking me awake as I realized we were covered with some kind of white dust that was still filling the air.

"Holly!" Parker almost shouted. "Something blew up! We're being attacked!"

His words forced me awake as my eyes flew open and I sat straight up. Everything in the room was covered with that dust, and it was still settling. All kinds of stuff had been jerked off shelves and furniture. Something big had happened while we slept.

"What happened?"

"I don't know. Stay here. I'll go check."

"No! We stay together!"

Before Parker could answer, our door flew open. "Get to the family tunnel," TJ said. "Stay there. Wait for Byron." He was gone as quickly as he'd come.

We threw on the clothes we'd tossed off the bed, and started for the door. As I got through the living room, Parker turned and ran back into the bedroom. A second later, he joined me again carrying his family album and the picture of us that I'd given him when all of us gave him the suite for his birthday.

"I'm not losing these," he whispered as he shuffled them under his arm and took my hand. We headed out.

We stepped into the hall. Before we could survey the damage, we heard loud arguing. Behind us, Anna and Sarita struggled as Anna tried to get Sarita moving. We didn't even have to say a word. Both of us turned back toward them to help.

"Let go of me!" Sarita kept yelling. "Byron! Byron, help me!" she cried as Anna kept talking gently.

"We're going to Byron, Sarita," she kept saying. "He's waiting for us."

"Sarita," Parker said gently.

She turned and looked at him like she was trying to remember who this man was. I think she always pictured Parker as a little boy anymore. It was hard for her to remember that he'd grown up.

"It's Parker," he said. "Want me to take you to Byron?"

From the look on her face, I think she finally recognized him. "This woman's trying to hurt me," she whispered to Parker. "Is she a vampire?"

"No, she's human. She's your nurse. She wouldn't hurt you. We have to go meet Byron."

Just then, we heard another rumble and part of the ceiling fell too close to us. Parker and I leaned over to cover Anna and Sarita as best as we could, and nothing hit them except dust, but she and Anna needed to breathe clean air. We needed to get them out.

Parker handed me the picture and family album he'd rescued from our suite. "Come on, Sarita," he said as he bent to pick her up in his arms, carrying her like a baby. She was so tiny, I think he hardly noticed her weight at all.

"Parker, you stop that. You put me down right now!" She half yelled, half laughed as I grabbed Anna's arm and we started running. Sarita acted like it was a silly game. She had no idea that the building might be falling down around us.

"We're gonna' find Byron," Parker said smiling down at her. "You know how hard he'll laugh when he sees me carrying you."

Sarita laughed and hid her face against his shoulder.

Everyone was running toward the family tunnel, crowding the hallways and common area, but it was strangely silent as we followed the flow of vampires down the hallway. Humans would have been screaming and crying, but vampires moved deliberately and quickly toward our only safety.

Obviously, someone had tried to drop the upper floors of Rule the Night into the residential basement, but something had gone wrong. At least wrong for them.

Parts of ceiling and walls blocked part of the hallway, but we all shoved and kicked stuff out of the way as we went. It hardly looked like our home anymore. The stairway going upstairs was practically gone, and the door at the top was now just a gaping hole. We all cringed and hugged the shadows at the side of the hallway as sun streamed through that hole. The upstairs must have been essentially gone.

Whoever had done this, had come awfully close to succeeding, but maybe the place was built more sturdily than they imagined, or maybe they failed to use enough explosives. Whatever it was, I didn't really care. All I cared about was that we were safe. We could have all been buried alive.

But I hadn't seen Chris, Lorna, Byron, Crystal or Luke. I prayed and hoped that they were safe, too, as we dashed out of our home.

Most of the clients were already in the tunnel by the time we got there, and everyone was just milling around or standing there waiting for instructions. Many of them looked toward Parker as someone who might be in charge.

"Has anyone seen Byron?" Parker asked the crowd as he put Sarita on her feet and in Anna's care. I think seeing all those vampires in the tunnel made her forget about seeing Byron. She wasn't comfortable surrounded by vampires, and I sure couldn't blame her.

"Not since he and TJ were telling us to come here," someone answered.

"What about Chris and Lorna?" I asked.

"Here I am," Chris hollered from the crowd as he was moving toward us.

I hugged him really tight. "Where's Lorna?" I asked.

"Helping Byron and TJ make sure everyone's out. Luke and Crystal stayed with them, but they made me come down here."

"I guess we'll just have to wait," Parker told the crowd. "Everyone try to get comfortable." Then he turned to me and whispered very quietly in my ear. "Watch Sarita and Anna." I just nodded and moved back toward where Anna had moved Sarita into an isolated corner near the door.

Everyone knew that Sarita was off limits, but it's hard to completely trust a relatively strange, stressed-out vampire. Stress could cause hunger to flare very easily, and control was an individual thing. I'd watch both of them very carefully, and defend them with my life. Thank God neither of them was bleeding. Chris moved toward them with me.

Meanwhile Parker moved among the clients keeping them calm and making sure no one was hurt. If anyone was injured, they might need blood, and that would endanger Sarita and Anna even more. He was taking over for Byron and I had to smile slightly to myself to see how good he was at it. Byron would be proud of him. I knew I was.

The door to the garage started to open and clients were moving away from the stairs that led up to the outside. My heart skipped a beat realizing that we could be under attack at any moment.

"It's us," I heard Byron call down the tunnel. "Is everyone alright down here?"

TJ, Lorna, Luke and Crystal were with him. I felt like I could breathe easier now because everyone was accounted for.

"As you've realized," Byron said, "someone tried to blow up the bar. Thankfully, they didn't know how the residential areas were constructed, and only the ground floor was destroyed. We lost Anthony and Harlon who were on the day shift, and three clients who were still in a poker room. I'll notify anyone that needs to hear of their deaths. I've already called Constance."

"How long do we need to stay down here?" someone asked from the crowd.

"It's daylight," Byron said as if he wanted to say, *Duh*. "If any of you want to get to a vehicle, you can leave as soon as Constance gets here. I didn't check to see if any of them are damaged or destroyed, so it's up to each individual. Otherwise, we'll be here until dark."

"Why do we have to wait for Constance?" another voice asked.

"She wants to question everyone. I don't think any of you would know there was to be a bombing and then settle down for a good day's sleep, but she wants to make sure no one saw anything suspicious."

"How long before she gets here?" the same voice called out. I don't know what Byron was thinking, but that guy was starting to make me suspect he knew something. Or maybe he was just being an ass.

"Should be within an hour," Byron answered simply.

She'd left Rule the Night only hours before the bombing, but the clients didn't know that. She probably just got back to the Assembly and had to turn the helicopter around to come back.

There were no more questions, so Byron simply stated. "Everyone get as comfortable as possible and we'll wait."

Within a few minutes, all of us had gathered near Sarita and Anna. Sarita was sitting on a pillow in the corner with a blanket wrapped around her, which Anna must have brought with them. She was really good at taking care of Sarita.

"Hello, Sarita," Byron said quietly. Inside I knew he was really relieved and happy to see her safe.

"Byron," Sarita smiled. "Did you laugh when you saw that silly Parker carrying me?"

"I sure did," he answered. "You try to relax and get some rest." She settled back against the wall and I suspected she might fall asleep any second. That would be best.

"What about the police and fire department?" Parker asked. "I don't suppose they missed that explosion."

One side of Byron's mouth raised slightly at Parker's sarcasm. "Clyde Reynolds is handling them. He's said I'm out of town, and called me like he was telling me what happened. Dr. Jamison is coming to get Sarita and Anna."

Clyde was Byron's lawyer that helped Chris and me so much with settling things after Mom and Dad died. We still hadn't sold the house, but the auction was scheduled and it would all be done in about another month.

"Thank you, Byron," Anna said quietly. I don't think she was very comfortable being surrounded by all the stressed-out vampires, either. I knew for sure she was worried about Sarita and wanted to see her settled somewhere safe.

"Maybe we should take you and Sarita over to the garage stairs," he said quietly to Anna. "If necessary, you two can leave the building quickly from there."

Sarita was sound asleep, so Parker simply carried her again. Anna walked in the middle of us with me taking one arm and Chris taking the other. The reality of passing through all those stressed, worried vampires couldn't be minimized. No one could predict what might happen to the only two humans in the room if someone lost control.

Chapter 20

Dr. Jamison was there in about a half hour. Sarita wasn't happy about leaving Byron, but she knew Dr. Jamison well and trusted him. Byron told her he'd come get her as soon as possible, but I don't think she understood that he probably wouldn't get there very quickly. I hugged Anna goodbye, but we all knew that Dr. Jamison would take good care of both of them.

Then Byron, TJ, Lorna, and Parker moved through the guests and helped them make plans for their escape. Luke, Chris and I tried to help all we could, but mainly we waited.

"Clyde Reynolds, my lawyer, is dealing with the police," Byron announced to the crowd. "He told me that some cars were damaged, mostly from flying debris. We'll have to wait for dark to know for sure."

"Our cars?" asked one of the male vampires that I hadn't met.

"I'm afraid so," Byron answered.

"So how are we supposed to get out of here?"

"I have six cars in my garage. I'm hoping Constance can provide us with other transportation. Beyond that, we'll have to wait until dark to see what we need."

"I thought you guys killed Charles. Why didn't you warn us that someone was still after you?"

"We didn't know until this morning, and certainly didn't suspect this," he said, looking around the room. "We planned to move all of you out this evening, but were too late."

"Obviously," the guy answered with a sneer. "Any idea which sanctuary could take us?"

"I have no idea at all. Perhaps you should try making some calls."

Byron was starting to show his irritation with the guy and turned to walk away when a couple walked up to him. These two drew my attention immediately because they were the most beautiful vampires I'd ever seen. That's saying something, because all vampires are pretty damn attractive.

"I need to speak to you privately, Byron, if possible." He spoke quietly, but his elegant English accent floated right to me.

"Of course, Jonathan. Let's walk up to the top of the garage stairs."

The woman hadn't said a thing, but she held Jonathan's arm, and they followed Byron together. They must have both been incredible humans, but I could tell that they were very old, even older than Byron.

The three of them came back about twenty minutes later and approached all of us.

"This is Jonathan and his companion Audrey. I knew them centuries ago when in London, but they've recently relocated to the States. They need to give Constance some information when she gets here, but they have already planned to go to Gina in Indianapolis. I want you three and Lorna to go with them."

"What about you?" Parker asked. I knew from his tone of voice that he was ready to start arguing again.

"Crystal, TJ, Luke and I are going with Constance," Byron hesitated before continuing. "This situation has gotten too big for us to deal with. The entire Assembly needs to find whoever attacked us, and I will be there to plan with them. No one knows we have any connection to Gina, but I called her, and she will keep you hidden there."

"But we want to stay with you," I said quietly.

"I know, Holly," Byron answered. "But this is beyond us. The time has come to retreat until we know what we're dealing with. You'll be hidden at Gina's and we'll be safe at the Assembly. It will be the full force of the Assembly that confronts our enemy, and I will come to you when they finish it."

"When *they* finish it?" Parker said. "I have the feeling you'll be part of that *they* while we're hiding. We can't leave that to you, Byron."

"Then you'll need to trust me. Constance almost had me convinced that we should all hide out and leave the battle to the Assembly. This explosion finished the argument for her. I won't endanger everyone I love again, or myself. TJ and Luke can choose for themselves, but Crystal and I will be safe at the Assembly."

I couldn't believe what I was hearing. Byron was actually going to do what I wanted, what Parker and I had argued about. We were all going to hide while the Assembly took care of whoever was fostering bloodthirst. It was all I could hope for, but I still wished we could hide together.

The sound at the garage door announced that Constance had finally arrived and our conversation was cut short. She brought Bartholomew and two others I didn't know.

They all looked like they were in pain, and I realized they must have parked away from Rule the Night to walk into the garage. It must have been some distance in the sunlight to have made these strong vampires look like it pained them so much.

After short greetings, Byron let Constance know that she needed to start her investigation with Jonathan and Audrey. They must have told Byron something.

"What did they tell you?" I asked Byron once Constance had moved Jonathan and Audrey to a private corner.

"Jonathan left the poker room a short time before the explosion and heard noises behind the bar as he passed. He assumed it was an employee on the dayshift, but now thinks it could have been someone planting a bomb."

"Oh, my gosh!" I gasped. "How could they have gotten in?"

"They couldn't have. At least not once we closed. They were probably already here. Might even have been a guest. Unfortunately, Jonathan didn't look to see who it was." He paused while looking around. "I'm going to help Constance sort through some of these people, the rest of you can just relax here."

It was a strange numbness that seemed to be passing through all of us, as we sat on the floor leaning against the wall. Parker had his arm around me, and I rested my head on his shoulder. Slowly, the reality of our situation was sinking in. Rule the Night was gone.

The bar where I worked serving and socializing with the customers every night. The private rooms where we all fed. The suite that we all decorated for Parker, but that he now shared with me.

I knew our lives would never be the same as I gazed around at all the clients standing and sitting in our family tunnel. They were dusty, dirty, and some had bled from rapidly healing scratches and cuts. Most of them looked as lost as I felt.

Their things were mostly destroyed or lost, too. But Rule the Night wasn't their home. It was a temporary resting place to them. To me it was the place I thought I'd be living for decades, or centuries.

I didn't know where we would live now that Rule the Night was gone, but did know that it wouldn't matter. The *where* didn't matter a bit as long as we'd be together. I wished again that Byron and Crystal were going with us to La Sang Rouge.

Hours later, I could finally sense the sun setting. People started to move quickly and quietly out through the garages. Mr. Reynolds had called Byron and told him that the police were gone, and the place was surrounded by that yellow tape to keep everyone out of the area. Byron had to go talk to them as soon as he "got in town".

"It's time for us to leave," Jonathan said as he and Audrey walked up to us. He looked into each of our eyes as if he was honestly concerned about us. That made me feel more relaxed, safe. "My van wasn't damaged, and I've pulled it around behind the garage."

"We need to see Byron first," Parker answered.

The four of us moved to the corner where Constance was questioning everyone that was left, and Parker caught Byron's eye. He came to us.

"Are you sure about this, Byron?" Parker asked. "We'd all rather stay with you and help the Assembly as much as we can."

"We're safer apart," he answered. "I have to help Clyde deal with the police and insurance agents, and I need to know you are with someone I trust. I trust Gina completely. I plan on coming to La Sang Rouge myself soon. And Lorna's with you. She'll protect all of you."

"I'm more concerned about you," Parker said with that concern showing in his eyes.

"Don't be, Parker. TJ, Luke and I will be with Constance."

"What about Crystal?" I asked.

"I've already sent her to stay with Sarita at Dr. Jamison's. I don't think there'll be any problems, but I want a vampire there to watch over them."

"Then we'll call when we get there," Parker said.

"Good," Byron said quietly. There was no emotion in his voice or face. Nothing at all. He must have been as numb as I felt.

We all hugged goodbye and moved out to the garage. I thought about this being the last time I'd pass through those passages that Parker had led me through way back when we were both human. Back when I had no idea that vampires were real. It seemed so, so long ago.

Jonathan had a black Honda van with really dark, tinted windows. Parker and I got in the third seats which was fine with me since I didn't feel much like conversation and I'd probably sleep the whole way.

Lorna and Chris got the middle seats while Jonathan and Audrey took the front. We moved down the alley and out onto the country road that would take us to Interstate 70. We'd stay on it all the way to Indianapolis.

I settled myself against Parker's shoulder as much as the seat belts would allow, and we drove away from Rule the Night, Adelle, and the only life I'd ever known, both my human and vampire lives.

* * *

The questioning was finally ending, and the family tunnel was practically empty. Byron had made arrangements for vampires to move to other sanctuaries, found transportation for many who had cars too badly damaged to drive, and offered countless apologies.

TJ had spent most of his time outside helping guests check their cars, contacting associates to pick them up, and making sure no humans noticed all the activity in the parking lot and garage behind a destroyed building. It was a difficult night, and it didn't help that his mind was constantly worrying about Byron.

TJ couldn't quite put his finger on what the problem was, but Byron was not his usual self. He seemed to be in shock. The decision to send the others to La Sang Rouge with Jonathan also bothered TJ. He couldn't imagine a situation that would cause Byron to send Parker away with virtual strangers. At least Lorna was with them.

After spending hours in the parking lot, TJ was finally able to go back inside. The place seemed empty as he walked toward Byron, Constance and Bartholomew. They were lost in conversation.

"Now that all of them are taken care of, I need to ask how you're feeling, Byron," Constance was saying.

"I'm fine," Byron answered with no emotion.

"You're fine?" she said with a tilt of her head. "Really?"

"What did you expect?"

"Anger. Desire for vengeance. Need to protect those you love."

"What are you getting at?"

TJ listened intently. Constance had noticed, too. Those were the very things TJ expected from Byron, but he hadn't seen them either.

"Your expression and manner have been calm and relaxed. You haven't expressed any desire to find whoever did this. You send those you love the most off to hide without showing any concern for them."

"I'm concerned for them. I don't know what you mean."

"And you have no reaction to my words." Constance looked at him very carefully before speaking again. "Who were you alone with before I got here?"

"No one," Byron shrugged.

"Jonathan and Audrey," TJ answered for him. "They said they needed to speak to him privately." Byron looked up at TJ as if he was talking about someone else.

Constance's eyebrows raised for a moment before narrowing her gaze to study Byron. He started to look away from her, but she grasped his face in both hands and commanded him, "Look at me."

After several minutes of staring intently, she dropped her hands from him and covered her own eyes. When she looked up again, TJ could feel her anger pulse through the room.

"TJ, look at me," she said. TJ never hesitated, but gazed directly into Constance's eyes. "You're fine," she said.

"But Byron's not? What's going on?" TJ asked while Byron looked back and forth between them.

"I never suspected that Jonathan or Audrey had such power," she practically whispered. "Byron, one of them has controlled you. They probably also convinced you to give up the fight and send the young ones with them."

"I don't know what you mean, Constance." Byron's voice was still calm and relaxed. TJ's anger was expanding with every word he heard.

"How long have they been gone?" Constance asked TJ.

"At least a couple hours," TJ answered with a dark, deadly expression. "Are you saying that it might be Jonathan or Audrey that set the bomb?"

"Probably both of them."

"Then they're all in danger." TJ was seeing the situation clearly, now, but Byron looked at him as if nothing was making any sense.

"I'm afraid so."

"It sounds like you're saying Jonathan would hurt Parker," Byron said calmly. "He wouldn't do that. He's protecting them."

"Byron," she said gently, almost like she was talking to a child. "You know that a few of us have the strength to control other vampires. You know that I am one. Since you mentioned Jonathan, I have to assume that he's the one who controlled you."

"No one controlled me." Byron was showing a little anger, but it was directed at Constance.

"I can feel his influence in you. I may be able to push it aside, but you'll need to help me. Open your mind, so I can try to release your true feelings."

"This is ridiculous," Byron said, sounding irritated, turning away.

Constance had to clasp his face again to force him to look at her, and still he seemed to be fighting against her. His whole body was so tense, it almost vibrated as Byron mentally fought against her.

"Byron. Look in my eyes," she commanded.

Their eyes were locked for what seemed forever to TJ. He and Bartholomew watched as Byron slowly relaxed and Constance tensed. Finally, they both closed their eyes.

Constance looked like she'd been through a hundred-mile run as she leaned against the wall.

Byron opened his eyes and raised his gaze to the ceiling. "My God! I've been such a fool," he whispered. "What vehicle do we have left?" Byron said, quickly turning toward TJ

"The Range Rover."

"Can we get any weapons from my suite?"

"I should be able to get through."

"Get anything you can. We have to go after them." TJ couldn't help giving him a grim smile. Finally, Byron was back to his normal self.

TJ took off, and Byron turned to Constance. "He plans on killing us all. I saw it in his mind, but he erased the memory and took control of my decisions. He plans on holding them somewhere isolated in eastern Indiana before calling me to come to the rescue. I have to go after them."

"We're going with you," Constance answered. "If he has enough power to control you, you'll need all of us."

"I think it was easier because I was so devastated by the explosion. But then, he knew that."

"Bartholomew," she said, "Sondra and Daniel are still guarding the outside. Go explain things to them, and have them take the helicopter to Indianapolis. Have them wait to hear from us, but tell them to be ready to move to our position."

"I'll bring some weapons from the 'copter," Bartholomew said as he headed up the stairs.

"Don't worry, Byron," Constance said. "We'll get them."

"What have I done, Constance?" Byron asked, showing the fear he was feeling. "He might have already killed them. I sent my son off in the care of a killer, and wasn't concerned. How could he have controlled me so completely? How could I be so weak?"

"It wasn't your weakness. He offered you everything you wanted. He created the danger with the explosion, then offered to take your son someplace safe, under the protection of a very old vampire. That kind of trick is one of the subtleties of controlling another vampire. He created a situation where you would want what he offered, so of course you fell under his spell. I should have kept better track of him and other powerful ones over the last century. I should know which of us is gaining in that kind of power."

"If he has injured them ..." Byron said quietly, not able to finish the thought.

"I think he's waiting for you, Byron. Powerful ones like nothing better than displaying their skills, and he has obviously hidden his for a long time. He probably wants to kill you all at the same time."

Byron looked up at Constance with a kind of pleading in his eyes. "Can you defeat him?"

"Probably. I don't think I would have been able to break his influence over you if I was weaker than him."

TJ returned with the weapons. Byron turned to him, and looked back at Constance. "Let's go."

Chapter 21

I woke up as the car was slowing down and expected to be in Indianapolis, but we were out in the country somewhere.

"Where are we?" I asked Parker sleepily.

"I don't know," he answered quietly.

"Jonathan, where are we going?" Lorna asked.

"We need to make a stop." Audrey answered.

I think we'd all been asleep. I didn't remember anything since we'd gotten on the freeway and had no idea how long we'd been driving, but we had plenty of time before sunrise. A little part of my brain wondered why we were stopping, but I quickly dismissed it. Jonathan knew what he was doing.

We headed into the woods, and Jonathan turned off onto a dirt road where the trees grew really close. We could all see well in the dark, but there really wasn't much to see, only trees.

Rounding a curve, we pulled to a stop in front of an old farmhouse. It would have been cute if anyone had taken care of it. Peeling paint, missing shingles on the roof, and rain gutters hanging toward the ground all made the place look like it was deserted long ago.

"Let's go," Jonathan said as he stepped out of the car.

"What are we doing here?" Lorna asked with a scowl on her face.

Jonathan opened her door and looked at her for a minute without saying anything. She began to smile. "Come on, everyone," she said as she turned to move her seat to let Parker and me out of the back.

"I want to talk to you, Parker. The rest of you go with Audrey to the basement," Jonathan said as we stood around in the muddy yard.

We all followed Audrey while Jonathan and Parker stayed upstairs. I noticed the inside was as bad as the outside as far as being run down. The place was filthy with thick dust and cobwebs. A big stain ran down the wall next to the staircase where rain had leaked in more than once.

The basement wasn't any better. It smelled awful with mold and something that had crept in and died. I didn't see any dead animal, but it was somewhere close. There were several old lawn chairs scattered around the room.

"Sit down," Audrey told us, "and look at me."

We all followed directions and gazed up at her. "Jonathan wants you to stay here in the basement. Stay in the chairs, don't move, and don't speak."

She walked away and we sat staring into the darkness. I watched a huge spider building a web in the legs of an old table against the wall.

* * *

"So, Parker," Jonathan said as they stood in the living room of the farmhouse, "how did you overcome bloodthirst?"

"I just did," Parker answered slowly.

Jonathan stared into his eyes. "The truth," he said.

Parker's face relaxed. "Constance did it."

"How?"

"She starved me. Then she fed me herself and taught me to feed again."

"Starved you? How long?"

"I don't remember for sure, but she said it was over a week."

"It is very painful for a vampire to starve."

"She helped me sleep so I didn't hurt as much."

"I don't understand how that worked. Did Constance explain it to you?"

"She said that my body used up all the human blood right away, then started pulling Charles's blood from my muscles and organs. When I was near death, she said it was like I was almost human again."

"So she changed you again with her own blood."

"Yeah."

"I had no idea that could be done. Very clever of her."

"She said Bartholomew thought of it, and they hadn't been able to try it on anyone before. I was the first."

"Did you want to drain the first human they gave you?"

"They had to pull me off her. I did it myself with the second one."

"Amazing. I assume they plan to use this technique on others?"

"I heard her tell Byron that they're going to keep it secret until they have the chance to try it again. I was made bloodthirsty on purpose. They want to be sure it'll work on those whose change doesn't go well."

"Then I'll need to make sure they don't have that chance. Go sit in the basement with your friends. Stay there, and don't speak."

Parker turned away from him and walked down to the basement. He smiled at Holly as he sat next to her. The four of them sat and waited.

* * *

Bartholomew pulled their car into a truck stop about ten miles after crossing the state line into Indiana. They parked at the back where they'd be out of the way and unnoticed. All they could do now was wait for Jonathan to call.

It had been almost five hours since Jonathan and Audrey had pulled away from Rule the Night, and Byron had to force himself to stay calm. All he could do was pray that Constance was right and Jonathan would be waiting to kill them all together.

He couldn't face the thought that Parker, Holly, Lorna and Chris may already be dead. They could be dead and it was his fault. He'd gladly sent them off with their killer.

Finally, the phone rang. Byron took a deep breath and answered, ready to pretend that he was still under Jonathan's control. "Yes?"

"Meet Audrey at mile marker 14 on the first county road going north after crossing the state line. Follow her to our location. Come alone."

Byron hung up and told the rest what he'd said. "So, now, how do we find him?"

"Let's go to the meeting place and look around," Constance said. "It's probably close. We should be able to find it before Audrey leaves to meet you."

They had to move back toward the Ohio line before they found the exit to the first county road. A few miles north, on the left-hand side, was mile marker 14. Just a few yards past the marker was a rutted dirt road that curved into the trees. It was probably the lane up to an old farmhouse.

"Let's leave the car and check that lane on foot," Byron said.

"Look." TJ said. "The mud in the road is undisturbed except for one set of tracks. I don't think anyone's been here in a long time until very recently."

"That's a good sign," Bartholomew added.

They moved silently along the road sniffing for any sign of vampires. They'd be able to smell their presence long before they saw the farmhouse, but would then need to back off. Hopefully, they'd back off before they were detected by Jonathan and Audrey.

There was the scent they were looking for. They all sniffed deeply to determine how many and hopefully who was hiding in the distance, then quickly turned to move back towards the SUV.

"That's where they are," Bartholomew said once they were back at the car.

"All still alive." Byron sighed with relief as he said it.

"We'll hide in the woods while you wait for Audrey," Constance said, "then follow to get as close as possible without being detected. We'll give you five minutes before we attack. Byron, this may not go smoothly. The battle may be difficult."

"What do you mean? The two of them against all of us ... "

"Byron, Jonathan must have them tightly controlled, so they might not be willing to fight against him."

"Are you saying Parker and the others would attack us? Parker would never do that. He'd never be against me."

"Under normal circumstances, you never would have sent them away with strangers, but you did. The safest thing would be to kill Jonathan immediately, but I need to question him. I need to know how far this has gone and who else he's controlled. Remember, we have strong evidence that he controlled Charles. We'll just have to be ready for whatever may happen."

"What about Audrey?" TJ asked. "I don't know her. How powerful is she?"

"Much younger than Jonathan, as I'm sure you could tell. She's probably completely under his control, so she'll fight viciously."

"Then Byron and I will take care of her," TJ said.

"No." Byron added. "I can handle Audrey. You help Constance and Bartholomew with Jonathan."

"That might be a good idea, TJ," Constance said. "I may need the two of you to hold him while I try to control him."

"You think he's as strong as you?" Byron asked.

"No, but I don't know for sure. He's hidden very well for the last century, so we can't know what we're going to face in there."

"I plan on killing Audrey and getting our four vampires out," Byron answered. "Other than that, you do whatever you need to, Constance."

"Byron," Constance said, "remember that they're under Jonathan's control. They might not be willing to leave with you. You might only be able to watch them until I can break Jonathan's influence."

Byron nodded to acknowledge Constance's words. He got in the driver's seat and waited while the others moved into the trees. They had to move far enough that their scents wouldn't be easily detected when Audrey showed up.

While waiting, Byron couldn't help but mentally beat himself up for sending the four of them away with Jonathan.

How could he have been so weak? Putting them in the hands of a killer, smiling as they piled into his car, not even realizing how wrong it was until Constance snapped him out of Jonathan's control.   He'd betrayed those he loved, and that was unforgivable.

It seemed forever before Byron saw the car lights headed toward him from the muddy lane. By that time, his anger was ready to explode, but he knew he had to keep his emotions in check and convince them he was still under Jonathan's control. It wasn't going to be easy.

He followed Audrey's car to the farmhouse. As soon as they went in, he saw Jonathan standing in the center of the main room. Byron's sense of smell told him the other four were in a lower level. Thankful that he didn't smell blood or fear, he concentrated on trying to convince Jonathan that he was still enthralled.

"So, Byron," Jonathan said without any other greeting, "where are Constance and Bartholomew?"

"Searching for whoever bombed Rule the Night," Byron answered calmly. He so wanted to say, *On their way to kill you.*

"Where are they searching?"

"I don't know. They went back to Assembly Headquarters."

"Come downstairs with me."

Byron didn't want to go downstairs. Audrey had moved to the basement while he was talking to Jonathan, but he needed Audrey back up here. It was obvious that the basement was where he would start the killing. With all of them together and controlled, it would be too easy.

Constance would come running to attack any minute, and the young vampires needed to be kept out of the battle if at all possible. Jonathan and Audrey needed to be on the main floor when they were attacked.

"Wait." Byron said. "I need to talk to you and Audrey.

"We can talk later," Jonathan said calmly, taking a step towards the basement.

Byron knew he couldn't be too insistent. He was supposed to be controlled. "I think one of you controlled me. I want to know how you did that, but I have to tell you that the Assembly suspects you."

"Why would they suspect me?"

"Constance wouldn't tell me, but she tried to get me to leave sooner for Indianapolis. She said I may need to protect the young ones. I heard part of their plans."

"Audrey!" Jonathan called down the stairs. "Tell us what you know," he said as he looked back at Byron.

"I want you to let my vampires go, first."

"Tell us what you know." Jonathan gazed into Byron's eyes and reached into his mind.

Byron felt the invasion. Jonathan was trying to force him to be truthful, and Byron felt the words forming on his lips. He wanted to tell Jonathan that Constance, Bartholomew, and TJ would attack at any moment. He wanted to tell him that Constance tried to help him resist Jonathan's influence. He wanted to tell Jonathan everything.

"Tell us." His voice was so powerful, so invasive.

Byron couldn't resist any longer. "Constance ... Constance knows you ..."

Jonathan's concentration snapped away from Byron as his face flew towards the door. He heard and smelled the three vampires rushing toward them. Before he could react, the door flew open.

Byron staggered against the wall as he saw Constance grasp Jonathan around the neck with one hand while Bartholomew pinned his arms back from behind.

Seeing that Byron was still disoriented, TJ leapt at Audrey, but she'd had time to defend herself. She was a powerful vampire, but no match for TJ's size and strength. After she landed several blows, TJ used his much longer reach, got his hands around her head, and snapped her neck.

Constance inflicted considerable pain on Jonathan's throat, but he was still able to break one arm free from Bartholomew's grasp and instantly struck Constance in the side of the head, making her stagger, but she never loosened her grip.

TJ ran to them from behind and reached around Bartholomew to seize Jonathan's skull between his huge hands. "One more move, and your brains will be nothing but bloody pulp in my hands," he snarled as he tightened his grip on Jonathan's head.

Bartholomew pulled wire from his pocket and reached under TJ's arms to tie Jonathan's arms back at the elbows and wrists. TJ never let up the pressure on Jonathan's head while Constance pushed him back into a small, wooden chair so Bartholomew could tie his ankles and knees.

Bartholomew took a gun from its holster, resting it against one of Jonathan's temples. Finally, TJ could let go of him and moved a step back. The whole attack only took seconds.

"Kill him," Byron gasped.

Constance and TJ both moved toward him. "Are you all right?" she asked gently.

"He had me again. He's so strong. Just kill him."

"I need information," Constance answered. "Trust me, Byron. I'm stronger. You and TJ go down to check on the captives, but don't try to convince them to do anything they don't want to do. I'll probably need to release them."

Constance went back to face Jonathan. He wasn't happy with his position, but there was still a hint of arrogance in his expression. He really believed he was stronger than Constance. Byron was afraid he might be.

Downstairs, the four captives sat around looking like they had no idea they were being held as prisoners. They all smiled up at Byron and TJ, but didn't say a word.

"Are you okay?" Byron asked them all.

"Fine," Lorna answered.

"Do you know what's been going on here?"

"We're just waiting for Jonathan and Audrey."

"Why?" Byron was very curious about what they knew.

"Because Jonathan told us to." Lorna's expression made it clear that she saw no problem with that.

"Do you want to leave with us?" TJ asked.

"No, we'll wait for Jonathan." Lorna seemed to be the spokesperson. The others simple sat there smiling.

"Okay. We'll be back," Byron answered, smiling at them, trying to pretend that everything was just fine.

"I've never even seen humans controlled like that," TJ whispered as they moved towards the steps. "Is Constance sure she can take him?"

"She says she is, but I don't know. He's so powerful."

"If Constance starts to lose it, Bartholomew will shoot his brains out," TJ said with assurance.

"Then let's get up there and give Bartholomew some backup," Byron nodded.

They found Constance and Jonathan in a mental battle. Staring at each other, the strain was visible on both their faces.

It was Constance, though, that held Jonathan's head and forced him to look into her eyes.

"Why destroy Rule the Night?" she asked with effort.

"To replace Charles. They killed him, ruined my plans."

"You wanted Byron to take Charles's place?"

Jonathan hesitated, obviously fighting not to answer. "I wanted both of them. Charles was supposed to bring me Byron."

"So you controlled Charles."

Jonathan almost smiled. "He was easy."

"Was it your idea to get him on the Assembly?"

"He wanted on the Assembly to fight bloodthirst. I changed his mind. Made him bloodthirsty."

"Why Charles?"

"He was strong, and you trusted him. He was the visible leader and I made him hate you. He took the chance of being discovered, while I controlled him like a puppet."

"After we destroyed Charles, you decided Byron would take over the Assembly for you?"

"No. Byron would work with me, but I would have killed you all. We don't need the Assembly telling us how to live. The old ways are better."

"You know humans would be able to track us and kill us. We can't kill them without fear of the consequences."

Through the conversation, Constance's face and voice showed the mental strain of controlling Jonathan's will. Jonathan showed the strain of trying to fight her, but the words came out of his mouth with almost no expression at all. Constance controlled him completely.

"We're stronger. We could control them all."

"That wouldn't be possible. Who else are you working with?"

"No one knows what Audrey and I planned. Once we destroyed you, then I would take over."

"There are others who practice bloodthirst. Who are they?"

"They stay hidden. They'd come out if you were gone."

"I'm sure they would. Who else did you control?"

"Only Samuel. The others followed Charles because they wanted to."

Constance couldn't help letting a small part of her brain think of Samuel instead of concentrating on Jonathan, and regret killing him. She could have broken Jonathan's control if she'd thought to look for it in Samuel's mind.

And Charles. Even he had been controlled. He'd been strong enough that Constance had seriously considered him for admission to the Assembly. He would have been good. What an incredible waste.

"Who else has the power to control vampire minds?" she asked.

"No one." Jonathan answered.

Constance knew that meant no one that had revealed themselves. Jonathan had hidden it so well, she had to assume others might be doing the same thing. She'd need to keep better track of the most powerful ones.

Constance still had her hands on Jonathan's head. She tightened her grip and snapped his neck. She was done, and let herself collapse into an old couch as Jonathan's body slumped and fell forward, only his tied arms holding him in the chair.

Byron felt Jonathan's death inside his brain. That part of him that Jonathan touched while they waited for Constance was finally released.

"Byron?" Parker called. He was the first up the stairs and gazed at the scene in front of him.

"Parker. Everything's fine now. We're all safe."

"What's happened?" Lorna asked. "Why did we come here with him?"

"What do you remember?"

"I remember everything like it was a dream," she answered looking confused. "Like it was someone else I was watching." They all looked confused and shocked.

"We need to get out of here," Constance interrupted. "We don't have much time before the sun rises, so we need to get to La Sang Rouge. Gina will find room for you, and our pilot is there already."

"The six of you can take Jonathan's van," Bartholomew said. "TJ and I will leave the bodies for the sun and follow in the SUV."

"Good," Constance answered simply.

They all headed out to the van and Byron drove down the muddy lane. The trip to Indianapolis was filled with a million questions and answers about what had happened and why.

* * *

The whole idea that Charles wasn't acting on his own evil thoughts, but had his actions controlled by Jonathan made my mind spin. If it hadn't been for Jonathan, Charles would have been the grumpy, hard-nosed vampire that TJ knew years ago, but he wouldn't have been a monster. Jonathan made him that.

It was others like Armand and Noel that were the really evil ones. They followed Charles because they wanted to. So, while Jonathan had started the whole ball rolling, there were those that would gladly follow him, gladly bring back the days when we all killed when we fed. How horrible.

My mind spun with the idea that all our problems had been caused by Jonathan. Well, I guess, not exactly all of them. I'd certainly gotten us in the middle of his insanity when I tried to drain Parker. While I still felt bad about that, I knew I couldn't do anything that would change it. The past couldn't be changed. All I could do was move on from it and keep trying not to make that kind of disastrous mistake again.

I could feel the lightening of the sky that signaled the beginning of sunrise by the time we got to La Sang Rouge. Byron had called Gina to let her know we were coming, so they were ready for our dash from the car to the employee entrance.

To my surprise, it was Joe who answered the employee door.

"Leave the car," he said. "I'll park it for you once you get settled."

"What are you doing here?" I had to ask.

He smiled. "I quit the force. I work for Gina, now."

"That's great," I answered without being very successful at hiding my surprise, but Parker and Chris had looks of surprise on their faces, too. There was too much on all of our minds at that point, though, to wonder about Gina and Joe.

The rest of the day, Constance talked to each of us individually. She needed to know what we remembered, but also looked into our minds to make sure Jonathan hadn't left any lingering commands that could cause trouble.

Constance spent the most time with Parker. Besides making sure his mind was clear of Jonathan's influence, she wanted to know how he was doing. It was her blood that re-made Parker, but there was still a small remnant of Charles in him.

Although everything Charles had done seemed like his own insanity, she figured the plot to make Parker bloodthirsty was a way for Jonathan to get to Byron. Charles and Byron had never been friendly, so pitting them against each other worked very easily. Sending Holly to Charles had created a horrible situation that exposed Charles to the Assembly long before Jonathan anticipated.

Jonathan still thought, though, he could create a situation with Byron and Charles under his control, working together. With Jonathan, the three of them could have destroyed the Assembly and plunged the vampire world back into the dark ages.

Finally, about noon, Constance was finished with us, and Gina found us rooms so we could sleep the rest of the day.

I snuggled next to Parker in the room Gina gave us. It was nice, but no where near as nice as our suite. "I'm just ready to go ..." Then I stopped and felt a tear roll down my cheek. "I forgot we don't have a home to go back to," I sighed.

"No," Parker said sadly. "But we're together and everyone's safe. It's finally all over."

"I said that to Constance," I whispered. "That I was glad it was finally over. She said that she didn't know if it would ever be over. She knows there are other bloodthirsty vampires hiding out there, and there's a few that could be as powerful as Jonathan."

"She's worried," Parker said as he stroked my cheek. "She feels guilty that she's lost track of so many of the oldest, but she knows better, now. The Assembly will contact them."

"I hope so."

"And no matter how many are hiding, they have no reason to be after us."

"That's true."

"Besides, it could be fun helping Byron build a new place and get it started." He was trying hard to make me feel better.

"In Adelle?" I asked.

"I don't think so," Parker shook his head. "I asked him that when we were in the family tunnel. There'll be too many questions from the police and arson investigators, and a lot more questions when they find the rooms downstairs. Byron won't go back to talk to them. We'll need to disappear somewhere and start over."

"So we're like all those clients who needed to wait around until they could start new lives."

"Yeah, we are. We could stay here for awhile, at least until Byron and Constance find a safe place to start building. Maybe see if Lorna and Chris want to stay, too."

"I'd like that. Gina's really nice, and Joe feels like an old friend. He really did save my life."

"He really did," Parker smiled. "We owe him."

"It doesn't matter where we end up," I smiled back. "Let's just concentrate on being together and living happily-ever-after like we've been planning."

"Now that's the best idea I've heard in a long time."

Parker squeezed me tighter and we both fell asleep knowing that troubles may find us in the years to come, but the worst was over. Whatever happened in our future, we'd face it together.

* * *

"I've been a fool," Constance said to Byron as they sat alone in Gina's office. Everyone else was sleeping except for the few daytime guards.

"You couldn't have predicted Jonathan's treachery."

"No, but I've been living with the belief that older vampires agree with my assertion that humans not be harmed. How many don't agree, but hide their true selves from me? How many are practicing bloodthirst while I pay no attention? Who will be the next one to believe he has the power to lead us back to bloodthirst?"

"You think there are others like Jonathan?"

"Others that *could* be like him. As old as I am, there are still some that are older and more powerful. How long before one of them tires of my rules?"

"I think Jonathan was an aberration. He had power, but also arrogance. It was the arrogance that led him to believe he could depose you and return us to the way we lived in the past."

"With power, comes arrogance. It has been my own arrogance that kept me blind to the danger, but I won't let that happen again. I need to keep in touch with those that are powerful instead of ignoring their potential."

"Could any of them control you?"

"Possibly. There's more to overcoming the will of another than power, though. There are skills involved that are difficult to teach. That's how I overpowered Jonathan. He was as strong as me, but his skills weren't as refined."

"I hadn't realized that."

"My skills were passed to me from my sire. He was incredibly powerful, yet was easily killed by humans while he slept. That was what led me to see what humans are capable of if we let them discover us." Constance paused for a moment before continuing. "Parker has my blood. Someday, he could be one who can control other vampires."

"He would never turn against you and The Assembly, Constance."

"Oh, I know that. I've seen it in his mind. In a century or so, once he's come into his full power, I may need to train him to use his skills. Until then, I'll need to look for others that could have the same ability. I can't go on foolishly believing those who don't openly oppose me are actually supporting me."

"So we keep fighting the same battle against individuals who use bloodthirst to satisfy their own desires while searching for those who use their power to spread bloodthirst and take us back to our old ways."

"Exactly. Our battle isn't over. It may never be."

About the Author

Ellen Fritz is a retired teacher and high school counselor. Over the years of teaching reading and English to students in grades seven through twelve before becoming a counselor, she had the great opportunity to discuss numerous favorite books with students and also took their recommendations for her own reading.

She finally found herself with the time to give life to the stories that have always been patiently waiting in her head for an audience. Ellen wrote <u>Mira</u> to appeal to those middle grade/teen readers that she found so inspiring through her career as an educator.

"I didn't start writing seriously until I retired and found myself with the time to spend a whole day in front of the computer. The ideas had been in my head for many years, but were undeveloped and unexplored. One day, several months after my teaching/ counseling career ended, I sat down and started.

Some days, the ideas, dialog, and characters flow from my brain and I can barely type fast enough. Other days, I have to walk away, occupy my mind with something else, and hash through what might happen, what might be said. But both days are valuable.

While waiting for a publisher to accept my first book, I discovered that rejections were okay. While I want young people to read and enjoy my books, I realized that the writing was more for me. It's a joy to develop the characters and situations, and I can't foresee a time when I'll be ready for it to end."